Philip Spires, born in 1952 in Wakefield, West Yorkshire, spent his first ten years in Sharlston, then a mining village, followed by eight in Crofton, a mile nearer Wakefield. He went to London University, where he obtained a BSc from Imperial College and a PGCE from King's. After two years as a VSO in Kenya, he taught in London for 16 years and devoted much of his spare time to assisting an NGO concerned with development and human rights. In 1992, after completing an MA, he worked in Brunei technical education. From 1999 he worked in Zayed University in the United Arab Emirates. Since 2003, he has lived in Spain, and has completed a PhD in education's role in Philippine development, and ***Mission***, his first published novel. ***A Fool's Knot*** is his second novel and expands a story mentioned in Mission.

www.philipspires.co.uk

ISBN: 978-1-905988-48-8

Cover design by Kelly Walsh
Cover photograph by Philip Spires

Published by Libros International

www.librosinternational.com

A Fool's Knot

Philip Spires

Libros
INTERNATIONAL

With thanks to all involved with Libros International and, in particular, to Carol Griffith for her careful editing.

For Willy Malukí, a man I never met

Character List

Anna Mwangangi – *John and Lesley's daughter*
Bill Goodman – *John Mwangangi's college tutor*
Boniface Njeru Muchira – *a teacher at Nzawa school*
Daniel Nzoka – *Janet's cook*
Helen Goodman – *Bill Goodman's first wife*
James Gitonga Kivara – *a teacher at Nzawa school*
Janet Rowlandson – *a British volunteer teacher in Migwani School*
John Mwangangi Musyoka – *Musyoka's son, British educated, returns to Kenya to become District Officer in Mwingi*
John O'Hara – *Bishop of Kitui, former parish priest in Migwani, boyhood mentor of John Mwangangi*
Joseph Munyolo (Munovo) – *one of Janet's students*
King Kabati – *Kabati town madman*
Lesley Mwangangi – *John's wife*
Michael Doherty – *Migwani parish priest*
Munyasya – *Migwani town madman*
Musyoka Mwangangi – *John Mwangangi's father, a traditional doctor*
Mutua – *Michael's cook*
Mwanza – *headmaster of Nzawa primary school*
Mwikali – J*ohn Mwangangi's half sister, much younger than him*
Solomon Musee – *a young man who danced with Janet at Kitui town dances*
Syengo – *John Mwangangi's clerk in Mwingi*

One

August 1976

England is smaller now. The sky is smaller. Daylight is softer, paler than memories of the harsh brilliance of tropical sun. There are people everywhere: there is no space here. There are no mountains, no heavy clouds, flat-bottomed in the sky and stretching to the horizon as if floating on the surface of a lake covering the earth. There is no distance here. The horizon is near and the sun does not shine.

A tremble of regret, an emptiness born of shock, passed through Janet's body. Her eyes stared blankly as mile after predictable mile passed by unnoticed. She was glad to be home again, but this happiness could not override the sadness she felt at leaving the place where she had lived so happily for two years. Though Migwani already felt a long way distant, it had perhaps felt more of a home than any other place that bore the name. Already it had become no more than a phase in her life, transformed by the hours of flight into a memory, outlived and outmoded. It was over and finished forever. How long will it be, she thought, as the drumming of the road filled her mother's car, before I begin to live facing forwards instead of looking back to a destroyed past? How long before it is really over?

She looked down at the seat beside her on which rested the jumble of a parcel she had made up so carefully the previous morning. Protruding from beneath the string-tied newspaper wrapping, which had been torn during her long wait in queues after disembarking in London, was a strange array of barbed arrowheads, polished cow horns and the three unvarnished legs of a stool. Tied to one leg, and now swinging over the edge of the seat, was a small gourd, a simple treasure, which meant more than all the other souvenirs and all the photographs with which she had returned. Of all the things she had brought home, this was the strongest reminder of everyday life in Migwani, an exact replica of those used in every household for carrying and storing water. She would polish it and use it as a vase for dried flowers. But protruding above and below the other trinkets and artefacts was the crudely fashioned but beautiful walking stick that had been Munyolo's personal present for her. Surely this was something to treasure.

Her eyes were heavy with sleep. For two days life had been hectic. It seemed that time had passed too quickly to be noticed, like an immense dream half-remembered between two clear memories. One was the joy she felt when she knew that John had accepted her invitation to come to the farewell party in the school. The other, from only an hour before, was the tearfully overjoyed embrace of her mother at the airport. She looked older, Janet thought. David Smythe, the neighbour and childhood friend, who had offered to drive her mother's car to the airport, had also changed, not that she had seen much of him in recent years. He remained the slightly overweight, goofy lad, who still lived with his parents over the road. But her mother's letters had referred at length to the help he had offered and the jobs he did for her. At least he was honest. He was both fatter and frailer than before. Both seemed to speak more slowly than she remembered. Was it really them? Had she really travelled those thousands of miles to return home with the feeling that she had never been away? She was not convinced - of anything, but there were truths that could not be ignored, truths locked into the trivialities of life, the very details of which, when remembered, make even dreams feel real. She had just come from the airport where her mother had greeted her arrival with such long warm embraces. She had felt great surprise when the car park attendant spoke to her in Swahili. Janet had insisted on paying the fee with the English coins she had faithfully kept for two years in a small box on her bedside table. Mistakenly she had included a Kenya shilling with them and the attendant, an Asian, handed it back saying, "*Habari ya Kenya*?" with a broad smile on his face. "Fine," Janet had replied taking the coin. The event itself had been bland enough, but the real awakening for Janet was how strange the Swahili sounded. It was 'foreign', no longer what she expected to hear. And how difficult it had been for her to answer in kind. She had sought the word but not found it; only 'fine' would come. Already a black face seemed a point of interest, an unexpected sight to be noticed and noted as different. Her suburban roots were already showing through.

There were things she would have to re-learn. She was sure of that. How long would it take, she wondered, thinking back to the hostess on the aircraft. A girl her own age, but Scottish and blonde, had set about her duties immediately the plane took off from Nairobi with a forthright confidence and clarity of purpose unknown to Migwani's lazy, timeless ways. Janet had been lucky to get a seat by a hatchway, where there was no seat in front and therefore no problem in setting down her large bulky parcel. Carrying an armful of trays to clip onto the aircraft seats, the hostess had approached Janet's aisle seat. She spoke with predictable politeness which, after another language's commands, seemed overstated. "Would you like a tray, Madam?" the hostess had said. Janet, lost in her thoughts for a moment, had naively answered, "No, thank you," causing the girl's consciously pleasant expression to harden slightly through the words, "But you're going to have something to eat." With the tray safely clipped on Janet's seat the hostess moved on to the man sitting next to her. Of course, Janet thought, it was not meant to be a question. Had the girl said simply, "Take your tray," and moved on, Janet would have understood, but another person, more used to 'normal' behaviour might have been offended.

But still the regret produced its confusion. As the car travelled south, town and country passed by outside, but inside a single picture lodged behind Janet's eyes and, try as she might, she could think of nothing else. In that picture, a collage of many scenes, two leafless trees stood out against a cloudless blue sky. Beneath one of the trees sat a group of women dressed in brightly coloured clothes, many of them wearing cardigans, though the sun was high and the day was hot. Spread out before them, on sacks laid down to cover the hard red earth, were neat piles of fruit: mangoes, green oranges and lemons, guavas and unripe tomatoes. Under the other tree sat a man, a shoemaker, surrounded by the sandals he had made that day from the tread and rubber of old car tyres. Nearby, undisturbed in his usual place, the town's madman, Munyasya, lay asleep, his spidery legs almost merging with the tree roots. The sun was hot, but in an instant the picture was sour, grey and cold. The shoemaker's tools lay on the ground beside him and his face was buried deep in his hands. The women, usually noisy, chattering or singing, were quiet and some were weeping.

How long, thought Janet, before I forget?

***

Father Michael pressed his foot hard on the accelerator. The sun was already low in the sky. He had an appointment with the Chief in Migwani that evening and there were still over sixty miles to travel. As usual, he had overslept. He always overslept in Nairobi. The beds in the Mission Centre were just too comfortable to resist. After weeks of discomfort caused by the springless wonder he called his 'unmade pit' in Migwani, the soft mattress and clean sheets at the Centre were irresistible. Add to that the likelihood that, for him, waking up usually meant waking up with a hangover, and the picture grows clearer. Nairobi was a place he both loved and hated. The hot and cold running water, the comfort of the Centre, the cinemas, the visits to friends and the occasional booze-up he enjoyed. On the other hand there were errands to be run, things to be bought, messages to be given and always too little time in which to do everything. He would never finish all of his jobs around town, but equally would never sacrifice a party or a long sleep to make more time. By the end of the second day he was always glad to be leaving it all behind. The worst part of every trip to the city, though, was this, the journey home. The road was a hundred dusty miles. When driving into town, one could look forward to the last few miles on smooth tarmac, with its promise of a hot shower in the Centre at the end of it all. But when going home there was only the prospect of a bucket of cold water and the creaking frame of the unmade pit.

Michael had something of a reputation. He was aware of it and often played to his gallery, sometimes consciously.

His fellow priests and parishioners alike saw him as something of an eccentric. He was perhaps just too vivid a character, too willing to accept a life of contradictions. Dedicated he certainly was, but ephemeral too. Wherever he worked, his positive influence could be traced right through the community he served. In Migwani, where he had been parish priest for more than five years, he had helped to establish a secondary school, three primary schools, adult literacy schemes and last, but certainly not least, a town football team called the Black Stars, in whose ranks Michael's white face invariably figured. Above all else he was a man of the people, a man positively loved by many. Not only was he a priest and a fluent speaker of Kikamba, the local language, but also a man who could talk about and understand the problems that beset the lives of ordinary people. Some individuals, however, regarded him with distaste. They would openly criticise him for drinking in bars, going to dances in the Unity Club and, above all, for doing 'the bump' with bar maids at those same dances. He drank too much, smoked too much, swore too much and probably worked too much. But his achievements were impossible to ignore and everyone agreed with that.

He was equally proud of his fame and his infamy. A tale he loved to tell which summed up his attitude was the one that he had retold to Janet the previous night, just before taking her to the airport. One day, he told her, he was driving to Kitui to play football. Since, as usual, he was late, he was in a hurry and driving too fast to remember that he was approaching a stony part of the road. The car hit the stones at speed and one of the tyres simply disintegrated, with the result that the car slid to a halt amid clouds of dust and grit. The jack, of course, was at home in the mission. He couldn't recall why he had taken it out of the car. Some ten minutes later, while he was fruitlessly trying to lift one side of the car in order to push a large stone under the jack point with his foot, a group of men came walking along the road and he beckoned to them for help. The men, however, simply stood and stared in disbelief at this *mzungu*, this European, clad in football kit and bush hat, who was trying to lift a car. Frustrated, Michael had then shouted in his broad Limerick tones, "You silly buggers, will you come and help me change this fucking wheel?" "Ah, Father Michael," replied one of the men. "We didn't realise it was you."

The previous evening that particular story had helped to clear the air, but only a little. He had planned to take Janet into Nairobi for one last night on the town before she flew back to England. In Nairobi they could do as they wished without worrying whether the Bishop of Kitui or people might begin to gossip. Michael had it all worked out. They would arrive in the afternoon, leaving time for a wash and a rest before a Chinese meal on Government Road, followed by an hour or so at the Swiss Grill, where they would have a dance or two. Janet's flight was not due to leave until half past midnight, so they would easily manage both venues before her check-in time.

What was to have been a great night out in fact deteriorated into a mere sad farewell over a beer in the airport lounge, where the fluorescent lights, if not flickering on faulty starters, made everyone look gaunt and ill. The best-laid plans can go astray, so it would probably be no surprise that Father Michael's tenuous idea turned out to be a non-starter. But on this occasion the failure was not his. He would still have liked his night out, but the events of that morning had overtaken them both. Janet, upset and close to tears throughout, had laughed a little at his story, but it was no more than a single moment to be weighed against the rest of the day, when sadness, tragedy and disillusion pervaded all.

The car rattled and bumped along the dirt road as Migwani's spectacular mountain backbone appeared through the gathering twilight. The long journey was almost over. A hundred miles was perhaps no distance at all, but on these roads you allowed four hours and the punctures often made it longer. He had been lucky today, unlike one occasion, when he had fixed no less than thirteen punctures of his tubed tyres and taken more than eight hours to do the trip. But still his repertoire of songs that he invariably sang as he drove was almost exhausted. Some minutes later, with darkness beginning to fall and headlights carving into the gloom, the car sped over the last ridge and the single light of Migwani after dark came into view. Michael sang a celebratory chorus of 'We're here because we're here', but at the end of this particular trip the words were tinged not just with resignation, but also with defiance and unease. Like a moth to a flame, the car left the road and careered down the small track that led towards the light of the mission house, his home. Mutua, the cook, who had been waiting for Father Michael's return, peered out of the kitchen window and waved as the car drew up by the back door.

When Michael entered the house, he was greeted not only by Mutua, but by two others, both not quite strangers. As Mutua pumped the pressure lamp that provided the only light in the room, he spoke to Michael in Kikamba. "These men have been waiting for you," he said.

Michael had expected to see the Chief of Migwani Location and it was he who first shook Michael's hand. Then, in English, he said, "May I introduce you to Bwana Joseph Kamau, who is the Chief Police Officer in Kitui town."

The second man then came forward and offered a

handshake. "I am pleased to meet you, Father Michael. Thank you for volunteering to come back from Nairobi this evening. It is best that we discuss these pressing matters today."

Father Michael sat down opposite the two men. In the years since his ordination as a missionary priest, he had experienced famine, disease and war. He had stalked death and it had lived alongside him. But throughout those years, he could recall no tragedy as sad as this.

Two

August 1976

As she stepped from the train, Janet swung her haversack over her shoulder. The train had been crowded, so she hurried along the platform with ticket in hand in an attempt to avoid the perhaps inevitable queue at the barrier. The ticket collector was black and, remembering the car park attendant, she paused for a moment after handing over her ticket, half expecting him to speak to her in Swahili. "Move along please," he said. She would soon have to get used to the idea that not everyone was Kenyan. And what difference would it have made if he had been Kenyan? A word of greeting and a single word of reply? What did it matter?

After a moment's indecision she walked towards the public telephones. From the inside pocket of her velvet jacket she took a tattered pink address book and looked up a number. The call took only a minute to complete.

An hour later she sat alone in a waiting room along one of the long meandering corridors of County Hall on the South Bank of the Thames. Her haversack was on the floor behind a hat stand in one corner of the room. Without it she looked considerably neater. Her jacket had weathered its two-year storage quite well. She had bought it for next to nothing in a jumble sale whilst at college and, having been told that

Kenya was a 'hot' country, she had decided not to take it with her. A white blouse, corduroy trousers and a pair of uncomfortably new shoes her mother had bought as a 'coming home present' completed the picture. She had hardly been in the country for a day before her mother whisked her off to the shops, intending to buy her a complete new outfit. Janet had refused the offer and had provoked an argument. A pair of new shoes, declared 'sensible' by her mother, was the pacifying compromise.

"Miss Rowlandson?"

Janet nodded.

"Sorry to keep you waiting for so long. Will you come in please?"

Janet stood up and crossed the rather cavernous waiting area into the adjoining office. She found herself strangely unused to the sound of English. Every statement she heard sounded like an apology.

"Good afternoon. Do sit down."

Two women faced Janet across a small cluttered desk. They might have been pictures of the same woman taken at different times, so precisely did they fit within the same mould. One, frail, middle-aged and grey-haired wore half spectacles. The other, slight and slim, wore a sweater and trousers. Her spectacles were large, round and thick-rimmed. Both were incomparably neat and polite, so much so that Janet's first thought was to consider her own relative shabbiness. Maybe this hadn't been such a good idea. There was a moment's organisation, during which the younger of the two arranged papers in front of the other, giving each sheet a title and function as she laid them individually onto the desk. The older of the two then spoke.

A few minutes passed in which introductions were made. Mrs Skemp and Miss Williams enquired after Janet's train journey. They had quite a discussion on the overcrowding on some routes. Mrs Skemp travelled from Notting Hill every morning by tube and her relationship with the Central Line was based more on hate than love. They wanted to know what she had done over the last few days and during her time in Kenya. Progressively Janet spoke for longer periods, no longer answering with merely factual information. After twenty minutes they had covered not only the two years in Kenya, but also the three years of her degree course in English Literature, her year of teacher training and even her school days, her membership of the Legion of Mary and the history of her holiday work in hospitals near her north Surrey home. Then came the real business of the meeting. Miss Williams spoke with a new directness.

"Can you tell us what it was that attracted you to Inner London, rather than, say, a borough closer to your family home?"

Janet answered as if her application had come about as a result of a long process of analysis and decision. In fact, some four months beforehand, she had suddenly realised that returning to England would involve getting some kind of job. Until then it had been a problem she could safely ignore. It was just too far away to deserve thought. When the time came round, however, she had realised that her two years of experience in Kenya would count for nothing. She would have to apply for posts as a newly trained teacher, still without having completed her qualifying probationary year. She had therefore placed a general enquiry to the Inner London Education Authority in the hope that such a large organisation would be bound to have at least something to get her started. At twenty-four, she had no designs yet on permanence.

"I've spent two years working with poor students in a poor area," she said. "I want to apply the same principles in my future work. Where my mother lives is solidly middle class. They even still have grammar schools. I have a strong belief in the power of education to change people's lives, so I would like to work in Inner London." Even as she spoke, she mused on the nature of self-deception. She surely did believe what she had just said. But how often in Kenya had she wanted to suggest to her students – especially the poorer ones – that they should think of doing something else with their time, something more likely to be of use and profit for them?

"I must say that you were very wise to have done something about finding a job before you got back," said Mrs Skemp. "Most impressive. And tell me what you might see yourself doing five or six years from now. Are you ambitious at all? Have you considered setting yourself some career goals?"

"I have no idea at the moment. All I want to do is get myself established somewhere. And complete my probationary year, of course. It will always look strange, I suppose, that I didn't achieve that until three years after completing my training."

There was a moment's silence. "I have a feeling that in your case it will have no long-term consequences," said Mrs Skemp. There was another long pause as Miss Williams and Mrs Skemp consulted one another in near silence. They pointed at a couple of documents, whispered a little and nodded. Then Mrs Skemp looked Janet straight in the eye, her gaze angled above her half spectacles. "How does Clapham strike you?"

"Clapham," Janet repeated. "It will be a long journey… A change of trains… but then I don't expect I'll stay at home with my mother once I have a salary of my own."

"You realise of course that all of the posts we are currently recruiting for are late vacancies. Jobs are normally filled during the summer term…"

"I realise that," interrupted Janet, not wanting to appear reluctant to accept the offer. "Clapham will be fine."

"It's a Scale 1 post in the English Department at St Mary's. You might even get some A-level work in that school," mused Miss Williams. "It's a really good opportunity. The post is vacant only because they have had a resignation on health grounds in the last two weeks."

"That's fine." And Janet was employed.

"There are a couple of forms to fill in. Miss Williams will give them to you on the way out. It's been a pleasure talking to you, Miss Rowlandson." Mrs Skemp rose from her seat, leaned across the functional, local authority issue desk and offered a handshake.

Over a coffee in a nearby café, apparently squashed beneath Waterloo Station, Janet sifted though the papers she had been given. Thank goodness that was all over. She had no reason to be nervous and knew it. But she had been nervous, so much so that her voice had trembled and her facial muscles entered spasm. And now she was employed. She would ring the school from home tomorrow and arrange to visit the head. In a few years would she herself be a Mrs Skemp or a Miss Williams, a clone of professional woman, safe, dependable, even conventional? And what wonderfully overt concern the English expressed for the plight of others! Had she really lived for the last two years amidst poverty, disease and starvation to find that, on her return, the cause for greatest concern was the comfort of trains? How parochial even the professedly sophisticated seemed to be. Despite the lip service paid to 'awareness' and 'education', people here seemed to know as little about the world and its problems of poverty as the poor in Kenya knew of the problems of affluence. People everywhere lived small lives in small worlds, it seemed. Everything seemed to be fine until something from outside this limited universe levered its way into their lives. Then, she thought, the result was at best misunderstanding and at worst direct conflict. In a way, this inability of everyone she had met over the previous few days to visualise the life she had led during her two years in Kenya helped her to live with the sadness of Migwani's tragedy. If the affluent in Britain could not visualise a 'different way', how could one expect an old man in Migwani to do it?

Outside, the rush hour was now in full swing. For some time she had been spared the experience of traffic jams and crowded trains. Now reunited with these joys, they somehow felt rather silly and pointless, perhaps even insane. Within a month she would be doing the same herself twice a day, without thought, without question.

Half an hour later she pressed the bell on the door of a semi-detached house in a quiet area deep within a west London suburb, after a rickety ride on a clanking District Line train. The door was opened by a tall red-haired man. He was plainly very happy to see her and shook her hand warmly as she stepped into the house.

"How did the interview go? Did you get it?" he asked.

"Yes. It was something of an anticlimax. It all seemed so easy."

There followed the beginning of a ritual. He introduced his wife, whom Janet had never met, but whom Janet knew to be his second. Then, after taking Janet's jacket and haversack and hanging them on the coat rack, he showed her through into the living room, which was comfortably floral, overtly safe. He opened the sideboard and offered her a drink, but Janet, still standing, ignored his question. There was a tear in her eye as she started to speak.

"Dr Goodman," she said hesitantly, "I have some bad news for you."

Three

January 1975

"Will you bring the arresting officer?" The sliding door over the small hatchway set in the wall snapped shut. The young man, who had been typing a record of the proceedings of the previous day's sitting of the magistrate's court, got up from his desk abruptly and left the room with perhaps over-stated purpose. The police station was only a stone's throw from the office, just across the main road. He walked briskly out of the District Officer's compound and crossed the road without looking. Traffic here announced itself noisily a minute or more before it approached. There was little else here to cloud the silence, save for an occasional call from a bulbul. Only the morning and evening bus to Katse and the occasional Ministry of Works lorry passed along that road, and both bus and lorry made so much noise and raised so much dust that you could generally see and hear them coming several minutes before they even reached the town.

After only a few seconds inside the police station, the young clerk was making his way back across the road accompanied by another young man dressed in the grey uniform and blue stockings of the Kenya Police.

"The arresting officer, sir," said the clerk, showing the

policeman through into the spacious, but largely bare office.

"Thank you, Syengo," said John.

Syengo closed the door behind him and then returned to his typewriter in the adjoining room. His office was small and cramped, but extremely tidy and well ordered. He took great care with his work and was proud to be the clerk to the court. After all, he had only left school a year before and only six of his classmates had managed to find a job at all. What had happened to the rest he had no idea. Many of them had no doubt returned home after finishing school and were probably spending their time tending their father's cows. This made him feel even prouder. Others would be walking the streets of Nairobi, drifting from one casual job to another, living from hand to mouth. This comforted him greatly as he sat down again behind his desk, taking care to rearrange the pencils in his desk tidy so that they were all parallel, all facing the same way. Above all else he was grateful. He was grateful to his teachers, to the Government for employing him and to his father, who had paid the school fees and also helped him to get the job. He was already earning as much as a teacher in a primary school and had already saved enough to buy four bulls.

"It is stated that you, Mulindi Kisuva, did on the third of January 1975..."

The slow untrained clicking of the typewriter filtered through the partition into John's office. The policeman and two other men sat facing John. The three watched in silence until he had finished. John, after reading through what he had just written, replaced the top of his fountain pen and put it into the top pocket of his jacket.

"Constable," said John without looking up, "since there seems to be some confusion surrounding the events in Nzawa last night, I have asked you to come here in order to listen to this statement which we have prepared. If this tallies with what you have been told by Mr Muchira, then we will have established that there is a case to answer."

John took up the papers and began to read. "I, Boniface Njeru Muchira, am a teacher at Nzawa Primary School in Migwani Location, Kitui District. I have taught in the said school for three years. On the evening of January 25 1975 I was in my house talking with my colleague, one James Gitonga Kivara."

The policeman, whose first language was also Kikuyu, could not suppress an intended quiet chuckle to himself becoming quite audible at this point. The name, Kivara, means 'baldy'.

"At approximately 9pm I heard the sound of shouting outside the house, which is within the school compound, so I went to the window and looked out to see what was happening. At this point a large stone hit the window, breaking the glass. I saw a group of about ten school students. There was a full moon and I could see some of them clearly. I shouted at them, telling them to go away or I would tell the police. Their reply was to shower the house with stones and shout obscene remarks about myself and my colleague. They continued to throw stones for about ten minutes. Mr Kivara –"

There was only a muted smile from the policeman this time.

"– and myself then decided to try to chase the boys away. Together we rushed from the house towards the group. We carried sticks to protect ourselves. Some of the boys ran away but others continued to throw stones. Five stones hit me before the rest of the children turned and ran. Fortunately I managed to catch hold of one boy and overpower him. I asked him to tell me the names of the others present. His only reply was to curse me. Two of the others turned round, came back and began to beat me with sticks until Mr Kivara chased them away. But to protect myself, I had to let go of the boy and he ran away. I then asked Mr Kivara to ride on his motorcycle to the police station in Mwingi to report the incident. He returned with a police officer at about 11pm and I made a full report to the officer. He asked me to come to the police station the following morning, January 26 1975, which I did. I found that he had assembled a large number of school students as a result of his investigations. He asked me to inspect each one and say which of them had taken part in the attack on my home. This I did. I feel I have done my job at Nzawa well and can think of no reason why such an attack should have taken place." John looked up. "Is that accurate? Does it reflect what you want to be recorded?" he asked looking from one to another.

"It is fine," said the policeman. The others nodded.

"Will you then sign the paper at the bottom, Mr Muchira? And you, Mr Kivara, can you sign your copy? I see no point in reading that one to the officer as well. It is substantively the same."

The two men signed the papers, despite the fact that in Kivara's case he had no idea what the word substantively might mean. They handed the sheets back over the substantial desk to John. Beneath each statement he printed John Mwangangi Musyoka, and then rubber-stamped the words, District Officer, Mwingi, at the bottom of each page. He then countersigned across his printed name and the stamp.

"That seems to be all," said John with an air of finality borne of relief. "I will write to you, Mr Muchira, as soon as a date for the hearing is fixed." Turning to the policeman, he continued, "Those boys you have in the police station can now go in the Land Rover to Kitui. They are to be held in custody until all the witnesses have been traced and have made their statements."

The policeman got up and stood to an overstated attention, the Prussian-style heel click of his boots following some seconds after the achievement of his fully stretched height. Then, stamping his foot with a great slap on the concrete floor as he turned, he marched out of the room as if performing a military tattoo. A brace of consciously dignified, but clearly hurt and rather belittled teachers followed. John Mwangangi watched all three leave his office, carefully filing their mannerisms and behaviour in his memory for future reference.

There was more to the case than met the eye, of that he was sure. But, as John collected the papers and filed them away in the neatly labelled grey cabinets along the wall behind his desk, his mind was initially filled with condemnation of the indiscipline of the children and their lack of respect for their elders. He had been taught to respect a teacher like he respected his own father. He wondered how many of the boys now handcuffed, and being ushered into the back of a police Land Rover with weld mesh over the windows, would have dared even to disagree with their own fathers, let alone stone them or beat them.

After a glance at his watch, he slid back the hatchway door in the wall behind his desk and told Syengo that he could finish work for the day. Syengo waited until the hatch door closed again – a full minute after John had spoken – before grabbing his brightly coloured cap and setting off home. He liked to make doubly sure that Bwana Mwangangi had no more work for him before he left. The District Officer was a very important man and he would hate to offend him.

Four

April 1951

Good things are seen during the rains, but this season the rains were poor, a bad omen for the people of Migwani, the pessimists had claimed. The good things, however, were all planned. Sugar cane had been cut and stored for some weeks and children had been sent to climb trees to collect the hanging seedpods. Then, two weeks before the first day of the celebrations, the town's old men had pulped and boiled the sugar cane with water, and set aside the liquor in large earthenware pots, which they kept for this one function each year. They ground seeds from the pods to a fine powder and stirred it into the liquor. During these two weeks the liquid fermented and matured to a fine, light sugar cane beer that would keep the gods awake. In every home, thoughts of celebration, dancing and music were paramount. Goats had been fattened for the feast and cows had been milked dry. All the beehives were empty, their honey brewed to beer, the special *uki wa nzuki*, and stored with care in fresh gourds. At one home in Migwani a high arch of banana leaves had been built by the parents of children who were to participate this year. The leaves were cut from the plants and carried by the youngsters. The adults sang as they built the arch, sang loudly, so the young children could hear the words which told them why, when and how, one day, they too would pass through this arch.

Musyoka, son of Mwangangi, had taken part in every ceremony since his own father died. How long ago that was he could not remember, but he did recall the first arch to be built before his own homestead. He had felt such pride that day, because it had not been until then that he fully realised what it meant to be the doctor in Migwani. Every year since then, the arch had been built during the month of the long rains, but on every occasion Musyoka remembered that same pride which, if anything, grew as time passed. This year, though, was to be a special time for him. This year his own first-born son was to pass through the arch into manhood and thereby become his rightful heir. Once a man, Mwangangi son of Musyoka could then succeed him as doctor, when finally his own work was finished and he was called to join his ancestors. The son was growing old: it was time. New days start when old ones end.

The dancing and singing stopped for a while and even the drunken reeling old men stood quietly to watch. Drums and horns, which had pulsed their rhythms during the dance, were silenced. The initiates began to assemble beneath the arch. As they stood motionless, young men moved along the crooked rows and hung garlands of flowers around their necks. Others threw chains of flowers over the arch. Their feet were caked with earth wet by libations poured in the honour of ancestors from every cup of beer. They took great care, though, not to pass under the arch themselves. That is not allowed, for that road is a way you take just once in your life.

On a far ridge, just discernible across the low, shallow valley, the entire scene around Musyoka's home was being mirrored. Over there were the girls, soon to be women, and these were the boys, soon to be men. Thus words were spoken and the process began. Girls and boys passed through their respective arches and there was no turning back. The girls walked as a group, followed closely by the women, all striding in time with the rhythmic chants they all sang. The boys ran. It was a race. The first to arrive would be leader of the age-set and, once upon a time, the head warrior and hunt leader of the group, the one who would lead the way to counter a threat to their people. But these days were long ago. Screaming, shouting and laughing, the boys ran up the steep hillside to Migwani with the mature and old panting on behind.

The small wooden church in Migwani stood only a few yards away from the cluster of mud-walled shops that constituted the town. The newly built mission house to the side of the church was a fine place indeed, built of cement blocks and corrugated iron. Just beyond the compound, just beyond the euphorbia hedge which defined its boundaries, there grew a large straight tree of such an age that even the old men remembered it the same. It was to this tree that the boys and girls would come.

Father John O'Hara knew when he bought the land that it bordered the holiest place in Migwani. Indeed that was one of the reasons why he decided to build his new church here, so that it might be a constant reminder of his teaching to those who walked near the tree. He disapproved of traditional ways, but did not criticise those who believed in them. His goal was to incorporate the fervour and devotion of those traditions into a new allegiance with his own church. This is why he had built on this site as an expression of coexistence, not domination.

As the sun sank low in the west, the giant silhouette of Mount Kenya thrust through the heat haze into rain-cleansed air. Earlier that day he had heard the sound of horns and drums from the valley. By then he had grown quite used to what they meant and in fact looked forward to the day each year when the boys and girls of the area came running to the giant tree near the mission.

First came the boys in a long, noisy winding snake, those forming the head deadly serious and competing, whilst in contrast the body ambled a little, accompanied by shouting and laughter. On hearing them, Father John left his chair and walked to the entrance to the mission compound, where he would greet them as they passed. He would keep his distance, but not because his presence was in any way resented. It was his own respect that intervened.

By the time the men arrived, most of the boys had recovered from their run. And it was half an hour before the girls and women arrived together, as a group. Men and women then formed a large circle around the tree and began to sing. The men sang of the skill of hunters, the valour of warriors and the need for all men to have a son who could carry their name. The women sang of marriage, of faithful and true husbands and the joys of bearing children. With friends and relatives in full voice around them, the boys climbed the tree to pluck off and throw down small twigs, which would be used at first light the next morning to indicate that the time for washing had arrived. The girls waited below to collect and bundle the wood. Eager to collect as much as they could, a minor scuffle broke out as each piece of wood fell to the ground as each girl tried to grab it for her own bundle. At some point during the long rains the ceremony would be mirrored in every centre, large or small, throughout the lands of the Akamba.

With enough wood collected and all songs sung, the procession set off as one. Boys, girls, women and men walked slowly together for the final initiation feast at the house of Musyoka son of Mwangangi. Only Musyoka's own son, Mwangangi, lagged behind. Troubled by something on his leg, he seemed to be trying to keep pace with the rest, pause to rub his leg and deliberately lag behind all in one. Then he stopped and sat, so that he could inspect the back of his calf. He then rose again to hobble towards the group, only to begin the process again with another pause. After a couple more minutes, he gave up his pursuit and hobbled back to the mission.

"Father John?" he said timidly, knocking lightly on the door.

O'Hara peered out from the dim interior, but he had already recognised the voice. "Come in! Come in, Mwangangi," he said warmly. "What is it that you want? Shouldn't you be with the others? I thought you would be well on your way by now."

"Father, I have cut my leg on a thorn up in the tree and it is bleeding. Can you look at it?"

O'Hara inspected the wound which looked bad, but when he cleaned it he could see clearly that it was just a long scratch. It had bled quite freely, however, so first he cleaned everything with cotton wool and some iodine, and then took a bandage from his first-aid box to dress it.

Suddenly Mwangangi drew away, as if he had just been reminded he was doing wrong. "What about the bandage?" asked the priest, slightly puzzled.

"I think it will be all right now," said Mwangangi. "I must go."

With that he turned and set off towards the door. Before he had taken a single step, however, he stopped again and turned. "Father, is it still good for my baptism on Sunday? Now that I am a man and not a boy…"

"You are welcome in God's house at any time, Mwangangi."

"That is good," said the boy, a relieved wide smile

spreading over his face. “Thank you, Father,” he said and then left.

Father John’s gaze followed him through the fast fading light as he walked towards the valley. Shaking his head he turned back into the room saying, “What a shameful and barbaric custom it is.”

Just before first light the next morning, Musyoka’s first wife, Mwangangi’s mother, lit the pile of wood collected from the sacred tree. The party at last was over and everyone was silent. As the sky turned to the cold grey of half-light, the girls and boys with Mwangangi amongst them set off together for the last time to make their way slowly, reverently, even solemnly to the river bed. Though the rains this year had been poor, the river had not yet run dry and this was seen as a good omen. With a slow chant that bade farewell to childhood, the initiates parted on reaching the riverbank, men and boys going one way and girls and women the other, the latter, of course, downstream. The two groups would wash separately and, from that morning, as groups would remain apart for the rest of their lives. Until that day, they could intermingle, share beds, and even touch one another, but now as adults they must live by another code. Though many would eventually marry, never again would boys be admitted to these girls’ meetings and never again would one of these girls follow a hunting party, not even to carry a calabash of beer for the men.

Fathers now accompanied sons and mothers accompanied daughters to their segregated washing areas. All that remained of the ceremony after the washing was the circumcision itself. Both boys and girls were now afraid, but, as required by their custom, they showed no emotion. They had been taught to look forward to this moment with a mixture of joy and awe. They must be happy for their rebirth into adulthood is at hand, and yet afraid because the innocence of childhood is set behind them and they must learn to shoulder full adult responsibilities towards their families, their community and their ancestors. The same was true for each boy and girl. When the moment of pain came, when they sat on the ground with their legs held apart, intertwined with those of their parents, the knife would cut as quickly and as cleanly as possible. The child should not cry, should not even wince, should not strain against the embrace. The children should do nothing, save for whispering thanks to their forefathers for guiding them safely towards adulthood. Then they would walk to rest on a bed of fresh green leaves, where mothers and fathers would come to dress the wounds with axe-water, herbs and milk. And so the process started. The washing began.

As Mwangangi stepped down from the riverbank, his whole body shuddered. Water had never seemed so cold. He sat down in the water and began to wash all over. Then, unexpectedly, his father called him. Mwangangi was not sure what to do. Musyoka called again, louder and more sternly. Reluctantly the boy left the water and rejoined his father on the bank. His father was suddenly angry, terribly angry, angry in a way the boy had never known a man could be. He said not a single word, but there was condemnation in his eyes. He then bent down in front of his son and took hold of the boy's leg with an iron grip. For as long as a minute he squeezed and rubbed the boy's flesh as he inspected the neat line of crisp scab which snaked up the back of his calf. Musyoka rubbed and scratched at the pale red stain that was clearly visible around the entire wound. Mwangangi's heart sank as his father stood and stared scornfully into his son's eyes. For some time they stood, apparently locked in one another's stare. In Mwangangi's eyes there were questions, in his father's condemnation.

Then he hit him, hard across the face. It was in full view of everyone assembled there, but no one spoke. No one intervened. And with that, Musyoka turned his back on his son and walked slowly, dejectedly back towards his homestead. Mwangangi was hurt, not physically, but still deeply hurt and ashamed as he returned to the river and continued to wash.

One hour later his turn had come and he sat on the ground. Behind him, facing the same way, sat a man whose arms embraced him firmly and whose legs intertwined with and held apart his own. Mwangangi was not afraid. It would soon be over and he was proud. Then, dancing and chanting, came the doctor. Mwangangi looked at his father, but the figure now dressed in goatskins, beads and feathers showed no recognition. The boy struggled and cried as he was circumcised. It was meant to be fast, with the cut made cleanly and quickly, not this slow agonising tear. The boy struggled and cried again as the pain grew worse. And then he fainted.

When he awoke with a start his mother bent low over him and offered comfort. He was glad to see her, to feel her hand on his arm when he closed his eyes, to spread cold, thick milk on the wound, which still gave him such pain, to lull him to sleep.

Outside, the day had aged to late afternoon. Musyoka sat on a tree stump by his hut, whittling away at a stick with an old army knife. He had spoken to no one since the morning and had sat like this locked in thought, unable to acknowledge even the presence of another. When people had left his home that morning, giving thanks for the new manhood of their sons, they had talked and argued with one another. Some were ignorant and spoke of Mwangangi's shame and of how his cries of pain meant that he would abuse the office of doctor, and should never succeed his father. Others, who were wiser, had seen what had happened, and spoke of their fear for Musyoka and their disbelief at what he had done. Had the knife he used not been old, dirty, rusty and blunt? Had he not deliberately sheathed the sharpened knife before treating his son? Did he not gnaw and tear at the foreskin, instead of slicing it with one long cut? And had he also not cut the boy's legs? It was very confusing indeed and a matter upon which only God could now give judgment. This must be a test of Mwangangi's right to succeed his father. The ancestors must have been offended, because the boy's screams had been long and loud. Only they, the ancestors, could now decide what must be done. If the wound was infected and the boy's body poisoned, then God had made his judgment and the boy would die. If it were to heal, and thus return the boy to strength and confirmed adulthood, then God would have made his judgment, and once again Musyoka would embrace Mwangangi as his son and heir.

Only Musyoka knew the reality. The boy had let blood during the ceremony and had not immediately begged his father to clean the wound and cast out the spirits, which thereby had entered the body. Worse than that, he had tried to hide that special wound behind a white man's hand holding white man's medicine. Only Musyoka knew the reality. He had used a blunted, broken knife which the boy, himself, had last used to cut euphorbia from the hedgerows. The scratch had healed. It had been too late to say prayers, so the boy must die or soon the curse his body surely now protected would infect his whole family, clan and people, and that would be a dark day indeed for the people of Migwani. His knife tore another shaving off the stick. It fell onto a pile of others on the ground by his feet. It, along with the rest, would be gathered up later and burned on the fire. The stick in his hand would be oiled and cared for by his wife and become the trusted tool that she would use to grind maize to flour. The shavings, the discarded waste, helped to make the stick strong and true. This was the way of the world.

Father John had heard the gossip. The town, the market and the church were full of stories and conflicting reports of Mwangangi's pain. Some said he was paralysed and lay poisoned and dying in his father's home. Others claimed he had died under the knife, that his screams had stopped before the job was done and that his life had passed along the paths to his forefathers.

John believed all of the stories and yet none of them. He must see and know for himself. The path down the valley was rugged and steep. In places even walking was tricky and John's motorcycle slithered and skidded on dust and stones alike. When he switched off the engine, the Musyoka household was quiet. Musyoka, seated with his knife and stick, offered him neither greeting nor even recognition.

The hours that followed were confused. Musyoka said nothing to Mwangangi or to John, and not much to anyone else. He was morose and withdrawn, even with other members of his family. Though she knew and trusted Father John, Mwangangi's mother could not allow him to be taken to hospital. Repeatedly she approached her husband and asked his advice, but stolidly, sternly, he refused to speak. Father John was willing to wait no longer. Sometimes helping, sometimes maybe obstructing, Mwangangi's mother watched as John O'Hara seated the boy on the motorcycle pillion. Father John shouted at her, telling her to be quiet and help him to harness the boy to his own body with a length of rope.

It was three in the morning when Sister came back to the convent in Muthale. "Well, Father John," she began with a deep sigh, “I think you’ve saved him.” His eyes closed in a silent prayer. “The blood poisoning has not gone too far and we can treat it, so that should clear up. He has more than one wound. It was no accident, that’s for sure. They are all messy and they will scar. They will take a while, but they will heal. The blood poisoning would have killed him.”

Father John and the other nuns in the room each gave out their own sigh of relief. “Sister, when I go home on leave I’ll go to Kerry and tell them down there that your hospital is working miracles.”

“Tell them no such thing, Father,” she said. Sister had battled against prejudice, bureaucracy and sometimes her own will to finance and build the small brick-built hospital, but she wanted no credit for herself. She began to scoff at him, saying, “You can tell them that with hard work, sweat and the Grace of God we’re saving lives. And that’s enough.” With that, the vitriolic woman known for her boundless energy and quick temper, retired to her room to pray and offer thanks for another life saved before taking her rest.

Five

January 1975

The bus from Nairobi growled to a halt in the town, raising a cloud of dust high above the tin-roofed shops around the marketplace. With the usual blasts on the horn, it had sped between the two lines of concrete buildings which constitute Migwani market, before a screech of tyres had brought it to a halt opposite the Safari Bar, where travellers would always congregate to await its arrival. Scenes that followed were the same every day. Beers would be finished in a hurry as the rush to get on the bus began. Women who had sat all day next to their piles of fruit and vegetables in the marketplace would hoist their loads on their backs and, screening their eyes from the dust whirls cast up by the braking bus, would rush to the door in a mad scramble to be first to get on. No one ever did manage to get straight on the bus, because the man who sold the tickets always stood on the steps to bar the way. But it was the same every day. On Fridays, about half of the hopeful travellers might not even manage to get on the bus at all, and others, who did manage to secure the few square inches of space needed to be squeezed into the aisle, would later be ejected since they had not sold enough of their wares to fund the two-shilling ride home. With dignity offended, they would set off defiantly on foot to walk the five or possibly ten miles home. And all this took time, so some of them would already be half a mile along the road by the time the bus, having renewed its journey and, packed to the rafters, passed by on its way north. These ejected and thus rejected women, of course, would shout their obscene abuse at the driver and his companion as it passed.

Amidst this confusion, slickly dressed young men in Western clothes, with beer swilling in their ever ampler bellies, would run out from the Safari on the corner shouting, "*Ngoja! Ngoja!* Wait! Wait!" They would always pay the fare and always find a seat. If there was none, they expected an old man or woman or, more usually, a child to vacate their own to make room. If, by some strange chance, their pockets were empty when the conductor came round, they would make some empty promise about paying for the journey the following day at the bus company's office in Mwingi. The conductor might look deeply perturbed and might even issue a warning about what might happen if they defaulted, but he would probably not dare to question their word and certainly would never suggest they get off and walk.

Then, with sacks of grain, chickens and goats loaded into the vast luggage box on top, a shout of "*Twende!* Let's go!" would come from the loaders, who would still be trying to negotiate their way down from the roof. There would be a shattering clank from the gearbox and an indeterminate groan or two from some or other moving part as the driver's foot pushed the throttle to the floor and more clouds of dust started to fly. Someone would also have checked that the town's madman, Munyasya, had not tried to prevent further progress by lying down under the wheels, which he often did, requiring the bus to engage reverse for a few metres before manoeuvring around him.

As the abuse started from the walking women, the two young men, who had loaded the freight onto the roof, would swing themselves into the bus from the external ladders welded by the entrance. Ten minutes later, when the dust had settled and the noise of the engines had drifted on past Kyome rock, the town would again be quiet, its dose of madness over for another day, with time again moving slowly, as it had done for as long as anyone might choose to remember.

All this took place out of Janet's sight as she sat drying her hair in the sun and wind, but she still saw everything. She had seen the bus come and go almost every day for nearly six months and could picture without effort the confusion and chaos it brought. In her first few weeks, she had wondered why, when teaching in class, the sound of a bus or indeed any vehicle passing along the road in front of the school would provoke her students to stand for a moment to peer out of the window. As time passed, she learned to do the same herself, and like the others, she did it not because she expected to see anything, but merely because, in this place, time was measured by the sun and buses more clearly than by any clock. It was time to get out of bed when the morning bus rattled up the hill on its way south, bound for Mombasa. It was time for lunch when the midday blue and white *Uhuru na Kazi*, *Freedom and Work*, went out to Nairobi. With the arrival from Nairobi there was time to relax as the sun began to set, and when the night bus from Mombasa sped anonymously through the dark, it was time to put out the lamp and sleep.

Thus it was time to relax. Another school day was over, its classes taught, its new knowledge imparted and, she hoped, absorbed. The day had been like all the rest and she felt happy and contented as she sat on the miniature veranda beneath the overhang by the front door, with the town spread across the far side of the low valley before her. The classrooms were locked, having been swept with the straggling but effective twig brooms the students made themselves. Some boys were still out playing football, but most had walked off down to the dam to find water for washing before the evening meal. Now that the bus had come, the day students would begin their walk home and Janet would relax, surveying the town's unchanging landscape.

As she sat, Father Michael's motorcycle came rasping along the track by the mission. Her eyes followed his progress as he banked the bike around the last corner to enter his driveway through the gap in the hedge. She watched him pull up by the front door and go inside. She knew he would be emptying the haversack in which he carried his priest's robes, his bottles of Mass wine and the tobacco tin containing the thin slivers of the Eucharist. And then there would be the short trip to the fridge at the back of the room to get a beer before collapsing in a tired heap in a not-so-easy chair. But today he unexpectedly reappeared and she watched him restart the bike with a kick and set off along the road in her direction.

Concluding correctly that he would be on his way to see her, she rose from her chair. She was not quite decent enough to receive him, so she went inside to find an extra wrapper. By the time she had re-connected the gas bottle to the cooker, filled the kettle from the water bucket under the sink and set it to boil on the fastest flame, he was already drawing to a halt by the kitchen door. As usual he entered in a flurry.

"Right. I'll have a cup of tea and a slice or two of bread and jam before my dinner," he said, as he marched straight through the kitchen in search of an armchair in the other room.

"Will you have a beer instead?" she asked.

"No, I'll have a beer as well," he replied, offering a gigantic yawn as accompaniment. "No. No. I won't," he said, now rubbing his eyes. "If I have all the enjoyment now there'll be nothing to look forward to later. Just the tea, please. And can I stay for dinner? Mutua had to go home this morning. His wife took sick."

Janet laughed at him. She thought he was a very funny and very sweet man, and truly looked forward to the days when they were able to eat together and talk during the evening. "Of course you can stay. Daniel always cooks far too much anyway."

She brought in the tea on a tray, which she set down on the low coffee table next to the priest's feet. Michael was stretched out with his bush hat over his face.

"Two sugars and plenty of milk, please," he said through the hat and making himself even more comfortable. "Oh Jaysus, that reminds me," he said, suddenly springing to his feet. "I've got a letter for you." From his trouser pocket he produced a rather crumpled blue airmail envelope. "It's from that little fellow from Nzawa in Form Three. What's his name? William? I was over there this afternoon," he said, as he handed the letter to her. "He said it was something very urgent." There was a hint of ridicule in his voice, indicating that he believed it was nothing of the sort.

Her student had definitely written something important. Janet knew that immediately, because the envelope was sealed, thus precluding its reuse. She took the single sheet of paper from the envelope and read the contents. "Michael," she began after a lengthy silence, "please listen to this. It sounds important." Janet waited until he was obviously ready to listen. "Dear Miss Rowlandson, I greet you with happiness and hope that you are well. I am at home in Nzawa, trying very hard to find the school fees for the term, but my father is very poor. I am writing this letter to inform you of the great trouble in our village. The police have come and taken away some of our friends. They are now kept at the prison in Kitui town. One of those taken was Joseph Munyolo from your class at school. He accompanied me here from school last Friday. Miss, the trouble is serious and I fear that Joseph will stay in the prison for a very long time if you do not help him. His mother has tried to see him, but they say that now he is at Kitui and she has no bus fare. Father Michael can tell you what has happened here if you ask him. Yours sincerely, your student, William."

As requested, Father Michael told the full story he had learned just that afternoon from his parishioners in Nzawa. It appeared that it had all started from some trouble in the primary school. Someone had written in charcoal on the Standard Four classroom wall a very abusive and obscene remark about the pedigree of one of the school's Kikuyu teachers. As a result, the teacher and his colleague had become incensed and had systematically beaten every child from the Standard Four class to try to find who had done it. This had all started in the middle of the previous week and the beatings had continued over three days. Of course, when the parents found out they were displeased, to say the least, but it had not been until market day, when lots of people met, talked and realised that every child had been beaten by these men, that the animosity grew. Then, so the story went, a group of men who had been drinking in one of the bars decided to do something about it and went to the school compound to teach the teachers a lesson. They threw stones at the house and broke the windows. One of the teachers then went to the police and made a complaint. A detachment of police came in vans and went to various homes and took people to Mwingi. It seems that the two teachers involved had given them a list of names. Initially they took about thirty people, but then released most of them when the teachers, now probably sober, realised that they couldn't accuse them all, because neither of them could positively identify anyone by name. The police detained six people in the end, because one of the teachers picked them out in a parade. He claimed he knew who had taken part in the stoning of his house. Joseph Munyolo was obviously one of the six.

"Joseph would never have got involved with something like that," said Janet, scoffing at the very idea. "He wouldn't hurt a fly!"

"That would have been my opinion," said Michael, taking a sip of his tea. "But the younger brother was one of those beaten by the teachers. Anyway, that's the story."

"So what should I do? What *can* I do?" asked Janet.

Michael thought for a while. "It's not something I have that much experience with. I have only dealt with criminal things a couple of times, and never in Kenya, not once in the last six, seven years. But there is someone you could probably trust, though he will do you no favours. He's not that kind of man. The kids were taken to Mwingi. That's where the case was lodged, so that will probably be where it will be heard. So that's the place to start, and in Mwingi, for my money, there's only one man to see. Don't go to the police. Go straight to the District Officer, John Mwangangi. His office is the large compound on the other side of the road from the police station. If he can, he'll help. He's a good Catholic."

Janet smiled again. He was always joking, this priest, but fundamentally he was never flippant. His advice was always precise and considered. Without another word, since Michael's advice had effectively concluded the point, she rose from her chair and took the four steps needed to reach the kitchen, where she lit the oven, in which the food Daniel had left was waiting to be re-heated, having first, of course, made sure that the connection to the gas bottle was sound. Daniel had finished early today, Janet having granted him some time off to attend to family matters. She hoped his wife would enjoy the unscheduled visit. She selected two clean glasses from the draining board by the sink and a bottle opener from a box in the cupboard. As she re-entered the living room, daylight was beginning to fade and it was time to light the lamp. Janet's attention was taken for a few seconds by the noise and dust whirl of the orange and white Mrembo from Mombasa. This Mrembo, this handsome young man, was of course a bus, owned by a division of Mulonzya Enterprises of Mwingi, the family firm that also owned the petrol station in Mwingi, the petrol station that was just along the road from John Mwangangi's office, an office she must visit urgently.

Father Michael had reclaimed his place on the settee and once more was feigning sleep beneath his bush hat. "Fancy a beer?" she asked.

"Is the Pope Catholic?" he replied.

Six

February 1962

John was already more than an hour late. Dr Bill Goodman and his wife, Helen, discussed for a moment what they ought to do, but decided to wait on, though the food keeping warm in the oven might spoil. It was not as if they really had a choice. Bill was convinced that John would arrive soon. After all, he had only been in the country for a few months and everything must still seem very strange. He had probably got himself lost on the tube.

Bill retired to the lounge and to his work. On the copious arms of his easy chair were balanced various things that he had gathered about himself that evening. On one side there was a wad of papers and a pen, an empty coffee cup and a half full whisky tot on the other. Carefully he threaded his body into the chair and took the papers onto his lap.

They were not a bad lot this year, he thought, as he scanned through the first written offering of the term from his first year tutorial group. University teaching could be a dull affair without the stimulus of some bright and interested students. In this year's intake there was one student in particular who seemed not only quick to learn, but also eager to teach his tutor and fellow students about things they would otherwise never even consider. A person like that could dominate and destroy a group, but if guided could also be its enduring stimulus.

Bill worried about this student, however. John Mwangangi Musyoka was surely talented, but he was finding it hard to settle into college life. He seemed not to make friends easily and spent every night studying his law books in his hostel room. It would be such a shame, Bill thought, if John's undoubted potential were to go untapped as a result of a breakdown or illness. John was clearly a candidate for such an eventuality, being quiet and timid in college, withdrawn and intensely studious away from it. As part of a strategy to draw him into things, Bill had endeavoured to build a relationship with John that could be stronger than the usual teacher-student mould. Though John hardly drank, appearing to regard the consumption of a glass of beer as more of a personal vice than a source of possible enjoyment, the two of them had already gone to the bar together on a few occasions after lectures. Time spent with John had soon begun to prove unexpectedly enlightening for Bill. He had taught many overseas students, of course, but they were nearly always from middle-class, professional families, representatives of a local elite. But John Mwangangi Musyoka was different. He was clearly from a poor family. He was not at all used to city life and was patently unaware of social mores and other cultural trappings, an ignorance that often seemed to leave him isolated, a reaction or two behind his peers. It was only during these chats in the bar that Bill came to realise how little 'European' or 'Western' life John had ever experienced.

Bill had found it quite incredible to learn that a large number of people in at least one part of the world believed that all European men were priests and all women nuns, because nearly all the white people ever to have lived in that area had been missionaries. But if all Europeans were priests or nuns and therefore celibate, Bill had asked, then how could it be that there were still Europeans? Didn't people see just a slight contradiction here? Bill had thought that John would see the intended joke. Surely he would retract and qualify what he had said. But John answered quite seriously. People did not believe that nuns and priests really lived apart. They had other lives behind closed doors. And besides the word for a white man, *mzungu*, also means a wonderful machine, so who knew what techniques of reproduction these white people might use?

The doorbell rang. John offered no apology for being late. Noting his wife's hackles on the rise, he found himself apologising to Helen on his guest's behalf. He was starting to protect this young man from himself, almost as if he were a son.

Bill had envisaged a long evening. He was quite keen to 'show off' John to his wife, and for quite a while he found himself feeling more than a little nervous as to how she would react. This nervousness was expressed as a constant fussing over John's comfort, offering him drinks he refused, plucking books from his shelves, directing him towards snacks that would only further postpone the meal that was probably already spoilt. John accepted only water and sat with a glass in one hand and one of Bill's selected books in the other, unable to pick up any of the savoury snacks. With Bill in such a socialising frenzy, it seemed that neither Helen nor John could slip in a word edgeways. The less they spoke, the more Bill extemporised, the more he dominated their exchanges and the more Helen allowed her attention to wander. Finally, Helen left the room without a word and served the food.

At table John was served first and immediately set about his meal with a dessertspoon. It was only after Bill and

Helen had exchanged glances and exaggeratedly taken up their knives and forks that John self-consciously licked the spoon clean and followed their example. With obvious embarrassment, he tried to explain that he had still not grown used to using knives and forks at the same time. Bill was sympathetic. Helen was not. She was obviously beginning to feel increasingly uncomfortable in John's company and Bill grew progressively more aware of the tension that was being built, and thus created more via his own compensatory manner.

After a while, however, John noticeably began to relax and talked more freely. He began to ask questions, some of which Helen found quite astoundingly naïve. She found his English difficult to understand and several times switched off her attention whilst he was speaking. Bill again sensed this and effectively repeated everything for her benefit, as if translating, but this only added to the young man's confusion. He asked, for instance, whether all houses in England had running water. Helen, who had heard that question, immediately gave him directions to the toilet, mouthed slowly in what were tantamount to vocal phonetics. "But I think you have not understood," suggested John after a moment's thought, during which he turned his attention back to his food. "Is it really true, Mrs Goodman, that women here do no work? And is it true that few people bother to grow food to eat? In my village every family has a farm and tries to grow all of their own food. Women do a lot of the work. They do the weeding. The men do the ploughing and planting. Everyone helps in the harvest. All of these houses here have gardens, but nobody grows any food, and yet I understand that many women are mainly just staying at home."

"I don't quite understand what you mean when you say 'just staying at home'," said Helen, her voice tinged with both defensiveness and obvious impatience. The man was such a contradiction. Was he being utterly naïve in asking such questions, surely more naïve than any first year law student ought to be? Or was he being provocative, implying that people in suburban Britain ought to be more aware of their privileged status and how little they had to struggle for existence?

"You see, Mrs Goodman, besides bearing children, women in my area must carry wood and water for the household, sometimes from very great distances, sometimes more than five miles. I have lived in Nairobi and seen that for many people life is different from this. But in Kenya, nowhere else is like Nairobi. It is a special place. But here it seems that everyone lives that way. For a Kenyan man, it would seem strange that English men do not require their wives to do more work." Perhaps John did not realise what he was saying. Perhaps.

Bill, who considered the proposition with some humour, interjected. "I suppose it is rather strange, isn't it, dear? Fancy turning over the front garden?"

"Yes, dear. How interesting. I'll bear that in mind."

On one occasion John came close to offending and alienating Helen completely. From the start he had insisted on drinking only water. He seemed to regard the wine they drank with sufficient distaste to want to distance himself from it. He was clearly a thirsty man, however, and soon finished the whole jug of water that Helen had provided at table. He was speaking at the time, trying to describe some aspect or other of his home area to Bill, whom he faced. He reached for the jug and began to pour before registering that it was empty. Almost without breaking the flow of words directed at his tutor, he cast a glance aside to Helen and said, "More water." His stress was placed on the start, with the intonation falling across the words, the flat ending making the phrase a command in Helen's ear. She was visibly and immediately startled, despite her beginning to fulfil the request before pausing to show her shock. But, not wanting to make a scene, she took the jug and refilled it from the kitchen tap. Meanwhile Bill stopped John and explained how he must follow certain rules of politeness in British society and learn to use them constantly. When Helen returned, John apologised, still not understanding what he had done.

"I am sorry," he said. "I have much to learn and hope that you can help to educate me. 'Please' is not a word that exists in my language."

The explanation, though acceptable to Helen as an apology, reinforced her developing opinion that had formed as a result of other things that had transpired. When John spoke of a Kamba woman's life of hard labour and of what she interpreted as his people's lack of politeness, she found it hard to believe how anyone from that background could possibly be regarded as 'educated'. In fact, John had said nothing to create these images. The meaning was entirely in her imagination and, perhaps, in the collective imagination of her own people, a code of assumptions that few were ever called upon to question.

Later, with the meal finished and the evening still quite young, Bill suggested that the three of them should adjourn to the lounge. John rose, picking up the napkin he had completely ignored until then and used it, after dipping it into his glass, to wipe his hands, as if it were a small towel. Like any other skill, this was another he would have to learn. Immediately, and to Bill's consternation, he expressed his desire to leave.

"Well actually," said Bill, "I had wanted to talk to you about this piece you gave me today..." So saying he walked briskly into the other room and returned with his sheaf of papers.

But as he re-entered the dining room, a confused-looking John Mwangangi Musyoka confirmed that he must leave. "It is right," he confirmed. And go he did.

"What did he mean when he said that? 'It is right'," asked Helen.

"I have not the faintest idea," admitted Bill. It was not until fifteen years later that Bill would understand. Then, seated in John's father's house and having eaten rice and soup, he watched as the host stood up to announce the end of the meal. "We must leave now," John whispered to Bill. "It is an insult to the cook to stay when the food is finished. It is like saying the meal was poor and you expect more."

Seven

January 1975

Oh Mwanza, John thought. If only life were a mirror! What image would you see of yourself?

Mwanza lived within a whirlwind of his own making. It accompanied him wherever he went and sucked in those unfortunate enough to come within range. To spend time with him was to contract activity like it was an infectious disease. No one was immune, but each person he knew had found an individual way of coping with the challenge. Janet, who saw a lot of him socially, found it best to head straight for an armchair after showing him out. There she would sit for ten minutes or more to convince herself that she was still capable of relaxing. She thought him rather like a dog chasing its own tail, living life by turning ever decreasing circles, always on the move and preferably in two places at once. Nevertheless, he was always warm and hospitable and had invited Janet to eat with his family at home on several occasions. She valued these experiences because it gave her the opportunity to sit and talk with Mwanza's wife, Rose, in her own home, where she felt relaxed. Rose was the opposite of her husband: quiet, restrained, thoughtful and considerate. She was also wise, and Janet had learned much from their conversation.

For Father Michael, who had known him longer, Mwanza's novelty had worn off long ago. The two men met very often, too often for Michael, since, besides being headmaster of a primary school sponsored by the Catholic Church, Mwanza was also a tireless worker for the project, involved in committees for fund-raising and sports events, as well as the compulsory school governors. Invariably, ten minutes of Mwanza left Michael either exhausted or angry. In search of any respite, Michael would make excuses or tell lies about having an engagement with someone else, just to get away from the man. Michael would bid goodbye, usually three or four times out of sheer necessity, and then, without risking a single backward glance, would make a dash for his motorcycle, muttering, "Stupid whore," under his breath. On a number of occasions, a mile down the road with his throttle full open, Michael had realised that he had left Mwanza alone in the mission, having offered the excuse that he, Father Michael, was in a rush to get home. One could rest assured, however, that Mwanza would simply move on to his next appointment without ever registering the contradiction. Mwanza's fame was universal and everyone would express the same opinion when his name was mentioned. "That man talks very much."

John, on the other hand, had only recently met him and had grown quickly impatient. He had tried repeatedly to impress upon him that the District Officer was a very busy man, that he had business to attend – a rank untruth that day – and that he had expected him to have prepared a written statement that could be read verbatim to the court. But no, Mwanza had monopolised the morning and left it, along with John Mwangangi, tired, limp and unproductive. John had been informed about the productivity of each family's farm and the headcount of goats and cows owned by each of the farmers. He had been told about a brother of one of the accused, who led the singing in church every Sunday by beating time on a five-string guitar, which he had traded some years before for a copy of the Concise Oxford Dictionary made redundant by his leaving school. John had heard more, and more and yet more.

Eventually John had raised his arms and demanded he stop, following this with a sharp slap of the palms on his desk. "Mr Mwanza!" John had pleaded. He found the silence that followed such unexpected bliss that he refused to break it for some time, but when he continued, his words were almost shouted. "I invited you to this office today in your capacity as head of Nzawa Primary School. I stated clearly in my letter that I wanted you to provide character references for the students from your school who are now in custody, and also for the two teachers who have brought the action against them. Since it is merely an administrative matter, please return to Nzawa, write the references and send them by mail to me at this Office, DO Mwingi. If you can manage to complete them by tomorrow, then you can send them to me via my Land Rover, which will pass through Nzawa in the afternoon on the way back from Kathiko. I will instruct the driver to call at the school and ask for you. Thank you, Mr Mwanza."

And with that John rose to his feet and offered his hand across the desk. Mwanza shook hands and left, giving the door an unintentional but almighty slam. He mounted his bicycle and set off along the road, ringing his bell almost constantly and greeting all passers-by, like some be-wheeled town crier. Before he had cycled a quarter of a mile, he met Janet, dismounted, and set off back along the road with her to return to John Mwangangi's office.

John heaved a massive sigh of relief when Mwanza left. He sat quietly for a minute or more to collect the thoughts that Mwanza had scattered and then, half-turning in his chair, he leaned back to push open the sliding door in the wall. "Syengo," he called, "you can take lunch now."

Syengo replied quickly, causing John to turn just a little more so that he could see through the hatch and scan part of Syengo's front office. "Sir, there is a teacher here to see you." John's heart sank as he caught sight of Mwanza hovering in front of Syengo's desk. "Shall I send her in?" There was no answer. "She has come all the way from Migwani to see you, sir. It's about the disturbance at Nzawa School."

John looked at his watch for a moment, relieved that at least it wasn't Mwanza who again wanted another audience. "Send her in."

Janet entered the office to find John reopening the file on the case. It was already thick with papers. On seeing her, he stopped abruptly, his impatience instantly changing to a warm smile of recognition. "You are... Miss Rowlandson from the secondary school in Migwani?"

"That's right. I am very pleased to meet you again, Bwana Mwangangi."

There followed some minutes of light conversation. "We met about a month ago, I think. Yes, it was after your school's *Harambee Day*," he said. His voice had a lightness of tone that almost communicated relief. "Father Michael introduced us." He enquired about her impressions of Kenya, of how she had come to teach in Migwani and how she found teaching Kenyan children compared to English. They even shared a few words about London, a place both of them knew intimately, it seemed. It was Janet who feigned impatience this time.

"Bwana Mwangangi," she said, "do you think we could get down to business? A friend of mine is waiting for me outside and we are going to have lunch together."

Remembering his own impatience with Mwanza, John

apologised and invited her to state her business.

Janet explained that she had been told a student of hers had been arrested following the disturbance at Nzawa. She had come to ask whether the student might be released so that he could attend an important interview for a place in the Village Polytechnic in a few days' time. She, herself, would provide any bail that might be necessary. She had brought the money with her.

"Let me first check if we have in fact arrested your student. A lot of those originally detained were sent home after the identification parade. What is the boy's name, Miss Rowlandson?"

"Joseph Munyolo," she replied, straining in her chair in an attempt to read the names on the paper John held.

"Let's see," he said as he prepared to read the list. "Kiloo Mbiti, Mbusya Mwanga, Kimanzi Munovo..."

"That's him," said Janet.

John said nothing, He looked at her across the desk in some confusion. "I thought you said his name was Munyolo?" He stressed the second name and then spelled it out.

"His Kamba name is Kimanzi," said Janet. "Joseph Kimanzi Munyolo. That's him, all right. The police officer who wrote down his name must have spelt it wrongly."

John scanned every paper in the file, seeking out every reference to the boy. It took time. Janet suspected that he was deliberately stalling. She started to fidget, running her thumb along the edge of the desk. "There is some mistake," he said. "The name is Munovo throughout, not Munyolo. I cannot make an order for release on bail if there is any confusion over the prisoner's identity." He began to flick back through the papers.

On the outside, Janet remained calm. Inside she had begun to boil a little, heated by what she considered to be trivial bureaucratic nonsense. "Would it help if I checked with the police officer who took the boys' names? He might have made a mistake."

"Yes, we could try that," said John still fingering through the papers. He then leaned back and banged on the hatch door. There was no reply so he banged again, much harder than before.

Now we'll have to wait for the inquest on why there's no answer, thought Janet, her frustration growing. This is just to put me off. "Shall I go across to the police station?"

"I think you had better," said John. "My clerk has gone for lunch."

Janet rose from her chair and left the office, the increased speed of her movements giving away her lack of trust in the current process. Outside, she broke into a run, telling the waiting Mwanza that she would be back in a minute. She did not stop to reply to his enquiry.

Across the road, she had some difficulty locating the officer who had made the arrests. The policeman on duty was convinced that he had gone for lunch. The officer in charge, whom she immediately demanded to see, was in the adjoining room. He declared that the officer in question was away 'investigating'. The action was left open-ended, as if the policeman had embarked on a mission to seek out misdemeanours. Janet's impatience became visible as no progress was made. After ten minutes of more indecision, the man she sought appeared. He had simply been to the toilet at the far end of the compound and had stayed on for a quick cigarette. One by one the runners sent out to look for him returned with their negative reports stifled in mid-sentence by his presence. Still more time was needed, however, to establish once and for all that this officer was the one who had documented the case and taken the boys' statements, and more still to establish the veracity of the claim that the District Officer wanted to see him, there being, of course, no documentary evidence of this fact. But eventually Janet's persuasive attributes overcame the collective reluctance and the officer crossed the road with her back to the DO's compound.

John explained that there might be some confusion over one of the names on the Nzawa list. The policeman answered in Kikuyu - no wonder he got the spelling wrong, Janet thought - confirming that he had written the names exactly as each of the accused had instructed. Munovo was the correct name.

John turned to face Janet. She thought he looked sincere, but was not convinced. "Well, Miss Rowlandson, I am afraid I cannot issue a bail notice for this boy. I suggest that you come to the preliminary hearing on Friday so that you can identify the boy in person. If you travelled to Kitui to do that, then the officer in charge would have to notify me of the result in writing before I could act. It would be Friday at the earliest before I received his reply. So come to the hearing on Friday, speak on the boy's behalf and then I will consider your request for bail."

Janet agreed, but her calm exterior was a conscious mask to hide an inner fury. "Of course it's the same boy" went around and around, unspoken in her head. In a final attempt to convince Bwana Mwangangi, she went out to the reception and returned with the boy's mother, who had accompanied her from Migwani and who had waited patiently and silently throughout in the waiting area. There followed a protracted argument between her and John in Kikamba, but there was no change in his position. The aging woman, who spoke no English and only a little Swahili, scoffed and left in a temper without waiting for Janet.

John watched her leave, shook his head and said, "I am

sorry, Miss Rowlandson, but I simply cannot do it. These are simple people …" he began, raising his arms to signify what Janet interpreted to mean all people outside the confines of his office, "and it is difficult to explain the law to them because they have no concept of how it works."

They are not the only ones, thought Janet, scathingly.

"Come to the hearing on Friday with the boy's mother and we will see what can be done then." There was a finality about his tone.

Janet got up and left the office, bidding John Mwangangi a curt goodbye and not offering a handshake. John placed the wad of papers in a file and locked it in his cabinet. As he closed the office door, pulling it hard to ensure the latch engaged, his thoughts passed from Nzawa School and came to a rueful rest on contemplating the half-hour of his lunch break he had just lost.

After rejoining Mwanza and Munyolo's mother outside, Janet suggested they go into town and find a teashop. She felt disinclined to talk about what had happened, regretting most of all the waste of a whole morning and the necessity to devote perhaps another whole day on Friday. The three of them took lunch together. Janet spoke very little Kikamba and so could communicate with the boy's mother only via Mwanza, who revelled in his position as interpreter.

"The woman is saying, Miss Rowlandson, that the man is doing something very wrong because in Kikamba the names Munovo and Munyolo are the same."

Janet's impatience was obvious. "He's obviously just another of these jumped-up government employees sitting in his office and creating bureaucratic complications to help justify his position. He has to do that, otherwise he would have nothing to do!"

For once Mwanza remained silent, Janet's tirade being

beyond his translation skills. When he did speak, Janet's attention wavered at first, as it always did when Mwanza piped up, thinking that he might be changing the subject and starting to gossip in his usual way, but she soon began to register what he meant and was deeply shocked.

"Miss Rowlandson, I would love to ride a motorcycle like Father Michael's. I have a friend who can sell me one at a very fair price. He has bought it, but does not have enough money to buy petrol for it, so it just sits at his house not being used. He has asked me several times if I want to buy it, but I have said no, and I have said no because of one reason. I have enough money to buy the motorcycle, but I do not yet have a licence to ride it and I would not be able to afford to pay the bribe needed to get one. This man today is not making trouble because he feels that there is any difference between the names. He is using the policeman's mistake to ask for a bribe. There is no difference between the names."

Janet felt suddenly enlightened, but not comforted. "If that's true, then he might not even grant bail on Friday if I do not bribe him."

"That is true," Mwanza agreed. "Let me tell you the experience of a friend of mine..."

Janet nodded from time to time but was not listening.

The journey home to Migwani was hotter and stuffier than ever. The bus waited a full hour in Mwingi market while more than two hundred people jostled and pushed to get on. Though she had travelled on such packed buses many times, her unacknowledged desire to preserve a personal space, and her deeply felt though unconscious revulsion when it was not granted, added to produce a sum of great embarrassment and discomfort. She was lucky in that, as usual, the crowd parted at the first sight of her white face to allow her to get on first, a favour which on most occasions she refused with a sharp but polite shake of the head. But today she simply accepted, because she knew she would get a seat. An hour or more later, after being squashed hard up against a jammed window on the sunny side of the bus, she wished she had refused, stayed outside and tried to beg a lift from a passing truck or Land Rover. Perhaps she might have been home by now.

Mwingi market had been packed that day. The marketplace resembled a nest of human ants without the soldiers. People had brought their cows and goats. It seemed that everyone wanted to sell these days. People needed the cash to buy food to supplement what their *shambas* could not grow. Famine caused by the failure of the last rains was starting to bite and it was now very much a buyer's market. So the hopeful had stood all day in the sun with their animals, repeatedly turning away the small but canny band of purchasers. By the end of the day, prices had fallen to rock bottom, and goats were being hurriedly sold for as little as twenty shillings, the thought of walking home to an empty cooking pot having got the better of many sellers. As businessmen brought around their lorries and pick-ups to load up the animals they had bought, animals whose meat would sell for ten shillings a kilo in a Nairobi butcher's shop, those people who had rejected all offers began to untie their animals ready for the long walk home. Few had bought, but many had sold, and it was they who queued for the bus holding the half sacks of maize or, for the lucky ones who had sold a bull, sacks of beans to fill their families' bellies until the next market day, when the entire scene would be repeated, repeated that is until all of the family's animals had been sold. Then there was not much to do except find a suitable tree, sit, and wait for the next rain, not due for some months.

The woman who shared the seat with Janet and Joseph

Munyolo's mother had sold two goats for fifty shillings and had bought a nearly full sack of maize. She entered the bus when already more than sixty others were crammed onto the seats. Noticing immediately that Janet was smaller and of slighter build than most, the woman made straight for the seat which, of course was only meant to accommodate two, and, finding an unoccupied corner onto which she could place a small percentage of her behind, she sat and lifted the sack of maize onto her lap, panting loudly, as rivers of sweat ran down between her ample breasts. She made a comment about the heat and fanned herself rapidly with a loosened corner of the wrapper she wore around her upper body, and gave out a long deep sigh. Over the next few minutes she carefully adjusted her position, each time nudging a per cent or two more of her buttocks onto the seat, using her significant weight to ease the other two occupants marginally closer to the window. By the time the bus reached Migwani, she had found enough space to have also planted the sack of maize on the seat beside her to ease the pressure on her thighs, leaving Janet so squashed against the window that her own behind was actually against the side of the bus, with only a small portion of one leg actually in contact with the seat. The woman would have been put off the bus back in Mwingi had Janet not paid her fare in a vain attempt to try to get the show on the road. Even Janet's poor Kikamba was enough to follow what was said.

"Where to?"

"Kwa Siku."

"Four shillings and eighty cents," ordered the conductor, beginning to write the ticket.

"But I have no money," replied the woman with an air of total innocence.

"Either you have the money or you get off," said the

young man, still commanding. He seemed to be very angry indeed, having already dealt with several people who were trying to get a free ride.

"*Aiee*," said the woman in feigned total surprise. She eyed the slightly built young man from within her enormous frame, peering over the top of the sack on her lap. She seemed to suggest that it would take an army to move her if she refused to budge. "But you can afford to take me. Look at all these other people who are paying you their fares. What does it matter to take one more person?"

"And at least sixty of them have the same story as you. You have money," said the man, pointing at the sack.

"But I have stood all day to buy this food for my family," she pleaded. But the tone of her voice said much more than this. She knew that the bus was already overloaded, that the company was rich and could afford to take her for nothing, that the man was asking her family to go without food so that the bus owner could make more profit.

At this point Janet interrupted. As she saw things, the argument could easily go on forever. He demanded the fare. She was not going to pay and neither was she going to move. And she was too big and heavy to be helped off the bus. So Janet produced a five-shilling note and paid the fare, indicating that the woman could have the twenty cents change. This unfortunately did not help matters. An old man sitting in front, who had just gone through the same routine with the conductor, only to have eventually produced the money for the ticket from a knotted handkerchief inside his shirt, stood up and shouted to announce to the whole bus that this was not fair. If this European woman was so rich, then she should pay for everyone. This fat woman, he said, pointing to the seat behind, should not get special treatment. With the two flat yellow pennies, the change from her fare, nestling in the palm of her hand, the woman also announced her delight to the entire bus and held up the twenty cents as evidence of what had transpired. The woman then turned to the side and thrust the coins into Janet's hand, indicating that they were a gift that could not be accepted and the general argument began to subside, ignoring the fact that the woman kept hold of the ticket. The conductor moved on to the seat behind to begin a similar process all over again. Janet sighed out of frustration and tried in vain to doze off on her shrinking seat.

And so it was with great relief that she finally made her way off the bus in Migwani, negotiating her way down the central aisle, stepping over buckets and sacks of maize, stooping to avoid bundles of sugar cane propped against the overflowing luggage rack, pausing on the way to avoid stepping on a trussed chicken or a goat's leg. With a perfunctory wave to the window where Joseph's mother now sat to continue her journey, she set off despondently towards the mission to tell Father Michael the details of her fruitless journey. As she passed in front of the south-facing bus, her clothes wet and her face dripping with sweat, she had to step aside as two of the luggage men violently pulled to one side the wiry frame of Munyasya, who had lain down beneath the wheels. He protested, shouting at them in his strange spitting voice. But he could move only slowly, so once he was clear of the bus, the men knew it would take him a minute or more to get to his feet.

As she crossed the road, the bus set off and by the time it had travelled the thirty yards to be level with her, it was already trailing a high swirling cloud of dust, which added a light ochre coating to her entire frame. And then, for good measure, the driver clanked at the gears and revved the engine in neutral, producing a puff of black fumes to add flavour to the cocktail. The mission was empty when she arrived, but thankfully the door was unlocked, so she went inside to find an easy chair and within a minute, she was asleep.

She awoke with a start when Mutua dropped a knife on the floor. Michael was sitting opposite her reading *Time* magazine. He looked up and said, "So you've returned to the land of the living. You must have been whacked."

"What time is it?" she asked drowsily.

"Eight," he replied, anticipating her surprise.

"What? I've been asleep for three hours," exclaimed Janet, as if she had lost something irretrievably.

Michael turned to Mutua and asked him to bring in a beer for Janet and then serve dinner. Raising herself in the chair to accept the beer bottle, she groaned loudly as the stiffness of her limbs resisted movement.

"You look like you've been raped," said Michael. Janet cast him a knowing look. "What's wrong? Did Mwangangi give you a hard time?"

"He did, but the reason why I'm so shattered is the journey. It was…"

"Mwingi market day," interrupted Michael, nodding, "and the bus was somewhat more than full."

"The bus was full - full stop!"

"So what happened?" asked Michael, sitting back.

She felt the first cold mouthful of beer run down inside her. It was one of those blissful occasions when you could feel the progress of the liquid all the way down to the stomach. And with it went the dust of the journey, the taste of fumes and the thirst of a day. She felt immediately refreshed and revived. And then, after a long sigh, she related the events of the day, finishing with, "Mwanza reckons he wanted a bribe."

Michael looked thoughtful for a moment and then spoke. "Mwanza would, the stupid whore. No. No, I don't buy that one for a minute. Mwangangi would never ask for a bribe. He's above that. Mwanza should have his mouth sewn up."

"So you think that if I go on Friday as requested, I will get Joseph out on bail?"

"If Mwangangi finds no objection and, if you come up with the money, of course, he will do nothing to prevent it. I'm sure of that." Again he thought for a moment before continuing, somewhat more slowly and pensively. "But there might be a problem. The case has become quite serious." Michael listed the charges against the defendants, counting them out on his fingers: creating a disturbance, damage to property, actual bodily harm on one of the teachers, using abusive language. "Knowing Mwangangi, he might not allow any bail at all. He tends to get very impatient with that type of case, the type where people try to take the law into their own hands. He is very keen to make an example of people who don't use the proper channels. Had people from Nzawa gone to him with their complaints about the teachers, he would have investigated. He would have been down there like lightning and he would not have let it go until he had got to the bottom of things. But if people act without authority… He gives people a fair deal, and he doesn't take bribes. He has probably concluded that they will have to stay in custody for their own and others' safety."

"Then why didn't he say that instead of making so much of the spelling of the kid's name?" asked Janet, her frustration flooding back.

Michael laughed and shook his head, saying, "He might be a young man, university educated and all, but he's still a Kamba! You know, they're just like Kerrymen. They can never give a straight answer to a straight question. Ask a Kerryman the way to the post office and he'll answer, 'Oh, so you want to buy stamps?'"

“And what about Limerick people?” asked Janet, laughing.

“They’re all the same. We’re all people and we’re all a crowd of stupid whores!” And with that they both got up and crossed the room to the table where Mutua was laying out the evening meal.

Eight

May 1951

Contrary to Sister Mary's belief that Mwangangi would recover quickly, the boy appeared to make only slow progress. The wound produced by his father's deliberately barbarous treatment during circumcision had completely healed in no time. Sister Mary grew progressively more concerned, however, as it became clear that, as well as blood poisoning, there was evidence of complications one would only associate with a chemical poison of some sort. If this was true, then the boy had been deliberately poisoned. He had scratches over his thighs. They were not deep, but each one had become red and inflamed with pustules that reminded her of nettle stings. And the effect seemed to be spreading. She tried a number of treatments which seemed to work for a while, but then the inflammation returned.

And then one of her junior nurses suggested that she knew the problem and knew a cure. Much to Sister's fascination, the nurse went off into the bush for an hour and came back with a bagful of leaves. These she steeped in milk and then applied the infusion to the affected area, repeating the process every hour or so. In a day the redness had gone. After another day the pustules vanished and by the next the boy was cured. Sister Mary asked the nurse to explain the process. The young girl did not have enough English vocabulary to communicate the details, so she led Sister by the hand out of the hospital and along the road for a few hundred yards where a large patch of succulents grew amongst rocks. This was the plant, the nurse explained. She described its white sap that could be dried and made into a poison. It was used to poison hunter's arrows, being applied as a sticky resin to the barbs that were shaved back just behind the small head. The pin-like barbs always made a graze on the animal's skin, even when the arrowhead itself did not pierce the hide. If the hunter waited and followed the animal, the poison would work into the wound and slow it down within a couple of hours, so that he could finish it off. Because the barbs were sharp, the nurse told her, the hunters themselves were always pricking their fingers and so regularly poisoned themselves. But there was an antidote, which was the infusion of leaves and milk she had used on Mwangangi. Sister asked her if the poisoning could have been an accident. She said it might be possible.

The boy's health did return. When Father John O'Hara paid his visits, Sister would make sure that he was fully briefed on what had happened, that the boy had been poisoned and that without the contribution of the young nurse his condition might have got much worse. "The only thing that matters is that he's getting better, thanks be to God," was O'Hara's only comment. Privately, however, he was wrestling with what to do when the time came to reunite the boy with his family and his father.

After two weeks in hospital, Mwangangi was discharged and returned to Migwani on John O'Hara's motorcycle. The boy himself had only a suspicion that his illness had been deliberately caused by his father, but he knew he had done wrong and he accepted that he deserved to be punished. What he did not understand was how severe that punishment might have been had it not been for the contribution of a young nurse, whose name he would not remember. Father John O'Hara, who made a second trip to the hospital to collect the boy, was apprehensive about what would happen when he took the boy home, so much so that he had already made enquiries and drawn up a plan as to what he should do if Musyoka would not readmit him into the family.

They stopped on the way at the mission in Migwani, where Father John and Mwangangi sat and talked about the future. First there was his postponed baptism into the Church. John asked him a couple of questions to test his knowledge of the catechism. They were answered perfectly and in full, of course, the boy explaining that he had used his time in hospital to do some extra study from the copy that Father John had given him on his first visit. The boy explained further that he had been very bored in hospital. Having nothing else to do, he had memorised the book. John O'Hara laughed at this, but then began to realise that the boy was serious. He chose two paragraphs at random, prompting Mwangangi with the first few words. In both cases, he continued word perfect to the end of the section, leaving the priest quite speechless, impressed, perplexed and immediately considering how this talent might be developed. The two remained silent for a minute or more.

"You have an excellent knowledge of the Church's teaching, young man," O'Hara said reassuringly. "I can arrange the baptism for next Sunday, if you want."

The boy was immediately proud. "I also want to ask you, Father, about the name I will take as a Christian. You said that it should be Pat… Pat…" he could not pronounce the name. There was no letter 'r' in his language.

"Patrick," said John. "It's a fine name to choose, my boy. Your church is dedicated to him and a finer saint or more Christian man it would be hard to find."

Mwangangi's small body, lost in the large armchair, heaved a little as he continued nervously. "But Father…" He looked up to see O'Hara's eyes glaring at him across the room. He was afraid. "Father, I want to have the same name as you. I want to be called John."

John O'Hara was deeply moved, but tried not to show it. His love for this boy had always been strong, but had intensified to an almost paternal affection since his illness. He was not quite sure what he might say or feel. Thus he said nothing for some time as he fought to control the tears that he wanted to cry. His face was set in a stern unchanging expression, but his colour changed. Gradually, and much to Mwangangi's growing fright, the priest's skin turned from light pink to bright red. Mwangangi had never before seen a white man blush and found the red skin, standing out in contrast to his prematurely silver-white hair and black bushy eyebrows quite frightening. And through this the priest's clear blue eyes seemed to pierce him with their steel gaze. It was hard to look at blue eyes, thought Mwangangi, who swore that when he felt them meet his own gaze, he could feel them piercing his head. Why did Father John remain silent? He had gone too far. He had offended him. To share someone's name is a difficult thing to ask.

Suddenly John O'Hara rose from his chair and walked out of the room. Mwangangi half rose to follow, started to ask what might be the matter and then sank back into his chair feeling dejected, already constructing his apology. He was not sure what he had done, but he knew it was wrong.

In his own room, Father John O'Hara wiped the tears from his eyes and knelt before the crucifix on his desk.

Aloud, he begged Jesus Christ's forgiveness for crying, for feeling such misplaced pride. He prayed for the boy's future and then bent forward to kiss the cross and whisper a repeated amen.

The door opened slowly. "Is it all right, Father?" asked Mwangangi timidly.

John jumped to his feet and shouted at the boy for coming into his room without knocking. Mwangangi felt sure that he would be beaten and cowered away in fear from John's outstretched arm. But the arm held him and embraced him. "Of course it's all right," said John after a moment. "Of course it's all right."

Mwangangi's face lit up with joy. He threw his arms around John's neck, embracing him as he would embrace his own father. "Thank you, thank you, Father John, thank you," said the boy, close to tears but not crying.

"But you must promise me something, Mwangangi," said John O'Hara a few minutes later. "You must promise me that you will never do anything to disgrace the name because, if you do, it will be my name that you will disgrace."

"Father, how could I do anything to bring disgrace on your name?" answered Mwangangi, still overjoyed. "I will try with God's help to do only good things in your name. I promise to work extremely hard at school and on my father's farm so that I can go to secondary school and become an educated man like you. I will work so hard that people will see that only good things can come from that name. More than that, Father," continued the boy, eager to justify his claim, "I wish to join the seminary and become a Father like you."

"Ah, boy, that is a very long way in the future. Think of today, and tomorrow will take care of itself." John was still close to joyful tears when the boy spoke again.

"Sister Mary told me that I might have died had you not taken me to the hospital," said Mwangangi with a confused and frightened look in his eyes.

"That is not for me to say," said John, "but it is for me to say that it is time we took you home, so go and fetch your book, we must set off now if I am to get back here before dark."

While Mwangangi retrieved his copy of the catechism, O'Hara, thinking that the boy might like to read some more, selected four volumes from his bookshelves – a Bible, a concise encyclopaedia, a history of Ireland and the complete works of W. B. Yeats.

Nine

December 1974

It must be a nightmare. Janet was very nearly running towards the mission. The disappointment that had grown all day had been overtaken by fear, perhaps an irrational, stupid fear that she scolded herself for feeling.

The day had begun perfectly. School had been dismissed for the term at lunchtime to enable the boarding students to complete their often long journeys home in daylight. With their usual keenness to depart, they ran from the straggling assembly lines to collect their boxes and set off in the direction of the town as a smiling noisy group with an obvious purpose and pace. Janet walked with them, very much at the centre of things, a haversack slung on her back, packed and ready for the lunchtime bus to Nairobi. After four months of long drop toilets and cold showers from a bucket, she was quite bursting with excitement at the thought of the city with its amenities and the long-awaited chance to spend some time with the other volunteers she had not seen since their training course.

For once, however, today's skies were dark with clouds. Clouds are a sign of rain, says a proverb, and the platitude had again proven true. For an hour a violent storm raged and the town was transformed. Huddled together under the overhangs of the shops' tin roofs the group of would-be travellers sat to witness the changes. With the first spots of rain people ran for shelter, leaving the marketplace, usually jammed with business and noise on a Friday, deserted. Even the goats, left straining at their tether throughout the storm huddled silently together, no longer bleating in vain for the return of their owners. The haste with which the change was made, at first, lent humour to the scene. Old women, whose day was usually spent in a toothless cackle of conversation punctuated by loud laughter, as they sat by their piles of tomatoes and fruit, jumped to their feet on feeling the first spots of rain and worked faster than any machine, tying together the corners of their sacking on which they displayed their wares for sale. With this done and the sacks slung over their shoulders, one by one they ran for the cover of the nearby teashop where the talking would continue over glasses of sweet tea and slices of dry bread. Initially this only added to Janet's and the students' amusement, but as the storm continued and the rain fell ever harder, their spirits waned from elation to boredom and finally to disappointment.

Here, rain was something different from anything Janet had known before. There were no drops of water. As if a sky-borne dam had burst, it fell in wide glassy sheets, obscuring even the tree in the marketplace, only a few yards from where they stood. There was no sound of raindrops hitting the ground or roofs, only the blank roar of a deluge, mingled with a growing trickle of the flow.

The road, hard, sandy and dry only a few minutes before, became a river, now carrying all manner of waste in its flow. From time to time, twigs, tin cans, beer bottles and paper melded with mud to dam the open gullies that served as roadside drains. These trapped the water which poured from the roofs, such as the one where Janet and her friends sheltered, and into this washed the cattle dung and goat droppings from the marketplace. Usually dung would remain where it fell and would quickly dry without smell in the harsh sun and dry air. After a week or so, after being tossed and ruffled by snuffling dogs and goats, or even eaten by a cow blinded by disease, faeces and any other rubbish left over from the market would be powdered, mixed with dust, absorbed and transformed, until it became dust itself. But today the detritus swirled together with a cocktail of red earth and rain water, and today it smelled, smelled so much it prompted Janet and her student fellow travellers to seek shelter elsewhere.

She had never seen rain like this. As they moved along the row of shops, braving the muddy gaps between, she noticed that small holes were starting to open in the softer earth where no puddles formed. It was just as they reached the restaurant front that some of these holes started to issue something else she had never seen before. Clouds of flying black ants started to emerge. Like geysers, the nests seemed to eject their contents from the earth. As if propelled by a great pressure, the dark columns buffeted by rain and wind thrust towards the grey sky. In an apparent silence of frenzied wing beats, the insects searched for a mate surely knowing that only one of their number would find the queen. Within a few short seconds, detached wings began to fall to earth, fluttering like black sycamore seeds. With their life cycle nearly complete in a few moments, the now flightless ants fell back to earth to land in piles, and then to be washed like dirt into the gullies.

As the rain fell ever harder, the entire marketplace was soon awash. Here and there the roadside gullies became torrents whose sides started to erode, with large clods of mud collapsing to form their own new dams. The travellers realised, but did not admit to one another, that within an hour the road would be broken. And so it was. A gaping trench grew wider and deeper by the minute, as a cascading flow of water, debris and grit followed the contour of the land across the road just beyond the last of the shops, and away into the valleys beyond. It became obvious that, even if the bus were to arrive, it would go no further than Migwani today. The travellers were no longer a laughing band. Now glum-faced they waited against all reason, willing the growl of the bus to appear above the hissing of the rain, but knowing that they would go nowhere that day.

When the rain eventually did stop, the only sound to break the air was the continued, but diminishing, trickling of the roadside rivers. In time, the goats began to bleat again and soon, ankle deep in mud, the owners trudged and slithered across the marketplace to reclaim their animals. The walk home would be long and difficult now, so market was finished for the day as its participants drifted away. Only now could the full extent of the damage be seen. Besides the trench across the road in the town, down towards the school at the edge of the town, just fifty yards from the marketplace, where the road was carried by a small embankment between the heads of two deeply rutted low valleys, a drain had dammed and the rain water from the town had flowed across the road, which had simply disappeared. Where it should have been, only a gaping hole remained, easily eight feet deep and ten across and looked, from the town, like a tooth dissolved from the jaw of the land. There would be no traffic through Migwani for some days, not until a Ministry of Works grader, a rare animal at best of times, had visited and left its mark. It would be a week, at least.

Resigned, but still reluctant, several of the students bid Janet goodbye and set off to walk home or to the next town, where they might find a lift to somewhere on their way.

Some of the group, providing there was no more rain, might be home in a few hours. As the students departed, some north towards Mwingi, others south towards Kitui and still others taking to the paths away from the main road towards Thitani, Janet was flooded with a new loneliness. Disappointment willed her to cry, but reason reshaped despair into mere undirected anger.

Only a few students stayed behind with her. They all lived too far away to walk and all needed at least two buses to complete their journeys, so they were resigned to the reality that they should stay another night in the school's dormitories and set out again early the next day, hoping that a few running repairs might just get a bus past the obstacles. Joseph Mutuli was the brightest of the group in every respect. The son of a Baptist minister, he had learned English by reading the Bible. As his teacher, Janet inevitably found that she punctuated every conversation with instructions to use 'you' not 'thou', 'your' not 'thy'. Joseph would shake his head and slap his leg, saying, "I am to be forgetting it all the time." How strange, Janet thought, that now she did not even try to correct the tenses of his verbs. The progressive present had become a norm that even she now used herself. "Even myself," she said over a cup of tea, "I am not to be using the correct English."

"Ah," scoffed Joseph, "but it cannot be true. It cannot be that an English person is not speaking good English."

Janet smiled and asked the owner of the restaurant to bring some food. She had been bound for Nairobi and had sent her cook home, having also not bothered to buy any groceries in the market that morning. So there was nothing to eat at home. Despite having been warned by many not to eat the local food, she followed the boys' example and attacked the plate of stewed goat and chopped doughy chapatti with great zeal. It was good food.

Michael Kitheka was from Kyuso in the far north of the district. He had been waiting for a different bus, but, of course, it too had not arrived. He was the tallest in the school, built like a pipe cleaner, and he was surely no boy. Janet judged his age might be anything between seventeen and twenty. In fact, she learned some time later, that he was twenty-six, four years older than his teacher. Dressed in khaki shorts and a simple short-sleeved shirt, however, he remained a schoolboy. Had the bus arrived, within eight hours he would have been transformed into the head of a household, the owner of a small farm, a few cows, a wife and four children. At this stage, Janet would never have believed it, had she known. To her he was simply a youth with immature ideas. Above all he was a discipline problem in the school. Several times he had been found drinking in bars and had been suspended from school or punished with bouts of manual labour. Had the school records carried his correct age, Sister Aidan, the frail nun who had administered the school since its foundation, might have better understood his behaviour. As it happened, this full-grown man was regarded as a naughty boy and treated as such. He did as she said and accepted punishments, because she was white and therefore *mutumea*, one worthy of respect. Had the head teacher been black, perhaps the salary he drew might demand Michael Kitheka's respect, admiration and even envy. He would soon learn, since, with the Sister now retired, the new term would see the school's acting headmaster take over the job full time. Michael Kitheka's desire for education and thus his entire journey through life was a quest for riches, a single-minded thrust along the wrong road toward a receding horizon he had never seen. The goat, however, tasted good and maybe he would now stay at school to study rather than try to make his way home. He would make up his mind tomorrow.

Michael always made decisions tomorrow, Janet thought.

James Maluki, on the other hand, was one of Janet's favourites. He was perhaps the only real child in the school. His voice was soft and light and his clear eyes were as innocent as his light brown skin was unblemished. Sipping his soup from his spoon with impeccable manners, he made a sharp contrast with Michael Kitheka at his side, who bent low over his own plate, gulping and spluttering, each spoonful raised by his lanky, almost mechanical arm. In Janet's eyes James Maluki was a sweet young child, exactly the kind of pupil she had imagined she would be teaching. In fact he was eighteen years old. His first few years of life had coincided with famine years in his home area and he had been lucky to survive. In Janet's eyes, however, he remained a smiling boy, whose model parents bought him a new uniform each term and always paid his school fees on time. In class, however, he was totally hopeless. He seemed to possess neither the energy to participate nor the intellectual facility to learn. It didn't really matter, she thought, because there were so many like him in the school.

The four sat and ate, sharing a thickly diced chapatti piled on a plate in the centre, from which they occasionally ladled spoonfuls of the bread into their bowls to saturate in the watery broth. Janet smiled a little, remembering a talk on health and hygiene from the orientation course she had attended. Never eat local food had been the message. Guard against infection at all times. Even if you have shaken hands with an African, they were told, be sure to wash thoroughly before touching food. How silly and superfluous all this advice now seemed. Talking to these boys, she began to feel for the first time that she was a part of Migwani, a member of the community. People no longer stood and stared as she passed. They had grown to accept the sight of her in the town, in the bars and the market and in the restaurants. Now she was simply *mwalimu*, the teacher, just as Michael was *muvea*, the priest.

With the meal finished, they knew no reason to leave. Outside, the rain had started again, recreating the same muddy scene of an hour before, so they ordered another tea and talked some more. Janet paid for all of their food with a ten-shilling note and took a sip of her tea. A man on the far side of the room, who had previously sat perfectly still as if asleep, saw this and began to rise to his feet, muttering. Janet had never seen him before, but in the coming months she would regularly notice him asleep under the tree in the marketplace, or in the teashop, or lying under the wheels of a bus. She would also learn to avoid him. He was tall and had a matted grey beard. He looked strange, but perhaps not significantly stranger than anyone else in the room. His wiry beard was matted with what Janet assumed were raindrops, but it was soon obvious that it was his own saliva. He was dressed in a torn and tattered raincoat, car-tyre sandals and a pair of ragged shorts. On his head he wore an incongruous flat-topped army hat with a shiny black peak. Still he muttered as he approached, looking straight at Janet. He said a few words more and then almost everyone in the restaurant started to laugh, including her own companions.

Janet looked inquiringly at little James Maluki. Embarrassed, his eyes fell from her gaze and he tried, with little success, to hide the smile on his lips. Tall Michael Kitheka shook his head and laughed out loud, slapping his thighs and offering a reply to the old man in Kikamba. Only Mutuli tried to explain to Janet what had been said.

"The man is saying that thou art very rich," said Mutuli.

Janet's face hardened into a teacher's call for attention. "…is saying that *you are* very rich," she corrected. She waited for a moment to be sure that he had understood.

“The man is saying that you are very rich,” repeated Mutuli, scolding himself a little for his mistake. “He is saying that if this is true, then you are able to buy tea for everyone here.”

Janet began to feel a little cornered and looked around at the faces that were generally turned her way. People were obviously waiting for her to say something. “Tell him,” she instructed Mutuli, “that I am not rich.”

Mutuli turned to face the man, who had approached to stand immediately opposite Janet behind Mutuli’s chair. His eyes were now fixed on her and, as Mutuli spoke, she felt their gaze begin to pierce her own in a strange, almost sinister way. The man did not blink – not at all. When Munyasya spoke, his answer this time was shouted, but in a surprising way, with his head bent right back, as if addressing the building’s roof.

Mutuli turned around. The smiles were all still there, but now they admitted questions. “He is saying that thou…” Mutuli winced at his mistake. “He is saying that you are rich because you have paid for all of this food and you are white and a teacher with a salary.” After a momentary pause he continued quietly, “I am thinking that this man has been taking beer.”

That was obvious, thought Janet. Since the man approached the table, the air seemed to be filled with the stale sweet smell of a urinal. “What does it matter?” she thought, looking around. “Bring tea for everyone,” she said turning to the owner, who was also watching with interest. A dozen or so cups of tea would only cost a few shillings.

Mutuli again turned to face the man and pointed towards the owner of the shop, who had already begun to fulfil the order. He had already lifted the large blue teapot, which usually simmered above his charcoal burner behind the bar, and was already in the process of filling the first glass offered in his direction. When Mutuli translated, it provoked a great roar of laughter and applause from everyone in the room, prompting Janet to believe that would be the end of it. One man stood, reached across the table and offered to shake Janet's hand, but the old inquisitor remained where he was. He did not move away. On the contrary, he moved closer to her, stepping out from behind Mutuli to stand at the side of their table. Again he threw back his head and shouted above the general noise. As he spoke, strands of saliva left his lips and settled unheeded and unwiped in his beard.

Kitheka laughed again. James Maluki got out of his chair and told Janet that he really must go back to the school immediately. He thanked her for the food and threaded his way with obvious haste between the tables towards the door, and noticeably avoiding going anywhere near the old man. Maluki turned to Janet and shook his head. "The man is very drunk, very drunk," he said.

Janet asked Mutuli what the man had said. "It is very bad, Miss Rowlandson. He is saying that if a white woman can do this, then white men can also buy food for everyone and then there would be no famine."

Janet could find no immediate answer to this. "It is very true," she said to Mutuli, "and I will try to make people understand that when I go home."

The decrepit old man spoke again immediately. Janet realised he could understand English perfectly, but clearly refused to speak it. "He understands everything you say," said Michael Kitheka, with a broad grin. "He used to be in the army and he speaks English very well. Everyone in the town knows him. He is just a drunk."

Muтuli again translated. "He is saying that you will forget when you go home. He also says some very strange things.

He speaks only in proverbs. I am not able to translate them."

Janet looked at the man, who had shuffled even closer. He seemed to sense that she was growing nervous and thus had detected a weakness he could exploit. She had hoped that her gesture would have satisfied him and sent him back to his seat, but she now found that each comment or action from her merely ratcheted up his interest and provoked longer and stronger replies. She was still the centre of attention. People clearly expected her to respond.

Before she spoke, the man's expression changed. The superior, if detached, smile vanished from his face and his lips set pursed around his open mouth. With eyes glazed, he stared at Janet like an animal ready to seize his prey. As he moved now uncomfortably close to her chair and bent over her still staring, she felt raw fear for the first time in her life. No one else seemed perturbed by his actions, so she still did not move. Everyone still watched, still smiled, apparently unaware of Janet's growing fear.

The old man's cloudy, bloodshot eyes stared down at her. Compulsively she returned his gaze. He raised his arms so that his hands rested directly over her head. Unnoticed until now was a length of string tied to his left thumb, but this now dangled uncomfortably close to Janet's face. A great shout of laughter filled the room as she tried to avoid it by moving her head to the side. Mutuli now seemed not to know whether to smile or worry, but Kitheka still joined in with the audience and laughed hard.

Breathing a laugh and a grunt, the old man took the end of the string between finger and thumb of his right hand and then stretched it out to its full length, bending lower over Janet at the same time. Then again he threw his head back and shouted whilst his hands tensed, slackened and re-tensed the string, before finally letting it fall with a flick of the hand. It looped, brushing Janet's face as it fell. As the man bent forward, he breathed deliberately directly into her face and she instinctively winced at the smell. Still everyone giggled, but now Janet was extremely frightened. Quickly she rose to her feet and, in the same movement, pushed the old man to one side. Everyone was suddenly silent as she sat down again.

"Mutuli, will you tell this man to go away? If he is asking for money then I will give him some," she said, trying her best to sound in control.

Kitheka spoke before Mutuli could speak. "Mutuli cannot give this man orders! He is *mwana wa mungu*."

Mutuli nodded in agreement. Janet did not have the time to ask what this meant before the man returned to stand over her again. Repeatedly he shouted at the sky and bent forward, each time pulling out the string attached to his thumb to its full length before letting it go. Janet again pushed him away, this time with some force. She now looked frightened and the man's expression changed again. Still the glazed eyes stared, but now the malice disappeared and the smile returned. It was as if he now felt he was in total control. Again he advanced towards her with his string and his shouts. No one seemed to take him seriously, she thought, as she looked around for support and finding only what she saw as gentle amusement on people's faces.

This time, the old man reached out and touched her. She tried not to flinch. Again everyone laughed. "*Mwana wa mungu*," said Kitheka again. Janet tried to stay calm and ignore him as the ritual shouting and string pulling started again. She asked Kitheka, by far the bigger of the two students, to tell the man to go away and leave her alone.

"I cannot," he said. "He will do whatever he wants."

"You are afraid of him," she said, her fear now turning to anger.

"No," he replied. "Not afraid…"

Hearing this, the old man quickly turned to face Kitheka and leaned across the table towards him. Kitheka and Mutuli immediately sped from their chairs and out of the door, howling with laughter. Janet watched them go, trying to call them back, but no words came. Before she could think, the man took hold of her head and with some force rubbed her face into the folds of his raincoat. Janet screamed. She thought she felt the string around the back of her neck. He was trying to strangle her…

She hit him as hard as she could. He staggered across the floor, collided with a table and fell heavily onto the concrete. Though stunned, Janet turned and watched, but still she could not move. The old man tried to get up, but fell back groaning. Everyone else laughed, including Kitheka and Mutuli, who peered through the open doorway to watch the show. She was too confused to react. Instinctively, she wiped her hair and touched a wet patch. He had spat on her hair. On the point of tears, she snatched up her haversack and ran. As she dashed outside, she caught a glimpse of the old man on the floor, propped on an elbow, watching her and smiling as he cast another incantation to the roof.

She continued to run, but her progress was far from quick and far from straight as she slithered through the mud. Behind her, Mutuli tried to follow, shouting, "The man is very drunk, Miss Rowlandson. Do not be afraid." Behind him was Kitheka, loping along, still laughing, but Janet did not look back and so neither saw nor heard her friends. She went on her way, her run soon slowing to a safer brisk walk. Kitheka and Mutuli returned to the restaurant to retrieve their boxes. The old man was still on the floor and was still laughing to himself. Everyone else still laughed as they recounted what they had just seen.

It must have been a nightmare, she thought, as she ran the last few yards to the mission. She entered without knocking and called for Father Michael. As she rushed blindly through the door, Michael appeared in front of her from around the kitchen corner and she fell into his arms and cried, her head against his chest.

"You smell like a sewer," he said. "Did you get wet?"

When Janet answered only with sobs, Michael's voice grew more serious. After trying to console her, he pulled up a chair and sat her on it. A minute later, Michael gently helped her hands from her eyes and offered her a glass.

"Drink this, my love," he said quietly. "It'll warm you up a bit."

Janet drank, coughed, drank again and coughed again. The whiskey warmed her and quietened her as Michael crouched before her. His eyes silently asked what was wrong.

Feeling better, Janet explained what had happened in the restaurant. Michael did not try to interrupt as the story flooded from Janet's lips. Not until she had obviously finished did he speak. "This fellah, did he wear an army hat with a peak on it? And did he spit a lot?"

"Yes, that's him," she answered.

"Oh, don't take any notice of him. That's only old Munyasya. He's a nutter, a real nutter. What he did to you was what he does to every European who visits Migwani. He probably got closer to you than to others though, by the sound of it. He cursed you to change into a snake, that's all. That's why he keeps pulling on that string," said Michael, sounding flippant.

Janet was suddenly very serious and looked pensive. Then, as Michael's words grew clearer, she began to laugh.

"I thought he was trying to strangle me."

"The old fool was probably so drunk he could hardly even see you. Don't worry. He won't even recognize you. If he sees you again he'll go through the routine again as if it was the first time. He didn't try to touch you up?" asked Michael. "He has been known to try that one with a few of the girls."

"No," she answered. "But I don't understand. Why do people just stand around and laugh at him? If everyone dislikes him so much, why don't they just chuck him out of the bar or at least tell him to shut up?"

"They wouldn't do that," said Michael. "He's a mad man. People will just try to ignore him. They don't put people like him away, you know. They just stay around the home and their families look after them. It's quite humane, really. It means that no one is ever left destitute or homeless, no matter how old or mad they become. No, people here will just let the old fool do as he wishes. If he asked for food in that restaurant, the owner would give him some. He doesn't need to buy anything. But his case is a bit strange, stranger than most, because he has no family. Quite soon after I arrived in Migwani, when he was still *compos mentis* and quite a figure in the community, he had an accident. I was out early one morning, contemplating my vocation, as we priests do, and found him in the marketplace under the tree where he now sleeps. He was drunk and had either fallen or had a stroke. If I hadn't taken him to the hospital in Muthale, he would probably have died. It might have been better for everyone if he had. Anyway, because he has no family, all the town supports him. Wherever he goes, he gets what he wants. All he ever asks for is beer and a bit of food, but he is never refused."

"But our boys, Mutuli and Kitheka, they ran away…" said Janet, sounding confused. "I asked them to tell him to go away and they just ran."

"Oh," interrupted Michel, "they would not want to order him around. They wouldn't do that at all. They will just want to leave him alone to do whatever he wants. They would not want to get in his way."

Janet thought for a second, trying to remember the name the boys had used to describe the old man. "They gave him a special name, but it wasn't Munyasya. It was more like Mw… Mw…"

"*Mwana wa mungu*?" asked Michael.

"Yes. That was it. *Mwana wa mungu*," she repeated.

"That's not a name," said Michael. "That just means a madman. Well…" Michael paused here to consider how he might explain. "It doesn't actually mean madman. Literally it means 'child of God'. People believe, you see, that these madmen become mad because they can see things that men should not see. They are really living in another world."

Janet felt very much better and her immediate anxiety had gone. The thought of being cursed to change into a snake ought to worry her, she thought, but Michael's flippant dismissal of the entire incident made it impossible to be afraid. "I wonder," she said, "if I had been a Kamba and Munyasya had done the same thing to me and delivered a curse, would I be worried?"

Michael thought again. "It's a strange question, because in his case he only seems to go for white people." He was silent again for a few moments. "I suppose you would be worried."

Ten

March 1976

John O'Hara was a man with problems on his mind. As he sat alone to eat his lunch, his thoughts drifted behind piercing blue eyes, whose fixed stare was trained through the window he faced, but whose focus was far beyond the mango tree that the opening framed. The material side of his diocese was taking care of itself. The problem of raising funds for the parishes was ongoing, but then it always was. The cathedral, which just two years before had been but a dream, was almost complete, the money coming from visits and lecture tours by himself and his priests to North America. They had realised a number of verbal commitments from churches and charities, and these had since matured into funding for the special projects that his priests planned and executed. He had seen the cathedral grow from an architect's model to become, already, the most prestigious building in Kitui town. Although unfinished, it was breathtakingly beautiful, astride its hilltop site almost completely shrouded by giant eucalyptus trees. Only the shining metal cross at the top of the tower showed above the branches, but because of its elevated position, this could be seen from almost anywhere in the town. The cathedral itself remained largely invisible until quite close, but already the lines were laid out and the eventual beauty of the building no longer needed to be imagined. When Father John – as he was still known throughout the district – had announced that he was going ahead with the cathedral, he had been concerned by the apparent lack of interest among the priests. Some doubted whether one could build a structure worthy of the name out of corrugated iron and cement blocks. More significantly, some questioned whether the Church should spend so much on a building when the Diocese was in the grip of famine. Nevertheless John had initiated the project and grew ever more committed to it. Gradually, as the building had taken shape and its final appearance became progressively clearer, resistance to it amongst the priests dwindled and eventually became transformed into positive congratulation. So it was clear that the mechanics of the diocese were running smoothly. This was not the area that caused O'Hara's deep concern.

He was returned to the reality of routine by an involuntary wince that shot through his entire body, a reflex reaction he neither initiated nor controlled. The cook had again omitted to soak the oranges in sugar syrup before serving them, and so the first spoonful of his fruit salad dessert was especially sour. John pushed the dish aside and left the table. Early afternoon was usually a time to sleep, to take an hour of rest before returning to his office at two to continue the day's work. Today, however, there would be no time to sleep, so he retired to an easy chair and opened a newspaper to pass the time before the arrival of his expected visitor.

Father Michael made a regular trip to the district centre each week. Kitui town offered facilities that Migwani could not. There was a post office which actually had stamps to sell, a grocer that stocked bacon and sausages, and then there was the Bishop, who held the purse strings. If these facilities were not essential to him, he would stay in Migwani, happy to spend the day visiting projects, talking to people and busying himself about his mission house where he had started a small but productive farm based on the house's waste water, whose flow he had directed away from the septic tank. But in Kitui he could meet with other priests from elsewhere in the Diocese. They could share ideas over a beer, or simply report how their own areas were coping with the famine.

Today, however, he had come to Kitui on another mission. In his pocket he had a letter, a personal invitation for a meeting with the Bishop. He had no idea what the subject of the 'chat' might be, but had a suspicion that he would be asked to leave Migwani to set up a new mission in a remote area to the south. There had been a lot of talk recently about the idea and Michael had been told unofficially several times that he had been earmarked for the job. So it was with a mixture of excitement and sadness that he drove to town that morning. The chance of opening a completely new mission was something that he relished, but still the thought of leaving the people of Migwani gave him little joy. Janet, who had been told about the scheme over dinner the previous week, had strongly encouraged him to take the job, if it was offered. The romanticism of the remoteness of the place appealed to her strongly, prompting her to use the phrase 'real Africa' to describe it. She had also immediately suggested to Michael that he establish a school there so that she could come and teach in it. They visited the place after Mass the previous Sunday. Though no more than thirty miles from Migwani, Yatta could not be reached at all by car and even a motorcycle would not get across the riverbeds after even the lightest of rain. Janet had been captivated by the place, completely carried away in her excitement at how Michael might make his impression in such a posting. He had brought her back to earth by reminding her that he had not even been offered the job yet, but the picture was already painted in her mind.

A noise from the kitchen woke John O'Hara, who had dozed off with his newspaper open on his knees. Startled, he jumped straight to his feet, but his concern was immediately eased by the appearance of Michael in the doorway.

"Oh, Michael, how are you, my boy?" said John, taking Michael's hand in his fierce grip and giving it a firm shake. John made every attempt to be sociable rather than managerial towards his younger priests, but invariably his manner grew more overtly paternalistic as a result.

"Nothing too wrong, my Lord Bishop," replied a good-humoured Michael. "Nothing, that is, that a glass of beer wouldn't put right."

Unexpectedly John's expression changed, hardened, and Michael realised that he had not been summoned for a friendly chat about a new job. "You don't change, Michael," he said. "Shall we sit down and talk first?"

Michael sat as invited, feeling somewhat confused. Behind Bishop O'Hara's friendly exterior there was clearly a matter of some concern and probably importance. In his own home he was usually so keen to be sociable that any request was answered without fuss or question, until, that is, the request was transferred to the office and money became the subject under discussion. Michael looked at John intently, trying to interpret the other's prolonged silence. Was the controlled expression a way of tempering Michael's disappointment? He is not going to offer me the job, Michael thought.

But what followed was a series of platitudes. O'Hara asked about Migwani and the severity of the famine. He wanted a report on Michael's work and then his general state of health. It was obvious that this was but a prelude to the real subject for discussion and thus Michael grew steadily more defensive as its appearance was further deferred. The overture had never lasted this long before.

"There's something I want to clear up," said O'Hara, after yet another short pause. Michael braced himself. This was it. "I've been hearing a lot of gossip recently. Now you know my attitude. If it reaches me, then it's already common knowledge everywhere else. I am always the last to hear."

Michael's eyes set in a fixed, cynical stare. He had heard the next part before.

"You are spending too much time in the bars around town, my lad. It's not good, you know, for people who are poor and have not enough to eat to see you drinking, dancing and enjoying yourself till all hours of the morning, especially when we tell people through our ministry that they should seek humility and discipline in God's Church." John paused to await a comment, but none came. "You must see the point, Michael?" said O'Hara.

Michael's voice was low, rather malicious in tone. "I see the point all right, my Lord, but I would find it a lot harder to justify a million shillings spent on a cathedral."

John's paternalism allowed him to ignore this almost personal slight. "Now, now, there's no need to talk like that. It's not as if they are alternatives. And you know full well that everyone, except for a few of our own priests, is filled with pride at the thought of this forgotten little town having its own cathedral. It's not just a building. It's a symbol of a change in attitude amongst the community. It puts the place on the map, so no one can ignore it, not even the government."

"The money would have fed half the district until the next rains," said Michael with a scoff. His views on the construction project were well known.

John still spoke quietly, calmly brushing aside the invitation to argument. "I see no point in going over old ground, Michael. When I was in your position, I was also a man totally involved in the problems of my parishioners and put them before any other consideration. But you must understand and accept what we are trying to do here. We are not just a charity to be used when needed. We're the missionaries of a living Church that represents a way of life and, in that respect, our mission is permanence. That's why we need a cathedral." John again awaited a reply.

Michael understood the argument, but he did not agree with it. A building could always come tomorrow, but a life must be saved today.

"After all," continued John O'Hara, knowing that Michael had just come from the town with a box of groceries in the boot of his car, "none of us gives up his own table to the poor…"

"And that's why we are always going to be a diocese of missionary Fathers contenting ourselves with the subservience of our congregations," said Michael, irritated by what he considered to be a lack of foresight. "On that basis, we are here to fill churches, not spread the faith!"

John was sterner this time. "We're here to do both, Michael. We cannot ignore either side of the work." John's heavy eyebrows lowered a little as he came to the point, abruptly. He eyed the younger man with all his authority locked into the silence of his stare. "There's also been a lot of talk around the town about your relationship with the girl in Migwani."

Michael was shattered, the shock running so deep that he was rendered quite speechless. John O'Hara seemed to interpret his reticence as an admission of guilt, or at least acceptance that there was an issue to confront.

"If the talk has reached Kitui, then goodness knows what it's like around Migwani. It's just not good enough, Michael." O'Hara's voice was now solid and pointed, and also louder than he himself realised, amplified by the inner rage he was trying hard to contain.

"That is quite ridiculous," shouted Michael. "If you are willing to believe a lot of senseless, puerile gossip, then I wonder how it is you have risen to where you are today…"

John was incensed by this. "If that's what you think of the sincere beliefs and fears of ordinary people, Michael, then all I can say is that you have no right to call yourself either a man of God or a man of the people!"

The two men thus began a loud and bad-tempered argument. Michael challenged O'Hara to believe his word as he described the friendship, and no more, that he shared with Janet Rowlandson. He believed that there was nothing wrong with their eating together, talking together or occasionally visiting friends together. As far as he was concerned, his friendship with Janet was the same as his relationship with his catechists, with his cook or with anyone else he called a friend.

O'Hara did not dispute Michael's word, but he strongly refuted the assertion that the relationship should be viewed like any other. Janet was young, attractive and white, and, her presence in Migwani accepted, that alone created a link with Michael, a link that had to be managed carefully, with always one eye on what people might think. The crime, he continued, lay not with people who rushed to adopt bigoted opinions, but with Michael and Janet for not having realised that they might fuel imaginations if they behaved without tact. Furthermore, Michael must not underestimate the psychological effect on himself of spending so much time with an attractive young girl. He had seen it happen before, he repeatedly pointed out, and the consequences could be dire for all concerned, including the Church.

Michael appreciated the argument and did not doubt John's claim to experience. Neither did he dismiss the last point. Only a few years before this same discussion had taken place between O'Hara and another young priest, who had become infatuated with a girl working for a year in one of the hospitals. On that occasion, the priest had become so angry with what he considered to be the warped minds of 'churchmen' that he decided there and then that he no longer wanted to be counted amongst their number. He left the Diocese and the priesthood, and then married the girl.

Michael, however, kept his calm. As the argument continued, he began to admit a strong disillusion. How could he, a young man with, he believed, the right ideas and the energy to put them into practice, work effectively in his own way when the people who controlled the institution he had joined held such obviously different views? Did John O'Hara really believe that Michael's beliefs were not founded on the interests of the Church? Surely he would never have joined a missionary order had that been the case. But he knew this dichotomy, even conflict, was not personal but institutional within the Church. The Second Vatican Council had created an agenda for priests like Michael Doherty. For older priests like John O'Hara, the Church as institution was paramount. It took the lead, was teacher to its flock and, in Michael's view, spoke with a one-voice-fits-all formula for salvation. It remained the individual's personal mission to live up to the model, to achieve its goals through a private aspiration to share a perhaps eternally unattainable grace. But for post-Vatican Two priests, the Church was a community. Faith and salvation remained personal, but expressed collectively the concepts now assumed a social dimension, a dimension that could be explored and perhaps fulfilled via social action. For priests of O'Hara's generation, the Church was the didactic teacher. For Michael Doherty and his kind it had become the heuristic learner. They were members of a single Church, but the worlds they inhabited shared no common universe.

After silence had cleared the air, O'Hara spoke again. Assertion was again edited from the voice. "Michael, my boy, don't worry yourself. There's no need to get worked up about it. Let me tell you what I want to suggest. Your leave is overdue. Is that right?"

"It is," said Michael blankly. He knew now what to expect.

"I suggest, then, that you take some months off and do a job for me while you're away. You can spend some time at home in Limerick and then I'll arrange a tour of North America."

Michael's thoughts rushed ahead to the time when he expected Janet's stay in Migwani to come to an end. He might not see her before she left. Suddenly he felt completely empty. The crudeness of the Bishop's calculations was obvious.

"I am sure you will prove to be an excellent ambassador for us, Michael," continued O'Hara. "There's so much goodwill to be tapped over there. I am sure that what we have achieved thus far is only a fraction of what is possible. The people are very generous."

Michael leaned forward in his chair and stared blankly at O'Hara. He had not been listening to the last comments. For a while he simply sat, quite motionless, his thoughts somewhere distant while Bishop O'Hara sketched the type of itinerary he might expect. He would arrive in New York and visit several of the large Catholic organisations before making his way to California via stops in Ohio and Illinois. The church in Santa Barbara, which had raised a hundred thousand shillings for the cathedral, would be his host for a fortnight, before he flew to Florida to begin his return journey to New York through the states along the eastern seaboard.

Michael, with his mind firmly fixed on August, got up and, without saying a word, walked briskly out of the house. O'Hara, caught off-guard by this, hesitated at first but then followed, offering first a sympathetic word and then, after this did not register, a stern shouted command that Michael should come back inside. With the military-like order ringing in his ears, Michael opened the door of his car and got in but he left the door open. The Bishop did not cross the kitchen threshold. He was clearly very angry, but his hands were clasped as if in prayer.

Back in the sitting room of his house, John O'Hara lit a cigarette. He drew deeply on it, the sound of his breath wheezing around the room. It seemed that the cigarette had become the focus of his thoughts. He would not chase after Michael, who would have to live with the consequences of his own actions and decisions, but he wondered whether he, himself, might have pushed too hard, been too forthright, implied criticism where opportunity might have spoken louder.

When Michael re-entered the room, neither of them spoke for several minutes. Michael looked at O'Hara and thought that a simple humanity had overcome and replaced the burden of authority. In his eyes, questions had replaced anger.

"I think you are a wiser man than I," said O'Hara at last.

"I am sorry, John," said Michael.

"It is not I who deserves your apologies, Michael."

Eleven

February 1975

The courtroom was crowded to overflowing. With windows shuttered to keep out the sun, the room vibrated with a humid heat and the assembled, seated on long plain wooden benches, sweated freely. Some occasionally mopped their brows with handkerchiefs and mumbled words of conversation beneath the muting cover of cupped hands. Others allowed their sweat to run freely and turned to whisper their words to their neighbours. Though a nervous silence pervaded all, the room was full of discussion held in whispers, spoken between the lines of time. As if with a collective bated breath, the entire room awaited the calling of the next case with a feeling of shared bitterness softened by apprehension. Over a hundred people had travelled from the scattered homesteads and *shambas* that comprised the village of Nzawa and fifty or more had crammed into the minute court room to hear the proceedings, the rest excluded only by the room's inability to accommodate them. People stood around the walls, sat on the floor between and beside the rows of wooden forms, while others pressed in groups outside by the shuttered windows, hoping they might hear what transpired inside. A group standing by the boarded window to the right of the magistrate's desk had encroached upon the section of open floor whose imaginary confines served as the defendants' dock. The sergeant at arms, a young and obviously inexperienced police officer, turned out in immaculate dress uniform, quietly, apologetically, but defiantly ushered them all to other parts of the room, other parts that were already crowded, so there was much jostling for position and whispered apologies as they stumbled along the blocked aisles.

In the very centre of the room sat Janet. Beside her was Joseph Munyolo's mother. They had no way of communicating verbally, so, as a means of offering reassurance, Janet held her hand and turned to her occasionally to smile. Janet looked down at the calloused and lined hand, which contrasted so sharply with the soft whiteness of her own. Munyolo's mother was a true *kiveti*, a housewife, whose daily chores started each day probably before sunrise and did not stop until well after dark, when the dishes from the late meal had been cleared away. She was probably only forty or so, but she looked at least sixty, her wiry body appearing to bear not an ounce of fat and the whole supported on ankles that looked incongruously slender above the plastic flip-flops, flattened almost wafer thin by continual use, their original bright green now masked by ingrained dirt. Munyolo's mother had loosened the cloth, the *kitambaa*, she invariably used to cover her head, to reveal close-cropped hair gathered into squares with rivers of sweating scalp between. Janet's discomfort was easier to see. Her neck glistened with lines of sweat and her light grey T-shirt was patched darker over most of its area.

The main door of the courtroom continually opened and closed as people came and went. No one wanted to leave. No one wanted to miss this next case, but the interior had become so uncomfortable that some people were prepared to suffer the embarrassment of threading and stumbling their way to the exit for a breath of fresh air. Thus a steady stream of people punctuated the expectant but near silent buzz of the room, as each of those coming and going turned at the door to face the oblivious and unconcerned magistrate to offer a silent and self-conscious, but carefully stated bow. These people were poor, but they bore their respect.

John concluded his report on the previous case by signing the document before him on his desk and rubber-stamping his official seal beneath. The defendant, accused of stealing from a shop, had flatly denied the charge, despite the combined and accusatory testimony of a procession of eyewitnesses. After being told by the magistrate that he was found guilty and that a confession would reduce his sentence, the man, still ignorant of the consequences, had refused to comply. In a voice heavy with regret and resignation, John had sentenced him to one month's imprisonment or a fine of four hundred shillings. The defendant, stricken dumb with shock, stood with his jaw sagging pathetically, trying in vain to equate the severity of the sentence with the meagre worth of the bag of sugar he had stolen. How could he pay such a fine? If he had money to pay a fine, would he not have simply bought the sugar in the first place? What would happen to his family while he was in prison? They were poor people and had no food. What else could he do?

Still mouthing the questions his body refused to ask, he was led by the handcuffed wrist, accompanied by the attached policeman who had brought him into the court. If the man had employed an attorney, most of whom were willing, at a price, to attend any court and fight any case, an appeal would have been lodged and the sentence then duly reassessed on compassionate grounds. With no money to finance such a defence, however, the man was led away and made ready for his transfer to Kitui prison, where he would serve his time. At least he would get a meal a day for the whole of the next month.

Syengo, self-conscious of his obvious youth, placed a new file on the desk in front of John Mwangangi and then turned to face the court to announce in Kikamba and English the title of the next case to be heard. "The disturbance at Nzawa School," he said, without expression. As John extracted the papers one by one from their folder, examining each of them methodically and closely before reassembling them in a pile, a tall neatly dressed young man, who had been sitting at the table beside Syengo and his silent typewriter, rose slowly and deliberately to his feet. For some time he stood there, fumbling with a pen, waiting to catch the attention of the magistrate, but John's eyes remained angled down, focused on the detail of his papers, detail which his agile mind merely needed to reinforce, since he had read them many times already over the preceding days. Eventually John looked up and the man brought attention to himself by holding up his pen. John nodded.

The man put his pen down on the desk and then stretched himself to his full height. Before speaking, he slipped his thumbs into his waistcoat pockets and took a deep, long and deliberate breath, whilst casting his gaze around the room to ask for total silence. Whether he had copied this attitude from re-runs of American courtroom dramas he had watched on the television he so proudly owned, only he knew. Most in the court were duly impressed. Janet thought him an obvious idiot. She could not predict how Mwangangi might respond.

"Your honour," said the impeccable young man in only

lightly accented English, "I am here to represent my clients Mr Kivara and Mr Muchira." Pauses here and throughout his speech allowed Syengo to translate each sentence into Kikamba for the benefit of the court. As Syengo spoke these words of introduction, a ripple of noise spread across the room as members of the audience turned to their neighbours to whisper, "Another Kikuyu."

The attorney, keen to conclude his business, continued above the murmur. He had accepted the case only reluctantly. Those who knew him would have realised from the terseness of his words that he resented travelling from Nairobi to attend such a lowly gathering in such a tiresomely bush area. Had the two teachers not made him such a generous offer, he would never have contemplated going to such trouble. "My clients," he continued, "have requested that the case should be adjourned until certain key witnesses, who are not present today, can be called." Syengo translated. The response was a collective, audible sigh from the gallery. They had come for nothing.

"The crooks are frightened to come here!" shouted a faltering voice from the back. It was an old woman, who had not found a seat and took support from the shoulders of the man in front of her. A wizened old man at the side of the room shouted his agreement and waved his stick towards the superior-looking attorney in a defiant gesture. John smacked his gavel on the table and called for order. After threatening the two hecklers with expulsion from the court, John turned to face the public prosecutor who, acknowledging the prompt, immediately rose to his feet.

"I have no objections, your Honour," he said, correctly anticipating John's unasked question. Syengo translated.

"The case is then adjourned until the next meeting of the court, which will be two weeks from today," said John, without looking up from the papers upon which he was making a handwritten record of the proceedings.

Janet stood up and raised her hand to attract Mwangangi's attention. All eyes rested on her as John continued to write. Though embarrassed, she continued to stand and to hold her arm high, afraid that Mwangangi would again refuse her request or, worse than that, simply ignore her and move on to the next case. She had decided not to try to see Mwangangi personally, where a suggestion of a bribe might be made, preferring to conduct all communication with him in a social arena. She now feared that this might have been a mistake. Her distrust of all officials suggested that the magistrate would conveniently forget to acknowledge her request for bail.

Without looking up, his attention still firmly fixed on the words he committed to the case's fattening file, John asked if there were any requests for bail. Syengo translated.

A man at the far side of the room stood up and confirmed that there were. Still writing, and without looking up, John invited him to speak. Munyolo's mother gave Janet a stiff nudge in the side, fearing that she would not speak up. Janet's nod offered her reassurance that everything was under control.

He has ignored me on purpose, Janet thought. She began privately to scold herself for not visiting the parents of the other defendants to see if they had offered bribes.

John granted this first request and levelled bail at three hundred shillings. Before Janet could speak, a second man stood and called out his request. This was also granted. Janet was worried that these men sounded so completely confident. She was convinced they had seen Mwangangi before the hearing. But then they spoke and made their requests in Kikamba. Being native speakers of the language, they could instinctively judge when the troughs and dips in communication appeared, and could occupy them. Janet's contribution would be in English and thus would not fit the same mould.

Frustrated, Janet spoke. Her request to be heard sounded a little impatient and John looked up from his papers with an expression of mild surprise. He then looked down again and continued to write.

"There was some confusion," said John, having anticipated Janet's request, "over the name of your student. Is this the boy whom you are seeking?" He looked up and turned to point his pen at the eldest of the defendants, huddled in a tight group in all that was left of their dedicated space.

"It is," said Janet. "This is Joseph Munyolo."

"Can you guarantee that if bail is granted, he will not visit Nzawa for any reason until the case is concluded?"

"I can," replied Janet.

"Bail is granted," said John, turning again to write his notes. Janet sighed with relief and, as Syengo delivered his translation, Munyolo's mother turned and smiled with relief and pride at her friends who were scattered throughout the room. "Bail is granted," repeated John, "at five hundred shillings."

Janet was suddenly furious. Why had Mwangangi not offered three hundred shillings like the others? Was it prejudice that immediately convinced her that he had increased the amount because she was white and could therefore afford to pay more? How she hated these paper tigers of officials who used every possible means to exert their pathetic authority! To think that people like this considered themselves to be educated!

Within ten minutes the courtroom was empty, except for John who remained seated at his desk collecting together the papers that still lay strewn over its ample surface. Janet emerged from Syengo's adjoining office after re-entering the building, having taken the refreshment of a minute or so breathing air that was not heavy with sweat and its associated odours. She had already paid the clerk the necessary five hundred shillings and held the receipt prominently so Munyolo and his relieved mother could see it. As Janet spoke to them, John Mwangangi collected his files and withdrew to his adjoining office.

"My mother wishes to thank you very much for what you have done, Miss Rowlandson. She says that we are poor and that she could not have found the money for my bail. Thank you again," said Joseph, as his mother shook Janet's hand. "I think you will accompany us to the bus," he continued, pointing vaguely towards the marketplace at the town's centre.

"Not yet," said Janet. "You go on ahead and I will follow. I want to speak with Bwana Mwangangi."

She stood and watched through the now opened windows as Joseph and his mother walked out of the compound and out of sight behind the high euphorbia hedges by the roadside. She then approached the office door and gave a sharp tap. She went straight inside without waiting to be invited.

"Ah, Miss Rowlandson," said John with what sounded like pleasant surprise. "Take a seat."

"No, thank you," she replied. Her voice betrayed an edge of contempt. "I wanted to ask you if there was a reason why Joseph's bail was set so much higher than the rest? Was the boy, perhaps, so much more of a risk than the others? And if so, why?"

John looked a little surprised, as if the question was so trivial it need not have been asked. "He is older, Miss Rowlandson. In the eyes of the law he is an adult, older than the other defendants, all of whom are primary school age."

She nodded and accepted this as *fait accompli*, without

actually knowing if this should make any difference. But she was not convinced. She was sure, however, that this man should not be trusted.

Twelve

November 1965

John looked out onto the street before proceeding. London was a dark and dreary place where people walked ant-like in columns, dwarfed by their surroundings, but what surroundings they were! Outside in the drizzle an orderly line of people edged towards a 68 bus, which had just stopped at the kerbside. There was a rush, but it was a controlled expectancy, measured by an unwritten and unstated but shared knowledge that people must coexist. There was no argument, only shrugs of acceptance with the odd word of dissent when the conductor barred the entrance and shouted, "Full up now!" and rang the bell with two sharp tugs of the cord above his head to tell the driver to move off. Those left waiting simply found another, shorter queue. Taxis raced along the street, their engines knocking loudly as their drivers changed gear to slow down for the traffic lights. Above all, the buzz of movement filled the air, other sounds becoming mere interruptions in the general hubbub.

But John hated the rush hour. After more than three years of living in this city, he had still not become accustomed to its demands. After four years in Nairobi, even that city, with its wide streets and lack of traffic, had still seemed as strange and alien a place on the day he left as it did on the day he arrived, a new graduate of Kitui School, ready to enter higher education. In his eyes it remained the capital of European Africa before the capital of Kenya. But compared to London it was little more than an overgrown village. The fine buildings, the cathedral included, were mere chicken huts compared to the stature of London's pride. Everything here felt like it had meaning, purpose above function. Institutions were respected not because they were powerful, but because they provided a service that people desired and occasionally even respected. In his eyes, universities in Kenya were showpieces, serving no more use to the nation as a whole than the statue of an old queen in the street. Here the university seemed to be part of life, its graduates were in demand and its work bore fruits. For John, London had become a symbol of wealth, of rationality, modernity and cooperation, a model worthy even of copy. From this perspective, Kenya seemed distant not just by miles, but by centuries, a trivial wilderness blinded by petty divisions amongst its people and an over-inflated self-image. If only everyone in Kenya could come here, he had said many times, to see for themselves that there are other ways of living, ways that don't involve scratching at the soil with a hoe. Only then, he thought, would Kenyans see the minuteness of their world, the smallness of their lives and the potential to which they ought to aspire.

As John stepped outside into the rain, as ever he was amazed. Drizzle created mirrors on the road. A line of traffic, waiting to crawl westbound down the Strand reflected its lights in the shining black below, giving reds, whites and yellows alongside the streetlights. The red buses, with their strange cutaway fronts and backs, like boxes with bites missing, clanked their gears and growled.

The sight of hundreds, probably thousands of people going about their daily lives with apparent independence, as if pursuing some known and long-held goal, filled him with wonder. If only his countrymen might live their lives this way, instead of clinging to the myths and pagan rituals of a bygone age. Then and only then might they share the same riches, the same prosperity, the same freedom as the people of this city.

The night was cold, windy and wet, but John felt warm. He had long ago grown used to the English climate with its unpredictable vagaries and surreal transformations, grown used to preparing for its demands and whims. Walking across Waterloo Bridge as just one element of the evening procession, he believed he looked and felt like everyone else, an illusion shared by few of his fellow travellers. Sheltered from the rain by a black umbrella, he wore a thick woollen coat over his suit. In his other hand he carried the now inevitable briefcase, packed tightly with papers he would study over the weekend in what he still called his 'free time'. Unlike most others, he looked around, rather than blankly following the flow. As ever, he found the view from the bridge breathtaking, no matter how many times above the usual twice a day he saw it. He had seen it hundreds, perhaps thousands of times, but it still enthralled him and prompted him to think of the others who had passed through the streets or along the river during London's twenty centuries. Turning full circle as he continued his walk, he scanned the panorama of the floodlit buildings and their rippled reflections in the muddy, tidal, wind-rippled water. To the left, St Paul's Cathedral symbolised a past glory, now superseded in importance and power by the tall obelisks of the business world, the cathedrals of the world's new, all-encompassing religion. Surely it should be to these altars of power that modern

Kenyans should offer their worship, not to the Stone Age ritual of the tribe or the outdated cross of the white man's church.

To his right was the seat of power, resplendently Gothic by the banks of the Thames. But its art was artifice, its identity imitation. He remembered studying the 'Mother of Parliaments' in his history lessons at school, just as he had learned to locate Buckingham Palace and the Tower of London on a map in the tattered nineteen thirties textbooks they used in Kitui School. As a schoolboy, not for a moment had he imagined that he would one day be close enough to touch these hallowed institutions and never once did he imagine that this proximity would question the respect for them he had been required to learn. Here in London, as a part of the city and a participant in its life, the celebrity of these places was in question, but strangely this only added to his perception of their power. Architecturally, the 'Mother of Parliaments' might be an impostor, but its power was real and its influence wide, aspects that the dog-eared textbook could never communicate to a naïve and trusting boy in a Kenyan school.

But this was not Kenya. John now felt further from home, further from his former self than ever before. He felt accepted here, as much, that is, as a black man could possibly feel in this place. His home village, his father's *shamba*, seemed mere blurs of memory now. Memories of the deep valleys of Kamandiu felt as real as fiction when juxtaposed with the sight before him. It was a lost memory, a scene from a dream that London had revealed as a nightmare. For John, life must never again become a battle against the insuperable odds of famine, disease and bigotry. The future must hold something better than that, at least for himself.

And his own future was very much in the forefront of his

thoughts these days. The first steps toward that new age had already been taken and he was happy with the direction his life had found. He had met Lesley in college more than a year ago. Their meeting had been by chance, a by-product of an administrative enquiry lodged by John in the office where Lesley worked as a clerk. The problem of John's grant for the new term had taken weeks to resolve. At first he visited the office once a week to check on possible progress, but later he went there every day during his lunchtime, when he would ask his questions, but then sit in conversation with Lesley over sandwiches and tea. And then he suggested that they meet one evening for a meal, and a few meetings later the venue was Lesley's flat in Lambeth, where privacy offered them an opportunity to get to know one another somewhat better.

Her job and its salary had been every bit of the liberation she hoped it would be. Her school years had been fraught with tension and disagreement at home. Her parents were not like her and she was utterly different from them. After years of consistent school reports, which had testified to her ability but condemned her disinterest, she emerged into the big wide world with modest qualifications, not enough to go to university, but sufficient to have opportunities. She did some training, took a secretarial and administration course at a technical college and found her current job immediately. Once employed, she blossomed into a responsible, dependable, trustworthy and conscientious worker. The initiative she lacked was never a requirement for her post, so she prospered. At last there seemed to be a reason for what she was asked to do and a real incentive for her to do it. She managed to save the deposit for a small flat off the Walworth Road, not the most upmarket area of London, but close enough to her parents if she needed some more of that comfort she had always taken for granted, and perfectly placed on the bus route to her job. And she could afford it, which was the main consideration. It wasn't very big, but she had modest tastes.

John took his seat on the bus. It was the same bus he could have caught outside college, but he liked to walk across the bridge, even in the rain, and he knew, after some years of making this trip, that there were always seats at the Waterloo Station bus stop, where half the occupants of the vehicle, packed at the end of the Strand, would alight to connect with their Southern Region for Surrey. From here the journey was short and at this hour not too uncomfortable. He could see no point in rushing and scrambling home at five when an hour later it was so much more comfortable. He used the time well, studying in the quiet of the library, an activity which often ran to two or three hours rather than the planned one. The more tedious of his papers, the ones that the others on the course often skipped or only half-completed, were the ones he chose for these hours of uninterrupted quiet work. Thus he had become a model student, who completed every task, sought perfection and, even in the assessment of his tutors, often came close to achieving it.

These days his extra hours of work provided Lesley with the time to prepare their evening meal. They had recently made the decision to live together, and every evening now they shared the meal that Lesley cooked. In the past they talked, sometimes they watched television, sometimes they made love before John left to make the short walk back to his own attic bedsit. But increasingly he no longer made the walk, Lesley's bed being more inviting, warmer, softer and more stimulating than his own. Their romance had an inevitability about it, a process that neither John nor Lesley felt they promoted, but one which they seemed unable to stop. They felt at times that their friendship, even relationship, as Lesley now called it, had a life of its own, a vitality that compelled both of them to strive for its preservation and growth. So what had started as a chance meeting had blossomed – as both of them were apt to describe it – and marriage seemed the next obvious and desired step. Unfortunately, Lesley's parents had other ideas.

They had repeatedly tried to persuade their daughter to end the relationship. She knew where the problem lay. John was an 'African'. Her father repeatedly made fun of John's name, pronouncing it as if it was some Edwardian music hall joke. Lesley resented this, was embarrassed by it from the start, but could find no way of communicating her feelings to her father. But each time she sensed her parents' opposition grow stronger, almost to spite them, she had taken the next step to deepen the relationship. And so they had now reached the stage where John was ready to move in with her. They would save on rent, of course, but the decision was not pragmatic, it was committed on both sides. Lesley had embraced him and said that she agreed on one condition, which was that he should never move out. And this was what brought the disagreement with her parents to a head.

After just two months of living together with pleasurable ease, they found that they had learned to care for one another, to love and be loved, and crucially they were ever more happy that they had made the decision, despite it being against the wishes of Lesley's parents. Initially they had reacted badly, the father's opposition moving from ridicule to anger. They didn't answer letters. They wouldn't answer the door when she called round and, for the first time in her life, she found herself shunned when she attended the Sunday morning church service that she could not remember ever having missed. She continued to go, continued to dress up in the requisite frills and finery, the hats and patent shoes that her family tradition demanded for this most social of events. She continued to walk back to the family home afterwards, but found that her mother and father had rushed off quickly, so when she knocked on their door the centre peep hole would open and then snap shut, to be followed by the clank of the top bolt being made into its hasp. If her parents were trying to bring matters to a head, they failed, because it only strengthened Lesley's resolve, made her more determined to marry John Mwangangi and heighten her desire to be with him. He was a Roman Catholic, of course, and she was not. Perhaps that was why her parents were so opposed. But for her it didn't matter. For her there was a God; that was definite and was all that mattered.

After some weeks, her resolve began to strengthen. She wanted to bring matters to a head. If they could reject her, then she could reject them. She decided that she and John must confront them together, but she decided that this would happen after they were married. Then her parents would either have to accept the union, or reject her for good, because she knew that they would never countenance the idea of divorce, her parents viewing this as synonymous with damnation. John was close to completing the qualification that would take him to the next stage of his ambition, when he would become an employee with a salary to continue his legal training on the job. So it was a good time for them to act.

The wedding invitation had cleared the air. An apologetic letter from her parents arrived almost by return of post. There was an air of resigned acceptance about what they said, but clearly the main problem had been their daughter's living in sin, which was about to be rectified. Lesley just shook her head, asking why they had never just stated the problems outright, why they always forced her to read their minds to understand their position. But the letter had finished with a suggestion that they should all get together to discuss the future and the appointed time had arrived.

So when John opened the door, he found the apartment unusually quiet. Inside, Lesley sat with her parents. A tension that understated words of greeting only heightened, held them all in total attention. John's arrival almost created a problem. Lesley's father, conscious of being on another male's territory, sprang to his feet in what might have been interpreted as an aggressive gesture. But John merely offered his hand humbly in greeting and, with a reluctance born of suspicion, the man shook it, but clearly remained ill at ease.

What happened over the next few hours was no less than a revelation for John Mwangangi. How could he ever hope to overcome such complete misconceptions? He tried in vain, it seemed, to convince Lesley's father that he was a Christian, a Roman Catholic, no less, that he would not marry another wife and relegate Lesley to second best, that he would marry her in a church, without recourse to witchcraft or curses. It seemed he could not convince them that he was just another person, flesh and blood like themselves. They seemed to assume that he was some dangerous throwback from prehistory on a mission to steal their daughter and transport her back in time, forever out of their reach. Try as he might to convince them that he had come to Britain to study and that he had almost completed the first stage, he felt that they still regarded him as a slave trader, who would sell their daughter as soon as she was his. They would not be convinced that Lesley's children would be treated like any others, that they would not go naked, and that if they were sick they would go to a doctor.

"I cannot understand why you think that life in Africa is so different," said John eventually, his patience beginning to run short. "If we were to go and live in Kenya, Lesley and I and our children would live a life just like we would in England. The main difference would be that it would be warmer and the garden would be prettier! In any case, I have no plans to return. I will start a job with a legal firm in a couple of months and I expect to develop my career with them."

Lesley's parents were eventually pacified, it seemed, though their fears were too deep-rooted to be dispelled. But they found themselves willing to accept John's word, which was in itself progress. Lesley, however, was still frustrated with their continued unwillingness to meet them halfway and still deeply embarrassed by what she interpreted as her father's ignorance.

"Anyway," she said, "who said anything about going back to Kenya, or having children, for that matter? We certainly didn't." Her pause proved too short to allow her father to interrupt. "We have planned what we are going to do and, up to now, you have got it all wrong. John has a good job lined up. I'm going to keep my own job and within a year we'll have enough to put down a deposit on a small house. Then and only then will we think about children."

"What do you mean, girl?" said Lesley's mother. "He's a Catholic. If you marry him you'll be pregnant for the rest of your life!"

Lesley could take no more. "I don't want to hear any more of your bigotry. You're bigoted against John because he's African. You're bigoted against Catholics. Why can't you accept people as they are? What on earth has John done to you to make you so against him? And if you were always so interested in what was good for me, then why did you bring us here? It doesn't seem to have done that much good for any of us. And you go on and on about John's people, his father and his family being backward or pagans, just because they are from Africa… I don't want to hear any more."

And with that they left.

"What do we do now?" asked John.

"We get married," shouted Lesley.

Thirteen

December 1974

Celebration was in the air. The small concrete box of a room was jammed with people speaking, shouting, singing, toasting their praise of the day's events, events that had unfolded beneath a scorching December sun, events that were now celebrated beneath the hissing shadows of a pressure lamp. The dancing, which women had begun early in the afternoon was now continued less energetically by men, whose drunken steps and tipsy words masked their fatigue. The women, who had previously danced and sung prompted by the ululations of their adopted leader, had sweated in the sun before an attentive crowd of four thousand eager to be pleased. The men, now repeating the songs with their voices flattened by beer, sweated in the heavy air of the bar, ignored by all, it seemed, save for a brace of geckoes, glued to the wall by their fear of movement. Some, trying to talk, sat with a finger in one ear, trying to ignore the noise. Others, more intent on conversation, shouted abuse at the rabble, imploring them to fill their throats with more beer and then either be silent or choke. Mbuvu, a caustic old man who drank only bottles of stout and had the stomach to testify, leaned on the bar, half-turned towards the dancers and half towards the barman, Mwinzi who sat, as ever, on a high stool with elbows on the bar, his chin resting in his hands, and his face frozen in the cynical but long-suffering smile with which he tried to tell his customers it was time to leave.

Mbuvu, an elder perhaps before his time, earned his living from a general store by the market, a store which provided sufficient income for him to devote much of his own time to local politics. His years of experience of council debates had cemented his face into an expression of cynical superiority. His mouth was curved like an upturned banana, and was heavily jowled with well-exercised and over-developed muscles, which tensed and twitched whenever he was forced to listen. When he spoke, his whole frame seemed to forge the words which flowed from him like a gale. In the past, the storms he spoke had cut all opposition to shreds, but recently his reputation had been harmed by a number of defeats at the hands of younger, more lively, more educated men, who withheld their respect for his age as a way of expressing how much they despised his ideals. Like an old dog in his kennel, he still ruled Migwani, but his influence was now smaller and shrinking. Janet only knew him as the overweight shop owner who took the money for the goods others served. Always seated behind his desk at the rear, his customers had to queue before him while he inspected his assistants' handwritten receipts, checked the prices and re-tallied the totals. Only then did he take payment, stashing it in the rattling bottom drawer of his metal desk before applying his personally cut rubber stamp to the bill. Only then could the customer go back to the assistant and claim the newspaper-wrapped bags of sugar or tins of cooking fat they had bought. Michael also told her of rumours that he had once been so abusive to one old man that his adversary had gone mad as a result and had never regained his sanity or his health, but Janet had no real idea what he meant.

In the corner of the room, below the place where the lizards hung to the wall, sat a group of people clustered around a square low table now overflowing with ash trays and bottles. The bar had long ago run out of glasses so beer was now drunk neat from the bottles, undiluted by the dregs of dirty washing-up water from the bowl behind the bar in which the glasses were habitually and fruitlessly rinsed. The laughing group had become the room's elite, the recognised and much observed high table one must be invited to join, around which the hopeful hovered. John Mwangangi, resplendent in the khaki uniform of his office, was partnered by Lesley, his wife, who drank little and listened rather than spoke. Across the table, draped across his chair as if melting, sat Father Michael, dividing his time between conversation with the group and impromptu solo renderings of revolutionary Irish songs, performances that in any case no one could hear above the general din. Janet, locked in a necessarily shouted discussion with John, perched on the very edge of her chair. Patches of sweat had spread across her back, dark staining her pink T-shirt. A drunk who had been dancing behind her, repeatedly tried to apologise, thinking he had splashed her with his beer. Having received her acceptance of his remorse on the first time of asking, he had expected to suffer verbal attack and had been surprised by her smiling politeness, interpreting her kindness as an invitation. Consequently, during the last hour he had repeatedly offered the same apology at regular intervals, prodding Janet on the shoulder to secure her attention. As time passed, his advances included graphic and obvious references to his belief that she wanted to sleep with him, but still Janet could decipher not a word of what he said, and chose to ignore the rather obvious gestures, believing them to be 'cultural'. So she continued to smile and nod, a tactic, which, of course, guaranteed yet another intervention from your man. The fact that through her smiles she was consistently saying, "Piss off, you drunken old sod," made no impression whatsoever across boundaries of misunderstanding, since he spoke no English and she had no Kikamba. Each exchange thus ended with prolonged laughs and smiles, only to begin again a few minutes later.

The last permanent guest at the table was Mwanza, the primary school headmaster, who, though never actually invited to any gathering, always endeavoured to muscle in to any function he deemed worthy of his presence. Tonight, as on most occasions, he was out of his depth and, listening with overstated interest to everything that was said, he played the role of spectator, feigning understanding by joining in with the other's laughter and mimicking their frowns of concern. Sometimes invited guests from another part of the bar would join the group to offer a self-conscious opinion on demand, only to return to their own places when the topic was changed or the point registered.

Occasionally singing, dancing and talking alike were halted by the re-emergence of a heated running argument conducted across the room between, at the bar, Mbuvu, and, in the opposite corner, one Councillor Ngandi, a younger, though by no means young man who had become Mbuvu's arch-rival both in official circles and in commerce. They pulled no punches in their waves of verbal attack, reason playing no part in either of the protagonists' rhetoric.

Though the parties themselves remained deadly serious, everyone else listened because it was entertaining, like a double act providing a floor show on this night of celebration. Mwanza, for Janet's benefit, gave an instantaneous translation, which probably made up in colour for what it lacked in accuracy. Michael and John listened to the original, of course. The proceedings were already at an advanced stage.

Mbuvu spoke.

"He is saying that the other man is no good," said Mwanza, his lips almost touching Janet's ear.

Ngandi replied.

"This man says that Mbuvu is a proud old man."

Eyes swung back to Mbuvu, who was overtly offended by this damnation with faint praise. His reply was spat towards the floor.

"Mbuvu is saying that Ngandi is no more than a boy and should respect his elders and not disagree with them."

Ngandi hastily countered.

"Ngandi says that Mbuvu can speak only faeces."

Mbuvu scoffed, spat, sniffed, slurped and swore before breathing deeply twice and offering his reply.

When it came, its succinct clarity brought this particular round in the ongoing bout to an end, with himself adjudged the victor by the volume of laughter and applause from his captivated audience.

"Mbuvu says that Ngandi's words prove that the only thing he owns in life is his wife's anus."

Mwanza laughed. Janet winced and checked with Michael, who suggested that Mwanza might have been a little out with the geography of his translation. Correcting the mistake, he caused Janet to laugh and Lesley to hide her face in an embarrassed smile.

With the show over for an hour or so, the bar buzzed with frenzied repetitions of the punchline before the singing began again. Ngandi would return before long to renew the verbal warfare, armed with a different flavour of abuse. The feud would not be settled tonight, nor perhaps any other night.

The conversation which had so engrossed Janet's group was renewed. They spoke of contrasts, of similarities, of contradictions, of concordances between different ways of life. Opinions expressed neither agreed nor differed, they merely stated realities, reactions or experiences. This was not debate, it was phenomenology, lubricated by beer, with each contributor offering personal experience as gospel, with each concentrating on the complexities of their personal experience, those unexplained details which form the basis of non-communication. And, as the evening wore on, they began to realise, much to their collective surprise, that far from relating difference, they were converging towards similarity.

John spoke of his years in London and Nairobi, contrasting them with his childhood in Migwani. What he accepted without question as a boy had suddenly been rendered meaningless, its currency converted to nothing. When education took him first to Nairobi, he learned what he thought were Western values. Then, in London, he quickly realised that they were no such thing. Janet listened with amusement and admiration when John described the English as an uncomfortably direct people, because they tended to ask for what they wanted and continue to do so until they got it. She cited their experience of Ngandi and Mbuvu's argument in an attempt to disprove his assertion. That could not happen in Britain without blows, she said. But John pointed out that, though the disagreement had been graphic and loud, not once had either party cited the real source of their conflict. When Janet looked confused, he qualified by explaining that Ngandi had been selling maize in his shop at a price below the official, government-controlled rate, undercutting Mbuvu, whose business had suffered. Mbuvu had gone to law, officially accusing Ngandi of illegal profiteering. Ngandi had countered by saying that he was suffering, not gaining from his actions and that his motives were entirely philanthropic in this time of famine. And anyway, Mbuvu had been doing the same with beans, on which the profit margin was significantly greater, and for months had thus been systematically trying to undermine Ngandi's business. The real cause of the argument was even more serious. Ngandi was now seriously undermining the monopoly of Migwani's trade, a monopoly that Mbuvu had enjoyed virtually unchallenged since independence. Neither would give way since Mbuvu saw this as a threat to his influence in the town and Ngandi interpreted Mbuvu's refusal to share the market as a personal slight, believing the other considered him unworthy of the status he had already achieved.

"Why didn't Ngandi just report Mbuvu to the ministry in the first place?" asked Janet. "Had he told them that Mbuvu was selling beans illegally, surely they would have taken away his licence?"

John laughed. "This is what I mean about directness. Firstly, I am sure the idea never entered Ngandi's head. He would be questioning the old man's right to make his own decisions and therefore not showing respect to his elders. In any case, Mbuvu remains a rich and experienced man. Had Ngandi initiated an action, I am sure a sum of money would have changed hands, ensuring that the matter would be forgotten. This would have left Ngandi defenceless and Mbuvu would have bankrupted him. So it just simmers on."

"But that has nothing to do with directness. That is purely corruption and can be overcome by law," said Janet.

"But why do you say the man is corrupt?" said John. He knew he was being provocative. "It is not simply materialism. The man in the ministry is an educated young man who fears a person like Mbuvu for the same reason that Ngandi fears him. He is worthy of respect. He is rich. He is old. To act against his wishes is the same as disobeying his own father, which one cannot do. The situation arises because the official is part of a system that was imposed from outside in contradiction of existing cultural and social relationships. That is why the officials are corrupt and that is why the system doesn't work. It is serving merely to amplify existing differences and bestow power upon people who are unable to exercise it for anything other than their own benefit. In a country like this, it is not governments that govern, but people like these old men, whose psychological hold over their relatives and the young in general enables them to manipulate the system. In the past they were paper tigers, no more than leaders of an age set, who competed with leaders of other sets and whose authority died with them. Nowadays their families grow rich and the power, now expressed economically, is passed from generation to generation. We are creating an aristocracy and no one can do anything about it. In Britain, a crook like Mbuvu would be put in jail. There would be structures, associations and even business partners who would object to his manipulation and exploitation of his privilege. But here, though we all know he is a crook, we allow him to run our lives."

The debate continued and Janet could almost feel the transformation in her outlook develop. What she had previously interpreted as a simple and perhaps natural life of subsistence was transformed by John's words into a mêlée of complicated relationships, a sophisticated web of political brinkmanship, whose operation actively hindered most people's ability to prosper or, to put it another way, to avoid famine. When people sold their goats and cows to provide money for the food their land could no longer grow, who bought them? Again, it was men like Mbuvu with their ministry-granted licence to transport animals to slaughter in Nairobi. There they would get ten shillings a kilo for the meat instead of six in Migwani. Having received their money, where did people buy their food? Mbuvu and the other traders simply reclaimed the money they had paid for the animals as people went to their shops to trade. So these people were buying cheap and selling dear with the animals, and then reclaiming their money on bought-cheap and sold-dear food. They probably doubled their money every time they transacted. And of course, when people had no more animals to sell, they still had to eat, so now families were parcelling off their land, selling it in pieces to fund their lives. And guess who was buying the land. Who, in this area, has the capital to buy land and the resources to manage it? It's Mbuvu and his kind again, of course. And what do you think these people then do with the land? Do you think they make it productive in an attempt to ease the famine? No. They lease it back to peasants for cash rental and the cycle is preserved. The poor peasant has to gamble on the land producing something. He has no other option. If he wants to buy land, he has to borrow money. And where can he do this? Only from the traders, and then only at an exorbitant rate of interest. "'A clever man buys a fool's cows' is what some people say when I discuss these things. But this 'traditional' attitude misses the point. No, it's not wisdom that has an advantage over stupidity, but capital that rules poverty. Welcome to capitalism," had been John's intended closing remark, but he thought better of it. "Well, to be accurate, let's call it mercantilism. These people are still at the stage of petty accumulation."

Janet mused for a moment on the word 'petty'. She associated it with smallness, triviality, unimportance, but to her nothing in what John had included in his cycle of wealth appropriation seemed anything less than deadly serious.

"There is great feeling amongst people," John continued, "that the government is ignoring the famine, that they should give more direct help to people so they might overcome the effects of the drought without having to sell off all their possessions and their land. But what can the government do? Mbuvu and his kind control this and every other place. He controls the right men in the ministry. If they were to act against his interests, he would have them removed. People in Britain might look at the problems we have in an area like this and respond by collecting money, buying food and shipping it in from outside. But that is utterly naïve, because it ignores the reality that trade in essential items is the largest determinant of local power, and you can't undermine those interests without creating instability."

Janet could think of no answer for a while. John's argument was quite new to her. It was as if he had opened a door to a new world outside of her experience. "But what about the politicians? What about those who are elected to represent the people of the area?" she asked. "What about people like the man who spoke at the *Harambee Day* this afternoon? People really seemed to be behind what he was saying. Can't he do something to change things? I'm talking about the man who donated ten thousand shillings to the school fund."

John laughed almost uncontrollably, attracting the previously wavering attention of Michael, who had been eyeing a pair of girls dancing together, though the music had now stopped. John was still laughing as Michael's raised eyebrows queried the source of the fun. John beckoned him to lean forward across the table and said, "Janet wanted to know if James Mulonzya, our beloved member of parliament, might provide some philanthropic assistance to a campaign to reduce the hegemony of local traders."

When an almost violent fit of laughter nearly launched Michael off his chair, Janet began to feel just a little embarrassed. Was what she had said so ridiculous? She heard Michael splutter something about low flying pigs as he tried to regain control of himself. It was John who continued.

"Please don't be offended, Miss Rowlandson. We are not making fun of you. What you suggest might make perfect sense, but James Mulonzya and his kind are the next step up from Mbuvu in a single system. If locally it's the traders who buy cheap and sell dear, then regionally it is they who have to enter a similar relationship with people like Mulonzya. Don't be taken in by his Mercedes Benz, his status, or his sophisticated, university educated son..."

"I've never met his son," she said, noticing for the first time that the otherwise silent Lesley Mwangangi was in fact listening to every word. "In fact, I have never seen James Mulonzya before today. I just thought…"

"Miss Rowlandson, don't worry," John said, touching her arm whilst casting another glance across the table at Michael, who was perhaps halfway towards recovery from his near fit. "It's just that you have touched upon a nerve. Father Michael and I have set up some projects to try and address just some of the simplest needs of our area. At the *Harambee Day* today James Mulonzya confronted us about one of them. He said it was harming his interests and demanded we close it down."

"What?" she asked, genuinely surprised. "What on earth have you been doing that would prompt a member of parliament to want it closed down?"

"We've been teaching women to read in Thitani," said

Michael, suddenly in total control. It was now John's turn to laugh. Janet had lived in Migwani for almost five months, long enough to become confused. John Mwangangi had impressed her, but she was not sure if she trusted him. He seemed to know all the problems and possibly a number of the solutions, as well. His opinions seemed to be those she wanted to express herself. At the *Harambee Day* that morning, he had made a speech of the kind that she wanted to make. He tried to suggest that education was no panacea, that people should invest in their farms before schools. But people had not trusted him. After all, he was himself an advertisement for that which he counselled against. He was educated, sophisticated, knew London, had a British wife, worked with Father Michael and the church. But this Mwangangi, this official who surely had the power to influence events, he stood back and analysed rather than acted. She sensed a superior air, an arrogance that claimed special treatment, at least in her judgment. So she was confused.

Mwanza still nodded a mechanical agreement. He had understood an outline of the argument and was determined to contribute. As ever he had missed the point, but nonetheless what he did say proved enlightening for both Janet and John.

"What I can say is this," he said, leaning forward. Then, as if addressing his assembled school, he bellowed forth an experience from his own life that he considered to be relevant. As ever, his judgment was wide of the mark. Earlier, they had been discussing cultures and traditions, and mistakenly he thought their discussion still occupied that territory. He was just not sophisticated enough to inhabit John Mwangangi's world.

He explained that his son, at the age of just one year, had contracted a serious illness, well known to the people of

Migwani. The child had been very ill and his wife had taken the baby to the hospital in Kitui for treatment, where the doctor had diagnosed malaria and prescribed quinine. After another month the baby was no better and the rash, which had covered half his face, had started to spread down his neck. Mwanza then related how his wife's father had gone to the hospital to see the boy and had scoffed at the treatment he was being given. Everyone knew, the grandfather had said, that the baby's illness had been passed on from the mother, because some women possessed spirits, which affected small children. He begged Mwanza to take the boy away from the hospital and allow a traditional doctor to come to their home and say oaths for mother and baby. He claimed that he had seen this done many times and that recovery always followed quickly. Furthermore, the woman would also be cured, ensuring that the next baby would not suffer in the same way. If it was not done, the grandfather maintained, the baby and any other male children borne by his daughter would die before reaching the age of two years.

Mwanza laughed at this but, to his surprise, the others did not seem to share his amusement. As his smile changed to confusion, his gaze darted from person to person, wondering why they had not understood. "I think you have not heard what I have said," he suggested. "The point is that the old man cannot accept that the new way is better." Mwanza almost implored the others to see his point.

"We are waiting for you to tell us what you did," said Michael impatiently.

"Surely there is no more to say?" His expression changed, suddenly realising what they were suggesting. "You are not saying that I should have done what my father-in-law was suggesting?"

"It is the way he would have chosen," said John. "Your

own father would have completely trusted the traditional ways and, unlike you, he had never heard of quinine."

"What's more," interrupted Michael, his voice now an inebriated drawl, "most people still ensure that an illness is treated by a traditional doctor, even though they might use the hospital as well."

Mwanza, who was privately offended at Michael's drunkenness, became suddenly very serious. "These people," he scoffed, "are still uncivilised. They are still too afraid of witchcraft to reject it and put their trust in modern European medicine."

"What does it matter," said Michael, much too loudly, "whose medicine it is? The only thing that matters is whether or not it cures. The only reason why you reject traditional medicine is because you are told to do so by the Protestant Church. It has nothing to do with being civilised. As far as you are concerned, it is just a matter of religious bigotry."

Mwanza was too furious to react. The same principles that demanded he reject traditional medicine also required that he did not drink alcohol. His only reply was, "The religion, Mr Michael, which allows its ministers to drink beer and smoke cigarettes is the one which is bigoted."

Michael smiled. Mwanza's constant refusal to refer to him as 'Father' had become an icon for their long-running argument. The Africa Inland Church, through its literal interpretation of the bible, implored its flock to call no man a father. The mid-Western American missionaries, who lived like settler families in replicas of the wooden houses of old America, added example to their teaching. Consequently, Mwanza's son would grow up to learn to call his father only 'Pa' or 'Dad'.

Michael was silent for a while, still smiling. The others watched him, knowing that he would have something more to say. With drunkenness apparently forgotten, he leaned forward to confront Mwanza. His eyes shone with enjoyment. He had tried many times to confront Mwanza on this issue, but had never succeeded in prompting an answer. “Mwanza,” he asked, “how will you circumcise your children?”

Innocently Mwanza replied without hesitation. “They will go to the hospital to be treated by the doctor.”

Janet did not react. John laughed a little. Michael laughed hard, knocking the table and causing several bottles, some full, to go crashing to the floor, frothing and foaming their contents. “Oh Jaysus!” shouted Michael. Instinctively they all jumped to their feet. Janet gave a little scream as beer flooded over her shoes. Mwanza’s arms and legs seemed to travel in every direction at once, as he rushed to stoop and pick up what was within reach.

“What on earth has got into you?” asked Janet, infected by Michael’s continued laughter.

Michael struggled to speak, but managed a few words. “I don’t believe it!” he said. Turning towards Mwanza, who was now grovelling under the table trying to locate his rolling bottle of soda. “Do you not realise that circumcision itself is regarded by these same Europeans as a mere pagan practice? Why do you not reject that as well?”

Mwanza, crouched on one knee, glared at Michael and thumped the table as he replied. “Jesus Christ was circumcised! How dare you call it pagan when it is a Christian act?”

“Jesus Christ wasn’t a Christian. He was Jewish. I suggest you go and see your American friends in Kyome!” Michael was deadly serious now. “Go and sleep with their women and tell me if they are circumcised – and don’t give me any of your shit about fornication. Remember that you got rid of your first wife because she gave you no children! The fact is, Mwanza…" Mwanza began to shout excitedly in Kikamba to the others in the bar, but Michael shouted louder. "The fact is, Mwanza, that you respect your 'pagan' origins when it suits your own purpose. When you want to show off just how modern and civilised you are, you would insult your own father with the name 'pagan' and despise him for respecting his own culture."

Mwanza could take no more. He stormed away from the table, shouting across to Mbuvu, who was still propping up the bar, having been an amused spectator of events. He was, of course, usually a participant in heated discussion and was clearly enjoying merely watching for once. "Councillor Mbuvu, I will come and talk to you, away from these insulting Europeans." He then made a sweeping gesture towards the group, prompting John to turn and face Michael, his eyebrows raised in surprise. It was only then they all noticed that Lesley had disappeared. Like everyone else, she had stood up when Michael upset the table, but now her seat was empty. They looked around, but she was no longer in the bar.

"Did you see where Lesley went?" John asked Michael, and then Janet.

"I've no idea," said Michael. "Maybe I knocked some beer onto her and she went outside to clean it off."

"She went just a moment ago. She seemed upset," said Janet.

John continued to look around. Janet noticed the sudden concern on his face and asked him what was wrong, but he offered no answer. She told him that she was on her way to the toilet and would check if Lesley was there. With that, she made her way to the yard behind the bar and crossed the small courtyard to where three doors were let into a concrete box by the compound's back wall. The three doors were all closed, so she waited for a moment. People did not spend long inside those places, which were just shrouds for holes in the ground that stank to high heaven. The night was drenched in moonlight and the air was cool and refreshing after the kerosene stuffiness of the bar. Every visit to the bar's toilets provoked a laugh, since the three doors before her were marked in English, 'Men', 'Women' and 'Special'. Behind the first two doors were the usual facilities of a large concrete slab with a one-foot square hole knocked through the middle, thereby allowing access to the twenty-foot deep earth pit beneath. Behind 'Special' was a gleaming white European-style porcelain water closet, Armitage Shanks vintage. The catch, however, was that in Migwani there was no running water to flush it, nor plumbing to purge it. After the last customer left the bar, Mwinzi habitually carried his bowl of murky washing-up water from behind the bar to cast it from distance into the pot. This washed whatever contents had amassed during the evening around the bend and straight onto the ground over the other side of the back wall where cockroaches and flies would be waiting to consume. In the local jargon, the standard conveniences were known as 'long drops', while the 'special' glorified in the local title of 'short one'. By this time of night, the drop was usually considerably shorter, so that particular privacy was something to be avoided.

The door marked 'Men' opened first and the occupant strode proudly out into the night, apparently oblivious of Janet's presence. From behind the door marked 'Women' came a low murmur of voices. Inside, John's young clerk, Syengo, was making the most of this day of celebration. Janet recognised the other voice as that of one of the town's choosier prostitutes, a girl who restricted the granting of her services to those who could pay cash up front: government servants, teachers or businessmen. The ten shillings she had probably already negotiated and collected would buy her cigarettes and beer, and also provide food for her children, who lived with the grandmother.

After emerging through the 'Men' door, Janet returned to the bar and told John that Lesley was not at the toilets. John had already looked immediately outside and had not seen her there. He said he would leave, saying that she may have wandered back to the mission where he had left the car.

"I'll come with you," said Michael. "I'll have to go and feed the cockroaches anyway and I'd rather do it in the moonlight under a tree than in those shit boxes at the back."

Outside there was again no immediate sign of Lesley, so they separated, John going to the left and Michael to the right, towards Ngandi's ever stationary tractor, which stood like a town landmark in front of its owner's shop. Michael had not fully registered John's concern and ambled towards the tractor with his own needs uppermost in his priorities. He went nonchalantly about his well-practised routine of urinating over the tractor's bald tyres, but in mid-flow was distracted by the appearance of a figure some distance away, silhouetted by the soft moonlight against the dull red earth.

"Lesley?" he called, trying to speed his task to its completion.

Surprised, the figure looked up and turned to face the sound.

"Lesley?" he repeated, as he emerged from behind the dampened machine. "Is that you?"

This time the figure approached with a quickening step. "Where is John?" she asked. She was in tears.

John, who had already had time to walk down to the end of the town and back, heard the words and spoke before Michael could offer his answer. Lesley went straight to him and buried her face in his chest. For some minutes she clung to him, unable to speak.

Michael stood alone and apart, suddenly sobered by Lesley's obvious pain. Though he was urged to offer consolation, he was at a loss as to what to do. Blank inaction was the only result.

Gradually, as her tears began to subside, Lesley tried to speak. The words were confused. They meant nothing to Michael, but much more to John.

"Father Michael," said Lesley, "please forgive me… When he spoke… Your father came today… with Anna…" And then she was quiet again. For a moment she could neither speak nor cry. The moonlight provided more than enough light for Michael to see the fear on her face. Then she began to cry again, saying, "We should never have sent her. We should never have allowed her to go there again…"

John's words were edged with suppressed impatience. "Lesley, he is Anna's grandfather. He wants to see her."

John and Lesley returned to the mission with Michael, collected the car and left immediately. A minute later, Janet and Michael heard the blast on the horn that announced to Syengo that it was time to go home. Janet wondered if the young man had finished his consultation in the toilet, but she could not be amused, since Lesley Mwangangi's sudden change of mood still dominated her thoughts. They had encouraged Lesley to talk, but she would say nothing. John also would offer nothing by way of explanation.

An hour later the bar was closed and Migwani town's other oil lamp was out for the night. The District Officer's Land Rover had left the mission compound and would probably be just arriving in Mwingi, its passengers, except for John and Lesley, feeling the effects of the day's celebration. John was driving, having decided that both his driver and Syengo were too drunk to do the job. Lesley was quiet, having said no more since they left Migwani. In

Migwani, Janet and Michael were still awake, still together, still sharing one another's company. They sat and talked by candlelight, the words now fewer, the silences longer.

"They were in Nairobi for a few days last week," Michael told Janet over a sobering cup of coffee. "John had some business in the Ministry, some course or other. Since it's school holiday time, their daughter was at home, but she didn't want to go back to Nairobi because she had only just arrived from there a few days ago. The plan was for her to spend the time with John's family in Kamandiu. She's been there a few times. She must have arrived home today."

"Lesley was certainly very upset," said Janet. "But wouldn't say a word while any of us were around."

"It must have been something I said. What was I talking about?" he said, his eyes searching his memory. "Something triggered it, something we were talking about…"

The two were silent for a while. The only sounds that crossed the room's shadows came from the ecstatic wing beats of a moth which hovered near the candle flame.

"I can't remember," he said scolding himself, "I can't remember what we were talking about…"

Fourteen

May 1975

The sun sets in contrasts these days. The western sky is vivid blue at sunset, an azure memory of daylight's intensity, melting slowly to the soft haze of grey-turquoise half-light before this procession of darkness from the east. Kirinyaga, as if reborn with each sunset, rises through the evening mist to show itself anew to unbelievers for just a few short moments before one's eyes, peering through the gathering gloom, cannot be convinced it ever existed. This mountain pap feeds the sky, gives light to the suckling sun it hides, so that new day might follow otherwise endless dark. It is evidence of land's motherhood. We, all living things, amid false pride and blinded pity, are again revealed as no more than we are: as yet unweaned pups crawling the thicket of our mother's belly towards the summit nipple that can feed us. For these few minutes each night we see our way. We plot our course and reflect on the fruitlessness of our day, when our task was forgotten and we slipped further from our goal. As if to stoke life's resolve to survive, the mountain comes now to give us hope, to replenish the energy to succeed, to point us toward the end of our path. But in our sadness, as we mourn the death of the sun, we see that, like the horizon, our nurture has receded, our path is still long and, until another day, we have lost our way. For how long can the mountain feed the sun? For how long can someone wander before his aim, too, is dead?

To the north and west rises Kirinyaga, pointed, a silhouette with a silver edge that swallows the sun. To the south and east is Kilimanjaro's distant cone, flat-topped, menacing and brooding, its summit snows lime-lit by watery daylight, its base already rejoicing in eagerly grasped darkness. Mountains cannot meet. They are eternally alone in their confrontation, but they are bridged. For no longer than it takes a man to stand, look and notice, cirrus clouds high in the roof of the sky glow yellow, burn crimson, fade grey to prepare for night and then, mysteriously, the air itself begins to shine. Incandescent, the paths to our forefathers bridge the peaks, pass intangible and separate overhead and disappear to a near-joined infinity beyond the horizon, growing ever closer, but never finding a place in this world to meet. Only souls may go there. Only the dead can walk these paths to the junction of earth and sky from whence they came to the place where the sun is re-lit and the harvest forever cut.

But those paths are only for the privileged, for those who have a family to mourn their passing, to remember a name for just long enough to re-energise the morbid soul. The way is long, the journey difficult, the pitfalls and dangers as hazardous as those in life. So the liberated soul must rest for a while to be nurtured by the memories of the living. But a different fate awaits those who cannot be mourned. They must wander this earth forever, without hope of even starting their journey. These are the spirits we fear, their eternal imprisonment firing them to envy, an anger they seek to vent on the living.

In darkness the world is transformed. No more is it the

land that nurtures men. No more does it offer the comfort and safety of a familiar home. Night is the world of the spirit, the time when the dead visit the living to see names continued, to see the unchanging preserved, to protect and reward the virtuous, to try and punish the wicked. Night is the time when people sleep, and thus themselves mimic death, so if it should come to them they are already close to knowing its ways and will not fear its call. And if it beckons, their souls will walk the paths in the sky led by those who already know the way. But if they should see death while waking, its clutches would be those of a claw, and their spirit would be cast down on the earth to wander, tormented, like one still alive. Some of those led along the celestial paths will join their forefathers to then watch over the safety of those who bear their name. Some cast to the earth will live on, trapped by the form of a snake or an insect. The dead, the ones who forged the curse, are powerless to break the spell. Only the living, and one appointed by descent, may free the soul from its bondage and relieve those who have survived it from the torment of evil. The names of the dead must never be spoken. They may not be dead and they may hear.

Had this been an ordinary day, Migwani would have dozed through the day. There had been no market today, no point to focus the life of the town. Buses would have come and gone in their clouds of dust bringing with them their momentary panic before vanishing again, leaving only an odd traveller and the smell of their smoky black Diesel in the still hot air. Barely fifty people would have walked the track between the shops today. A handful of women, released for the day from the necessity of working in the fields and having come to sit, ignored, in the shade of an acacia, would have returned home with their unsold handfuls of softening fruit. The cobbler would have sat patiently all day in the shade of the market shelter's tin roof, quietly fashioning his fabled pairs of 'squirrel catchers' from the stretched rubber and tread of old car tyres. As the sun lowered, he would have transferred the day's products to the shelves of a nearby and as yet unoccupied concrete box of a shop he had recently rented as a base for his trade. Tomorrow he would return to repeat the day, which would prove as fruitless as the rest, but, like everyone in the sleepy place, he did as he knew, repeated his chores, relived his role, with thought for neither success nor failure. Today, as ever, cows and goats were the town's most frequent visitors. Ambling down the hill past the shops to the point where the path dipped along the floor of a deep rain-cut gulley away from the road and towards the dam, they could find their way by instinct and practice. The small boys, whose task it was to drive their fathers' stock to water, strolled along with the straggling column, stick in hand, sometimes far behind the herd, often diverted for minutes by the sight of a man mending a bicycle or the sound of a blacksmith forging a hoe. For the animals, nothing had been strange today. Mulindu's cows had been driven to water and had returned to their grazing in front of the mission. The businessman Mbuvu's massive herd of goats, newly bought at the previous week's market for sale in Nairobi, had been driven to water and had returned to their grazing behind the chief's camp. But for Migwani, this had been no ordinary day.

At seven the wind had begun as no more than a breath of breeze. By nine it had grown to its usual howling gale, blowing dust like a blizzard. To sit beneath a tin roof in Migwani at night was to listen to a chorus of cracks and pings amplified by the volume of the room. When cooled by a gust of wind, the metal contracts, squeaking and creaking on the nails that hold it to the rafters. Dust on the wind plays a rain-like line as it bounces across the corrugations. These sounds are part of the night, part of every night here. They are as natural as the clicking of crickets or the electronic buzz of the cicada; that elusive noise one never hears until it stops.

All this went quite unnoticed by John Mwangangi as he sat alone in a room behind the Safari Bar, leafing through the wad of papers he had accumulated during the day's court sitting in Migwani. His magistrate's court was held in all locations of Kitui North in rotation and today, when the case against the boys from Nzawa School was to be heard yet again, it had been Migwani's turn. Thus, that day every shop had been closed. Every person living in or near the town – all thirty – had come to the chief's camp and crammed into the mud-walled, classroom-sized meeting room to hear the proceedings. Others had walked the dusty miles via hill and valley from Nzawa, Thitani, Kyome and Kamandiu. Friends, relatives and mere acquaintances of the accused had made the journey and many others, merely curious, had joined them.

The gallery was by now both used to and tired of its role. This was the fourth time the case had come to court since the boys' bail was granted. Each time the teachers' attorney had requested and had been granted a postponement. Surely today, with the hearing to be held in Migwani, itself, surely today there would be judgment.

Looking, as usual, incongruous in his surroundings, the young attorney stood to defend his clients, the two primary school teachers. He spoke in a voice calculated to express a model of efficiency, reason and professionalism. Listening to this young man, dressed perfectly in a three-piece suit with a gold watch chain for decoration, John showed no emotion, every word of his comment couched in a consciously impartial voice without expression. Beneath this, John despised the man. He was an impostor with no right to claim the status he demanded, nor the knowledge to inform the role to which he aspired. His clients had grown afraid of the action they had brought and he knew it. All reports John had received told the same story. The whole of Nzawa seemed to know exactly what happened and, indeed, why it had happened. The whole of Nzawa knew, except for Mr Muchira and Mr Kivara, the two Kikuyu teachers involved, who stolidly maintained their own independent version. When the statements were read out in court, everyone listened intently, many laughing openly, many scoffing criticism at what they heard.

In reality, the only solid evidence to incriminate any of the accused boys was Muchira's assertion that he had recognised the voice of one of them shouting from the road by the school soon after the attack on his house. Obviously at best no more than circumstantial, this evidence John now rejected out of hand, much to the consternation of the young attorney who laboured the point for some minutes, before the magistrate, in his matter-of-fact way, simply told him to shut up or leave the court. The young man sat down deflated and humiliated and, in sympathy, Bwanas Muchira and Kivara hung their heads, and thereby effectively admitting publicly that their claim was groundless.

Witness after witness endorsed a thoroughly consistent story. It stated that the teachers had been attacked not by these boys, but by thirty parents of children from the Standard Four class. Pupils had been mercilessly beaten each day for a week by these two teachers in an attempt to discover the culprit responsible for writing an abusive slogan in pencil on the classroom wall. It had read simply, "Muchira fucks only his mother" and the abused had been incensed. As the week progressed and each day their children came home in tears, still bearing the scratches left by the crude thorn switches the teachers had used to beat them, the parents had talked, shared grievances and vowed revenge. A group had coalesced around an agreement to act, to teach these Kikuyus a lesson of their own. Under cover of darkness, they had gone to the school, stoned the teachers' houses and then beat the two pleading men with sticks. These teachers, claimed the witnesses, knew the identities of all of the masked assailants who had delivered their justice and, equally, knew full well that none of the accused students were among them. In truth, they were now afraid to stay in Nzawa and, indeed, had immediately left the area to be re-posted elsewhere. So, afraid to return or to tell the truth, lest their educator's professionalism be questioned, they had fabricated charges against those they thought might be weak enough to bully, thinking that a judgment in their favour would cover their backs. And now even their calculated ploy had backfired.

Protesting, the teachers, now oblivious of the presence of their attorney, got to their feet and shouted that the court should not be dealing with these stories. The fact remained, they implored, that they had been attacked and that their own story was accurate. The court should be trying the defendants, they pleaded, not themselves.

John silenced them with a word of warning and then, without further hesitation, brought matters to a close by dismissing the charges, announcing that there was no case to answer. The court was immediately filled with an uproar of cheering that John did not try to silence. Even the public prosecutor clapped his hands high over his head in joy. He had been released from his task in this particular case by the presence of the teacher's private attorney and had voluntarily taken on the task of organising the boys' defence, stating openly that his interest was only to see justice done. Humiliated, the trio of Kikuyu men left the room in a largely unnoticed and hasty flurry. Publicly belittled, the two teachers immediately began to argue and, feeling that it would be unwise, perhaps unsafe, to wait in town for a bus, they set off on foot along the northward road towards Mwingi. In renewed silence and order, the public prosecutor stood and formally asked John to inform the defendants of their right to take action against the teachers in view of their false accusations. John did as asked, but the youths, all exhausted in their relief at the outcome, declared themselves satisfied with acquittal and rejected the proposition. The case had already taken almost six months to resolve. It had hung over them like a weight and they were now merely glad to be rid of it.

With the court dismissed, members of the gallery went their separate ways, their smiles and staccato comments testifying to their satisfaction with the outcome. Janet, obviously relieved, came forward to thank John and congratulate her student, Munyolo, who was overjoyed at the decision and deeply grateful to her for the support she had offered. In return, he promised that she would share the next harvest from his family's farm. Faithfully, four months hence, he would bring her a bag of beans worth more than two hundred shillings and an ebony walking stick he had carved himself. He had needed to save just to buy the wood. Janet would donate the beans to the church's famine relief service, but the stick she would treasure and, though clumsy and crude, she would prize it as one of the greatest mementos of her stay in Kenya, even when, years later, it would form the centrepiece of her display in St Mary's School library.

John, himself, had gained a lot of satisfaction from the case. Though he had tried to remain impartial, the more he learned about the events of that night in Nzawa and, indeed, those of the preceding week, the more he became angered by the attitudes and deeds of the teachers. Much as he condemned the action of the parents, he could not help but sympathise with them. It seemed that Muchira and Kivara, and others like them throughout Kenya, considered themselves, by virtue of their education and the salaries they drew, to be above reproach, above criticism, above even the law. These people despised the uneducated, illiterate poor of Nzawa, dismissing them as peasants, who knew of nothing other than the cultivation of their fields or the driving of their skinny goats and head-hanging cows. They seemed to assume that no one, save perhaps for the school's headmaster, had any right to criticise their actions. Since, in this case, their headmaster was Mr Mwanza, whose prime consideration was not the education of the children but their adoption into the Africa Inland Church, the teachers did not even respect his right to question them. John took great satisfaction in bringing these two arrogant men down to earth and his decision had clearly been popular with the locals, but he was equally aware that he was taking something of a risk. Without doubt the two aggrieved teachers would soon be knocking on the office door of a contact, a relative or a friend in some ministry or other, to complain that this Mwingi magistrate had not shown due respect for their status and had succumbed to pressure from the mob. Entries would be made in his file and if, one day, the gossiped claims of such enemies, though empty, developed weight out of sheer numbers, then surely someone would take notice and he would thereby have a new enemy, and one to be feared. But for John, here in Migwani, it was only justice and the truth that deserved any respect.

Now, save for a moth trapped in the room, he was alone. Today the District Officer and his entourage had not immediately returned to Mwingi, as they would normally have done. Tomorrow there would be a fund-raising *Harambee Day* for a Migwani primary school, a day of celebration, speeches and auctions that John was required to attend in an official capacity. As usual, there were to be four speakers. The chairman of the school governors would start the proceedings and Migwani's Chief would follow. John would be third on the rostrum, just ahead of the star attraction, James Mulonzya, the area's member of parliament. It was expected at such gatherings for the invited speakers to extol the still unquestioned virtues of education, to praise the Government's wise and effective policies in the sector and to list and elaborate the numerous successful projects throughout the region. Over three thousand people were expected to attend. It would be another day of celebration, a near repetition of the others he had attended during his time as Northern Region District Officer. But this was likely to be his last such occasion. Unknown to anyone in Migwani, John Mwangangi was about to leave his post. In a month or two he would move to Nairobi to reclaim his own legal career with a prestigious law firm.

Events that had appeared random at first sight had mysteriously combined to provide the lure of an opportunity he found attractive, alongside a push he could not ignore. It had been soon after the turn of the year that one George Nzou, a Migwani man, younger than himself, had sent him a letter of invitation. John knew Nzou from his time in university. They had shared a year in Nairobi before John left for Europe. When Nzou graduated, he joined a Nairobi firm and had stayed with them ever since. He was now a partner. Nzou's letter had suggested that he might consider joining the partnership himself, alongside, of course, a substantial input of capital. At the time, John had acknowledged the request, but declined the offer.

Certainly at the time, his priority remained public service in Mwingi.

But then two months later, Nzou wrote again, this time with better conditions and, crucially, recognition of John's superior qualification, experience and expertise. The conditions were easier, the capital input reduced and the potential earnings greater.

That same week, perhaps coincidentally, John found himself hauled before the District Commissioner in Kitui. He was a much older man, a more 'traditional' administrator, who at all costs sought to preserve order and respect among the elite of the District, though with younger elements, such as John, he could be pugilistically direct. There was a complaint, the Commissioner announced, from a respected man in Thitani. "Bwana Mwangangi," he continued, the verbatim transcript of the session having lodged solid in John's memory, "we public servants must not play politics. Teaching women to read and write is a commendable activity, but using that context as a vehicle to attack a political opponent is not an activity becoming of a District Officer." The words, clearly, were well chosen, well rehearsed, and delivered according to the script, whose authorship remained anonymous, but suspected. And so John was formally requested to withdraw his official and personal support for non-governmental activities. All of his joint ventures with the Church would have to cease. He would supervise them in his official capacity, of course, since that would remain his job, but he should no longer be a participant.

And so the knot tightened. His honeymoon was over. His official duties remained, but his interest in informal, community-based projects could only be furthered at arm's length. He could, of course, continue with his own projects, such as the farm, which were funded by his own capital, but that was a limited resource. But, and here is how the circle closed, it could be bolstered in the longer term by increased earnings from private practice. A carrot and a stick, offered in the right order. Too good to be true. There were forces at work here, but at all times he felt he could keep the upper hand. The reason why they acted was because he was succeeding. A tree by a busy road always bears scars. And in the future he could still succeed in exactly the same way, but from a different place. And so there were changes afoot in his life, changes that meant that his judgment in the Nzawa case could be made without fear of drawing extra attention to himself, for that was already accomplished.

And he had to admit that the bush was not a place where Lesley wanted to be. With their daughter now settled in a Nairobi boarding school, it made sense to move to the city, and so he was to leave government service and re-enter the private sector. He was by no means defeated and had ongoing projects in Migwani, which would continue to demonstrate how families could profit from the land. Details of the schemes, including his own farm in Kamandiu, would form the basis of his speech, on which he now worked.

The speech would, he hoped, be different from the others, different indeed from the norm. Whilst he expected the other speakers to express the usual, established position of the virtue of education, he wanted to encourage a different perspective. Whilst the mainstream would restate the platitude that schools and education were beneficial to students, communities and country alike, his own speech must introduce some practical realism. The received view, of course, was that through the amassing of knowledge a student could become qualified, could secure employment and salary, and thereby fund the education of siblings or their own children, thus closing the virtuous and expanding circle, strengthening the individual, society and nation.

John's view, however, was that this ideology was a trap that for most people in this poor place, ensnared them in worsening poverty. He would, as usual, grant the importance of education for the child and would recognise the potential contribution the school could make to the well-being of the town. But he would also stress the shortage of jobs, even for highly qualified school leavers. Parents could no longer think of education as being like a calf, an investment that would grow to a profitable maturity, if it was nurtured with care. To the old men he would offer the advice that they should never let their children forget their true heritage. They should see that traditions and values were maintained, even though the children might come to despise them as uneducated or primitive. They should encourage their children to stay connected to the land, to the farm, the resource that could offer food and nutrition, and thereby security and health. He would address the young and encourage them to turn back to their *shambas* after school, and become farmers like their forefathers. Did they know, for instance, that a crop of onions, destined for sale in the towns, could produce a profit of twenty thousand a year? All it took was water. If children used school properly, they could learn how to collect, store and use rainwater to grow such a crop of onions, or cabbage, or tomatoes. Education would always help, he would say, but he would temper his support with the warning that it could never be a guarantee of future prosperity.

The following day John's speech would be politely applauded and acknowledged, but not understood. After all, he, himself, was an educated man, an office-bound civil servant who owed all his achievements to his schooling. Surely this was proof that his words were mistaken? Why should they scratch a living from the land when Mwangangi, the one who advised them along this path, had himself branched onto the alternative way, that of education in the white man's school in the white man's country? And why should they heed these words if the one who spoke them did not live this life himself? If Mwangangi had farmed vegetables, would he ever have returned to govern them? No, they would not be fooled. A school, a fine rich school is what they wanted and Migwani needed. The future lay in employment, not agriculture.

So as the moth tried in vain to force a way through the glass of the oil lamp by whose light he wrote, he deliberated over the wording of a speech that was destined to pass over the heads of his audience. Outside there was only wind and dust and the silence of the town. Then he was aware of footsteps, short quick steps, stopping, walking, stopping again, walking again. And then there was a knock on his door.

It was Janet, alone, who entered the room. "I'm sorry to disturb you, Mr. Mwangangi," she said very quietly, her nervous deference lowering her voice as well as her stature, "but I wanted to see you about this morning's hearing. I didn't get a chance to say anything to you after the court was adjourned."

John invited her to sit down on the room's vacant chair. When staying overnight in Migwani, as was sometimes necessary, he always rented this particular room, known to Father Michael as the King's Suite because of its relative opulence. The ten shilling charge included not only the unlimited use of an oil lamp, a table and the usual bed and foam mattress, but also two chairs, rather than the usual one and also, on cold nights, a charcoal burner with fuel. "Certainly," he said. "What is it that you want to know, Miss Rowlandson? Were you not satisfied with the outcome?"

They both laughed before Janet answered. "Of course I was happy with it!" she said. "I was absolutely overjoyed with the verdict. Everyone was. And so was Joseph Munyolo. He told me afterwards that it was like being released from a prison that had got smaller and smaller over the months. Those teachers have dealt a real blow to his future, you know, but I am sure he will overcome it. He had wanted to go to the polytechnic in Kitui to learn motor mechanics, but at the interview he had to tell them about the case and the fact that he was waiting to be called to court. They told him that they could not consider his application until the outcome was known, so, by the time he can apply again, he will have wasted a full year. I think they will accept him, but he has suffered."

"I am very pleased, Miss Rowlandson," said John sympathetically, "that your student can at least pick up his life where it was left off. I accept he has suffered, but nothing further can be done by way of recompense unless the accused make a case against the teachers, and none of them want to do so." There was a pause here, a pause that signalled an end to the matter. "Can I get you something?" he asked. "Would you like a beer?"

She accepted, though feigned reluctance on the grounds that she had marking to do for the following day. But it clearly was no impediment and John went out to the bar, returning with a bottle of Tusker for Janet and a soda for himself. Settling in his seat again and pouring his drink, he looked up and asked what he could do for her.

Retiringly, Janet looked away, saying, "I've come to apologise. On those occasions when I came to your office in Mwingi, I was extremely rude. I didn't accept it when you told me that you were just doing your job. I thought that… well…"

"...That I would back the people with the social status, like every other small town official would do? ...That I would take the easy way out?" John let the silence provoke a reaction in his guest. It was one of surprise at his candour and directness.

"You remember the confusion over his name?" Janet asked, pausing herself to allow his acknowledgement. "His real name is Munyolo, but on all the statements – including his own! – it was recorded as Munovo. The policeman didn't even trust him to know how to spell his own name. Well, I thought that everything was going to work like that, with no one listening to what he and the other accused had to say and with every word of the 'educated' teachers taken as gospel."

John thought for a moment and laughed. "Oh yes, I remember. The policeman did think that way. The teachers had given the policeman a spelling of the name and he simply refused to listen to what the boy said. I also remember that you went to the police station and frogmarched the poor young man into my office, where he refused to admit that he had not checked it. He insisted, didn't he, that the boy had spelt it that way? He had to save face. I must say, Miss Rowlandson, that after watching you deal with that policeman, I am quite relieved that we meet tonight in pleasant circumstances. I think I would not like to be on the receiving end of your anger."

His attempt at small talk embarrassed her a little. "Do you mean to say that you knew the name was wrong and yet didn't say anything?" There was a hint of aggression in the end.

"I could not offer opinion," he replied seriously. "I was presented with a signed and witnessed statement. If the policeman says it is a fair and true record, then I must accept it as evidence. Later, when it comes to trial, when all the evidence is presented and considered, then it can be judged as true, false, relevant or not. I am a prisoner of my position. I must be seen to do only what is allowed and correct at each stage of the process. First I have to record, then consider, then conduct a hearing and finally judge. Incidentally, in Kikamba, there is no difference between Munyolo and Munovo. I had to give equal importance to every piece of evidence, since I was in no position to judge at that stage." He spoke with great precision, a quality that impressed Janet greatly. She had never before met a Kenyan who seemed to think so deeply about every aspect of his responsibilities, who was conscious of his power without displaying the slightest intention of wielding it to his own advantage.

"I hope you won't be offended," she said tentatively, "but I thought it was your way of asking for a bribe…"

John burst into laughter, provoking Janet to follow suit. "You flatter me," he said. "I don't think I am capable of turning a situation like that so quickly to my advantage. Believe me, Miss Rowlandson, I just don't think like that. I was just trying to do my job."

Three hours elapsed before Janet left the room. She had smoked a few cigarettes and had drunk a couple of beers, which John had bought, with his visits to the bar being carefully noted by the clientele. The conversation they had shared ceased to focus on the day's court hearing and had eventually meandered into many aspects of their lives. At last Janet had met someone with whom she could not only converse as an equal, but also respect as an intellectual superior. Though she might live through phases when one despised one's intellect and shunned its every call, as Janet had consciously done for months, its reawakening is quite involuntary and can be an enlightening surprise. John had been adamant. Janet had asked questions, offered alternative suggestions, but he would not be swayed from his assertion. By the end, Janet had totally succumbed to agreement. No matter how long she might live in Migwani, she could never be accepted as a member of the community, never be accepted as an equal by the people of the area. In their eyes, she must always remain special – white, privileged - and, as a consequence, rich. She was educated, a teacher and, that rarest of things, an attractive unmarried woman.

Janet had turned the conclusion on its head. What about himself? Forgetting the fact that he was not white, many of the same arguments also applied to him. He had lived abroad for years. He had grown up in a European education tradition, had learned to live a way of life different from his family heritage. He was also considerably richer than Janet could ever imagine herself becoming, and had recently become the owner of a large tract of land, which Father Michael had pointed out to her on a recent trip to Mutito. John, however, flippantly avoided answering her point. Donning an Etonian accent and sharpening the edges of his voice, he spoke with pure English phlegm. "Mind you," he said, as Janet began to smile, "I do speak their lingo absolutely fluently." Thus the evening ended on a high note with a laugh and, as Janet walked home in her torchlight, she was glad she made the decision to offer her apology and she felt faintly energised, renewed by an entertaining conversation that had meandered across several areas of common ground.

She had learned, for instance, that they shared an enduring love of London and that they had effectively attended neighbouring colleges. Janet had been at King's College on the Strand, while John, a decade earlier, had been just across the road and round the back in Lincoln's Inn. They discussed the 68 bus route, and how dour-faced

Londoners would take their seat and would say the single word 'Elephant' to the conductor as they handed over their fare. They both remembered the experience as absurd, perhaps surreal. She told him of her year in Kenya and how she liked to visit the dances at the Umoja in Kitui at weekends. And so the man she had met with Michael in a bar, on a night when some personal or family matter had brought the evening to an abrupt halt, had now become a friend.

Left alone, John first set about completing his speech, but soon he felt tired and decided he was no longer capable of concentrating. He decided to go to bed, but first returned the empty bottles to the bar. Back in the room and after undressing, he reached across the table to put out the lamp but, for some unconscious reason, he opted to lever the glass up and blow out the flame rather than simply turn down the wick. The moth, which had clung to the roof motionless for some time, again took to flight as the new breeze wafted the flame to a smoky flicker.

John's eyes were drawn by the movement and he waited, almost statuesque for a while to watch, the lamp's glass still raised. Suddenly all was a flurry. The moth's wings beat the flame to blue and then, rising quickly, it hit the ceiling with a crack, and then the wall and floor. He turned, but lost sight of it as it flapped to the edge of the room. Then in a moment it was flying again and he turned to watch as it stuttered across a wall. Back to the flame it came. This time a wisp of smoke near the wing was white, not black like kerosene soot. Then it hovered, working frantically to maintain its motionlessness. It rose again before dropping again like a stone to plunge under the lamp glass and into the flame. An orgasm? For a moment the insect seemed to be alive yet totally helpless, lying prostrate on the table with wings outstretched feigning death. Then complete agitation followed as it ran along the table, over papers, books, John's arm in an apparently randomly repeated path. Then it stopped again, holding the shaking wings out as if to cool its large soft body. The seemingly over-fat abdomen was cream with a brown spot above.

To the air again, as if to rediscover the path to ecstasy, like a child eagerly clambering back to the top of a slide he has just gleefully descended, it rose halfway up the wall and climbed, its wings beating out a violent excitement. Was this expectation of what was to come? Now he dropped to the flame again and there was a pop, sounding more like an explosion in the deep quiet of the place. This time it was stronger. He has played with death again, doing only what instinct tells him. He was an insect attracted to a light.

Now there is no restraint in his abandon. The violence seems stronger this time, deeper and closer to pain, stronger and further from control: a private ecstasy, greedily clutched. His gyrations roll him over the tabletop and onto the floor, surely now earthbound forever, never again to flirt with the flame he desires so much. A raised hand. His body is at rest save for a leg twitching involuntarily. As the hand moves closer, his fit begins anew. One finger presses. A slight crack – like the fracture of a peanut shell – brings life to an end without mess. A passing sugar ant, on some lone sortie across the floor beneath the cover of darkness, stops to prod the giant body once or twice with his antennae. He moves on his way, unimpressed. The gentlest of breaths puts out the flame.

Fifteen

October 1974

An old man's advice is always remembered. He speaks the wisdom of experience, not the half-truths of youthful self-interest. He is the one who can solve life's problems by telling of old ways now forgotten or ignored. He is the teacher of children and a kind and compassionate grandparent when the parents are away. He knows how to keep children happy and keep young boys from mischief. The stories he can tell them will all be the stories of long ago and the children will listen with amazement, learning from the parables he has lived.

The path was narrow and steep, but Musyoka, who had walked this way many times, knew it well and strode briskly and confidently along the ledges, which perched on the very shoulders of the hillside. Anna followed him closely, reassured by her grandfather's confidence. He helped her over the difficult parts, especially where the path dipped suddenly into a gulley whose sides were strewn with loose stones. In spite of his age, Musyoka was used to jumping straight to the bottom of these trenches, and thereby not making the sometimes treacherous descent, with its danger of sliding and slipping on the rocks. He knew how to choose the place to land, where the dust was deep and soft enough to break the fall. Surely he must convey this skill to Anna, his granddaughter, but today was not the moment and he held her hand tightly as he picked a careful way down the gulley sides, kicking away the piles of stones to make the footing sure.

The path took them away from Kamandiu and into the massive valley of Ikoo. Then, winding between the hills, it met the Vinda at the end of the valley and turned right towards Museve. There, beneath the hill, stood his son's new house, where Anna would be reunited with her parents after her short stay at her grandfather's house. There were nearly seven miles to walk but Musyoka, who had known an age when there was no other way to travel, thought nothing of it. He had scoffed in disbelief at the overt concern his son's wife had shown at the thought of her daughter having to walk such a distance. In Musyoka's eye, it was nothing, the kind of journey a normal child might make twice every day on the way to and from school. Had Anna been his own daughter, he told her, his words translated for Lesley's benefit by John, she would walk that distance every day from the age of seven to carry water from the well.

In fact he had been worried himself, but not by the length of the walk. As John and Lesley set off in their Land Rover to Nairobi, he and Anna began their walk up the valley towards his home. He was privately afraid that the two days she would stay with him in his household would seem like an age if the child proved to be undisciplined or frightened. All his fears, however, proved groundless. From the start, the moment he called his granddaughter by her Kamba name, Katuunge, the name of his own wife, he realised that the child had warmed to him and would more than enjoy her stay. He had been told many shocking stories of the ways that Europeans treated their children, of how they were not taught to respect their elders or even their own parents, and he feared that these ways may have influenced his son during his time overseas. He found to his satisfaction, however, that the girl was a fine child, who had been taught already many of the ways of her father's people. She could speak some words of his language, enough for them to converse about simple things. Though he would rarely admit it, he could also understand quite a lot of English and so, in a private mixture of languages, they learned much of one another. Initially it had been Musyoka who was the one held spellbound. She told him things about London and her school in Lambeth, about her other grandparents and the other people she called aunts and uncles when they visited their home. Many of them were in fact no relation whatsoever, being her father's friends, many of them Kenyan and some of them Kamba, who had met her father through his work. Above all Musyoka could not understand one important point. "Your mother," he asked, "she is English?"

"My mother always says she is British," Anna had replied, "but she was not born there. My grandfather and grandmother came to England when she was a girl, but she was very young and cannot remember the other place."

Though Anna's Kikamba was slow, inaccurate and confusing, it was good enough alongside the occasional English word for Musyoka to understand. "Ah," he said, as if a light had been switched on in his mind, "so they came to England from Africa, just like your father."

"No," she answered innocently. "They have never been to Africa."

The old man scratched his head. He could not understand how these people could not have come from Africa. They were certainly not English because they were black. Their daughter and their granddaughter were black, and black people come from Africa. He could not understand. Over the two days of her stay in Musyoka's home, Anna tried to explain many times that her mother's parents were not African and had never been to Africa, but still he knew what must be true, and so preferred to trust his own assumptions.

By the end of her stay Anna had become the centre of the household. All day-to-day tasks were neglected, or done by Musyoka's other wives to allow John's mother, Musyoka's first wife, to devote all of her time and attention to her granddaughter. Mwikali, Musyoka's youngest daughter - there had been no more sons - took time off from her work to walk with little Katuunge, to talk to her. At this time of year, Mwikali's days were usually a repetition of hoeing between the ripening maize to prevent the inter-planted beans from being stifled, so she was very happy that Katuunge had come to stay. Having completed primary school, Mwikali spoke some English and Anna enjoyed satisfying her endless curiosity. She had found the questions just as funny as the family found her answers. Previously, Anna had seen her grandparents for only a day at a time and always accompanied by her parents. When her father spoke Kikamba to others, she could not understand what he said. Her mother, on the other hand, spoke no Kikamba at all, having always maintained that she did not want to learn the language, because it would never be of any use to her. Until this visit, therefore, Anna had exchanged little more than occasional greetings with her grandparents, but this time it had all been different. They had been kind to her and above all had explained many things that were new and some others that she had never fully understood. For their benefit, she had tried to recall as much as she could about London, but somehow it now all seemed a long way away, and it was not easy to remember.

But she had played with the other girls. On the second day she had played with a girl of her own age from the next *shamba*, and she realised that this was the first real friend she had made in Migwani. Together they followed the goats to the dam and then drove them back again. What she would treasure from this short holiday, however, was her new friend's plain bamboo flute for which she had swapped a charm bracelet that her mother had bought her as a souvenir of a trip to Brighton.

By lunchtime the journey was over. Hand in hand Musyoka and Anna, who now wanted to be known as Katuunge, ran the last thirty yards to the house, laughing as they scrambled their way up the gentle incline.

Anna ran smiling to her mother, who had emerged from the house to greet her. The child laughed pure joy while her mother gently wept beneath her smiles, so great was her maternal relief. Within the embrace, Anna, as only a child is able, spoke a torrent of words with ebullient excitement. It seemed that she told the entire story of her stay away from home inside a minute. She listed memories of events, scenes and pictures, the whole rushing out in a jumble. Her grandfather's house was made of mud. And she had slept in another house also made of mud. It had a grass roof where bugs lived, bugs that fell on her during the night and woke her up. She had eaten such a mountain of maize she thought she might burst. She had driven goats to the dam and back, and had helped her grandmother to bring water from the wells, a job that required her to carry the heaviest load she had ever tried to lift. She had played with other girls and swapped her bracelet for a flute.

Lesley, in contrast, was almost too overcome with relief to speak. When she did, her quivering lips could mouth only a mother's questions, all focused on the mechanics of life. Was she all right? Had she eaten well? Did she have water for washing? Had she gone to bed at the proper time? Musyoka, standing some respectful distance from this meeting of mother and daughter, smiled contentedly, propping himself up on his stick, as he watched them hug and kiss.

After a while, Lesley pulled away and held her daughter at arm's length, looking her up and down, as if to check that she was all there. With a comforting smile she told Anna to go inside and wash. Anna protested strongly, but her mother simply shook her head and feigned a refusal to listen. "You've walked a long way this morning, my lady", she said, "and your dress is dirty. There is a pan of hot water in the bathroom ready for you and some cold in the bucket by the sink. So off you go and get washed. Put on the clean dress I've left on your bed – and be sure to put those dirty clothes in the washing basket." Anna, now reluctantly resigned to obeying her mother's command turned and spoke to her grandfather, much to Lesley's surprise, in Kikamba, before rushing off towards the open kitchen door at the rear of the house. The old man smiled, waved and said a quick "OK" in reply.

Lesley had never learned how to feel comfortable when left alone with John's father. Unlike Musyoka, she had always been highly self-conscious and embarrassed about their lack of a common language, since she had no Kikamba, save for pleasantries, kitchen jargon and simple greetings, all of which she had learned out of necessity rather than desire. Whenever she tried to speak the language, she felt only extreme embarrassment and tension, later always transformed into irritation and nervousness. Being tonal, the language held numerous pitfalls for one whose ear had not been trained to hear it from birth. A change of stress, a change of tone, a rise rather than a fall, a flat line instead of a staccato clip were all capable of changing a chair into a vagina, milk into lakes, and a fly to tits. One, like Lesley, whose ear had been trained to hear only English, would inevitably make numerous howling errors with every attempt to speak, guaranteeing great entertainment for all. White men seemed to stretch their lips in order to mouth the language's profusion of vowels and always seemed to speak down their noses. Even priests like Michael, who spoke the language with apparent fluency, would still fall victim to at least one howler per conversation, and the particularly harsh edges of Michael's voice, an accent produced by the encroachment of broad Limerick, rendered his speech birdlike in most people's ears. His nickname – *ngunguu*, a pied crow – reflected not only this similarity, but also mirrored, through the birds black and white markings, people's appreciation of the near schizophrenia of his character. Some people, Lesley among them, were not equipped to deal with the embarrassment that trying to use the language inevitably brought, and thus the tension strengthened, precluding any further learning.

Musyoka, himself, always tried hard to communicate with his daughter-in-law. Speaking an amalgam of Kikamba and English, a curious hybrid language in which every adjective was a gesture of the hand, he would try, often in vain, to say what he wished. His English vocabulary, however, was limited to the useless words that are commonplace in the army. If ever the subject of the conversation might shift to cleaning a rifle, doing parade, or the cooking of barracks food, he would be able to make his point with ease. This smattering of English, however, was usually used to the detriment of communication rather than its aid.

"A cup of tea?" mouthed Lesley, almost chewing the words as she offered generic drinking motions of the hand.

The old man nodded and mumbled the word "*Chai*" under

his breath. As he followed her into the house, his previous expression of uncertainty hardened into suspicion.

What annoyed Lesley the most was Musyoka's manner. She was convinced that he did not trust her and was resolved never to trust her. He would eye her, squinting from beneath the thin lines of his eyebrows, which he would draw up like crests on the protruding sharp bones of his brow. In truth, she was rather afraid of him. It was not a tangible fear provoked by some identifiable aspect of his demeanour, but a deep indefinable mistrust that she seemed powerless either to ignore or overcome. Again today Musyoka had begun to eye her in that way, his forehead all furrowed. If only they could communicate. She began to feel quite nervous. On most occasions when he behaved like this, unknown to Lesley, there were specific reasons that provoked his suspicion. His actions were intentional and expressed the misunderstandings that developed between them. Neither realised that the sources of the tension in their encounters were prosaic misunderstandings which, if either had even a modicum of understanding of the other's language, could easily have been avoided.

Today, for instance, though quite willing, even keen to accept the drink Lesley had offered, Musyoka wondered why she had bothered to ask. Lesley believed she had merely asked if he would like to drink tea. Musyoka, interpreting the question surely as anyone would, believed it was said to hide a personal slight. Anyone, after walking several miles to honour an invitation from a son, would expect to find a meal waiting for him on arrival. The person would not be asked to stay to eat because that would be assumed. To be offered something was therefore surely a way of saying that this would be all he would get. Lesley, via her strange, misinterpreted question had placed her father-in-law in some confusion. Did she really mean that there was only tea, or would there be food as well? If he accepted the tea, he ought to leave as soon as it was finished. It was rude to stay beyond what had been offered, for it was a criticism of the quality or quantity of the gift. But if he left he would still be hungry. Had Lesley been a European, he would have accepted her rude behaviour and lack of respect. All white men were the same, after all. But since Lesley was black, as far as he was concerned, she ought to know the correct way of doing things. Her parents, he concluded, must have been poor teachers.

Musyoka stood by the kitchen door, just accepted inside the house. He held his tattered hat close to his chest until Lesley specifically and exaggeratedly beckoned him towards the central table. Immediately he was rendered quite speechless by what he saw. This was his first visit to his son's newly completed house. He had seen it before only as a skeleton, unroofed and unplastered. Never had he seen a house like this. Lesley had modelled it on the desirable English home. The old man had never seen so much furniture in one room. In his eyes, the rooms felt like the inside of a shop waiting for customers to come and take items away with them. And the rooms were all too large. How would they ever be kept warm after sunset, especially since none of them had anywhere for the smoke to escape? Why did his son fill this house, in which they would only stay at weekends or holidays, with so many possessions? Surely he did not need them all. Possibly he had brought them to sell to other people in the area. There was far too much for one family, especially one so small, with only one wife and one child.

Lesley gave the old man his tea, which he drank from the saucer, much to her hidden disgust. He spluttered and complained that there was no sugar in it. Who in their right mind left tea half made like this? Lesley gave him a spoon and pointed at the sugar bowl on the table, but to her surprise he merely stirred the tea, as if he assumed that she already knew how he liked it. She tried to explain that he would have to put some sugar in the cup and then stir it, but not until he had winced at the bitterness of another sip did he realise what she meant. After all, the sugar, along with the water, tea and milk, should have gone into the pot to make the brew. What an utterly foolish thing to do. Cooking tea without sugar was like boiling meat without salt. Could it be that his son had made an unfortunate choice? Could it be that this woman simply could not cook?

As the old man finished his drink, he decided, if reluctantly, perhaps merely out of politeness and respect for his son's house, that he must leave. His stomach felt very empty indeed and he did not relish the thought of the long walk home. But his daughter-in-law had made it clear that there would be no food for him. So with great speed he stood up, bid Lesley and Anna goodbye and left the room. Lesley did not realise what was happening at first, thinking that he had seen something or someone outside as he walked towards the door. What about the food she had prepared? In a fluster, she rushed after him in pursuit and was relieved to see that Musyoka had met John, who had just arrived home for lunch. His car was parked some distance away at the edge of the compound, so she had not heard him arrive.

"John," she called, "could you ask your father if he is staying to eat?"

John put the question to his father, who scratched his head and looked utterly confused. In his frustrated disbelief, he struck his stick against the ground. Recalling Lesley's invitation to take only tea he said, "Your wife said there was no food, that there was only tea." John translated his father's answer as a question to his wife.

“I did not say that,” she replied with obvious offence.

John could not see how the misunderstanding had arisen and reverted to his usual tactic when things seemed a little tense. To clear the air, he took his father by the hand and led him laughing back towards the house where, on reaching the door, he put his other arm around his wife’s waist and kissed her. Then, holding his father’s and his wife’s hands between his own, he greeted them both with a simultaneous shared handshake. It was a gesture inviting reconciliation, but since neither party knew the source of the difference, it failed.

For Lesley, the meal turned out to be utterly traumatic. The stew she had cooked was perfect and much impressed old Musyoka’s palate. So she can cook, he thought. The old man ate in the only way he knew – with his fingers, ignoring the cutlery the others used so exaggeratedly. What he did not like was the fact that his potatoes, his cabbage and his meat were all neatly placed in separate piles on his plate, so he began by mixing everything together before plucking mouthfuls from the resulting pile with his fingertips. At the end of the meal he mercilessly pursued every last drop of gravy by lifting the plate to his lips and drinking the juices. When Lesley got up and turned away, he thought she was going to the sink to do the washing. His son had learned dirty ways in England, thought the old man. Neither he nor his wife had brought a bowl of water and soap for his hands before the meal. He had therefore had to eat with dirty hands. It was a very bad thing to do indeed. Lesley, of course, had thought the old man terribly dirty. He had eaten food with his fingers without first washing his hands. What disease, she thought, might Anna have caught over the previous few days? And what a mountain of food the old man had eaten! She found it all quite unbearable. He who says he is satisfied, thought the old man, abuses the cook. He leaned back in his chair, and patted his stomach after finishing the last of the stew from a pot, which Lesley had thought might do them two meals. At last Musyoka offered his cook a genuine relaxed smile. Lesley responded with her own, somewhat forced attempt, as she ruefully surveyed the splashes and debris that surrounded her father-in-law's plate.

The greatest contradiction for Musyoka had been the presence of Lesley and Anna at the same table. In his own house that would never have done but, here in his son's house, this foreign place, he was prepared to make this concession. He knew that European families always ate together at the same table. Though it was not good manners to do so, he was willing to grant the inevitability that his son, after living in England for so long, would have learned to accept some foreign ways out of necessity. An animal smells of the forest in which it slept, thought Musyoka, but now his son had returned home, surely it was time for common sense and good manners to reassert themselves.

John asked his father to come and look at the farm, especially the work he had been supervising that morning, and the two of them left the house to walk in silence towards the river bed which bordered the large plot of land. John had been occupied there since dawn supervising the construction of foundations for what was to become the pump house. By the side of the Vinda, which at this time of year was a river of sand, he had laid into the earth two courses of red earth bricks. Piled around the edges was the fine dusty soil which had been moved the previous day and on top of this lay strewn a hundred or more new bricks, some already crumbling or broken, waiting to be added to the structure.

John and his father stood on top of the pile of earth to survey the project. The old man was clearly very surprised that his son had already accomplished so much. He had said many times to John's mother that he was afraid his son would forget how to work in the fields, if all he did every day was sit in a chair and write.

"This," said John, pointing proudly to the small square of brickwork, "is going to be the engine house. It will be finished, roof and all, before the end of the week."

Musyoka gave out a hearty laugh and grabbed at his hat as it shook off his head. "I thought it was going to be the toilet," he said. "It seems to be about the right size. I was going to say that you ought to have dug the pit before you started the walls!"

John smiled knowingly and decided to give his father something of a shock. It is the young man who must teach new words to the old. "The toilet is inside the house."

"Inside?" retorted his father, as if suddenly burnt. "Are you telling me that you have paid money for a man to build a new house and he was stupid enough to have put the toilet inside?" He tut-tutted for a second or two and shook his head as his son continued to smile. "You finish a job, and then you see the mistakes. That house cannot be a home for you, Mwangangi. It will be very dirty, smelly and unhealthy for your children. And the smell will attract flies. The house will be full of them."

"Father, it will not be a long drop toilet," John explained. "It will be a European style with pipes that bend and stay filled with water. There will be no smell."

"What a waste of water!" scoffed Musyoka. "What will this place do?" he asked, jabbing the air with his stick in the general direction of the brick foundations.

"This will house a diesel engine," replied John with some pride.

"So what? A man is always satisfied with a skin from his own cow," thought Musyoka. Though somewhat impressed with the idea, he was still baffled as to why his son should wish to build a house for an engine. After studying the foundations with reverent ignorance, he turned to face his son and waved his stick towards the expanse of sloping fields before him. "And how do you propose to make this desert fertile? There is no rain here. That's why no one has farmed this land as far as I or your grandfather can remember." He continued to face his son, his wide-eyed expression suggesting that he had asked an unanswerable question. Any reply would be sheer enlightenment.

John pointed at the dry sand of the river bed. The old man looked and noticed for the first time what seemed to be an oil drum sticking into the earth. "Beneath the surface," said John with some gravity, "there is always water. The engine is going to pump that water. Some of it will go straight onto the fields and the rest will go into those tanks." He swivelled to point his father's gaze towards a cleared area nearby, where concrete foundations had been laid to support the corrugated iron water tanks that were already on order. "More than that," he continued, now with almost childlike excitement, "at night the engine will drive a generator to make electricity and, better still, the excess power will charge batteries that will power some electrical appliances, such as our fridge and the washing machine, during the day."

For some time the old man appeared to be studying the ground near his feet. "It will be very expensive to run," he said, his observation clearly the least of the problems he could envisage.

"Ah, no," scoffed John, his tone momentarily offending the old man. "I will run the engine, the pumps and the generator for about five hours a day. It will cost only forty shillings a week for the fuel. I will also have a small windmill up there on the ridge, which will trickle-charge the batteries from a car's generator throughout the day."

To Musyoka forty shillings a week sounded like a small fortune. The contradiction this aroused infected his words with what sounded like sarcasm. "I suppose we harvest what we plant. It seems strange to me that for generations we knew nothing of these things and yet rain came to water our crops."

"That's true," replied John, "as long as you also remember the times of famine when people died unnecessarily and, above even that, the fact that a generation ago this land supported less than half the people it does now."

"What you say is true," said the father. "I am an old man now. You must excuse me if I cannot learn new words. All I can say is this. When I was young, if our land had grown as bad as this," he said, turning to point vaguely towards the hillsides, whose surrounding parched brown faces bore no signs of life, "we would have moved to a new area and there would have been no famine."

John decided not to pursue the point and opted to change the subject. But before he had a chance to speak, his father continued. "There is famine, my son, because people are no longer allowed to live their natural lives. We are unable to move because our government forbids it. They told us years ago that we should support them, that they would rid us of the British so that we could return to the way of life which we all knew and which had been denied us. They said they would repeal the laws that limited the number of cows a man could own. Well, they did that and we were grateful. What they did not tell us was what they themselves really wanted. They just wanted to take the white man's place, to banish him and then replace him with their own. But, alas, they are only Kikuyus and cannot see that they are fools. The white men still control them with bribes. If you go to

Nairobi and look around, what do you see? You see white men – rich white men riding alongside these Kikuyus in cars. The only reason, my son, why there is famine here is because the government wants one. If we could move, as we used to, or if the government would give us dams and not schools, then there would be plenty. These Kikuyus, though, will only allow us the husks of the maize whilst they promise the grain. These people," he scoffed, waving his arms high to imply and include everyone who lived in the area, "have been blinded by the white man's religion, his schools and his water pumps. They don't seem to realise that they will get nothing of any use from their Kikuyu masters or, for that matter, from the white man. They have been educated into stupidity." He paused for a moment, as if to allow time for his words to sink in. His lips seemed to be bursting with examples he could use to illustrate and strengthen his case, but he calculatedly chose only one, and one which had direct relevance for his son. His words were intended to provoke, and provoke they did, but John listened in silence, if grudgingly, like he had done as a child, when scolded for criticising his father's advice. "Look at the people in the town," Musyoka continued, now almost shouting, pointing up the valley vaguely in the direction of Migwani. "The council said they would bring water, so they put one of your engines by the dam. And what has come of it? It has worked for about three weeks in the last two years. When the water comes it is undrinkable because it is so dirty and it is expensive. It costs more than buying a woman as a new wife to draw water from the well. The whole idea is stupid."

John could listen no more. "The water would be fine if people did not allow their animals to shit in the dam. And the reason why the pump doesn't work is nothing to do with the engine. You know yourself that the man who got the job to operate the thing is a drunkard. When the fuel for the engine arrives he sells it to Mbuvu at his shop to get money for drink and, when asked, he lies and says it was never enough and that it has run out. It is the people here who abuse themselves. But there are better ways, more effective ways to do things, ways that work. In fact, if everyone would listen to the 'white man', as you call him, and learn some of his ways, as I have done, then they might all be as rich as the Europeans you saw in Nairobi." The bitterness in John's words provoked an equally bitter reply from the father.

"One does not ask a fool to untie another fool's knot. If it were not for the Europeans, our land would not have died like this. How can we trust the one who killed it to bring it back to life? The one who casts the spell cannot be the one to undo it."

"I am doing this," shouted John, gesturing towards his farm. "Am I an Englishman?"

Musyoka smiled at his son and stood proud and erect before him, stretching a little to compensate for the smallness of his stature. "There are times when I wonder, my son." After a pause that seemed like an age he continued. "What a man is taught by life lives with him until he dies. You must ask yourself who gave you your life – the white man and his machines," he said pointing at the pump house foundations, "or this soil, your birthplace and your father."

John could not answer. He had tried in vain so many times to convince his father that the choice was not as he saw it, that there were no contradictions between the roots of his identity and the way he chose to live his life. He was not embracing the white man's ways or rejecting his birthright. All he wanted to do was acknowledge and use what was good in any way of life, any culture, any identity. He wanted what would prove best for everyone and cared little about its origins. Above all, he wanted what was best for his family. Though not prone to despair, John had often wondered whether his father would ever recognise this and stop interpreting every suggested change as a threat.

"Well?" asked Musyoka forcefully, clearly expecting at least some reaction. "Do I speak the truth?"

Frustrated, John turned aside, as if sidestepping the thrust, trying to find words that might bridge the confusion. "Of course you are right, but…"

"Then prove me right." His father interrupted, as if he had foreknowledge of the opportunity, as if things were conforming to a plan. An old bull fights with an aim. "Prove to me that you respect what I say. Prove to me that you respect your traditions, your ancestors and your family. Prove to me that you have returned to this place to live as my son, not merely like some white settler who fences off our land and calls it his own. Prove to me that you have returned to respect me, not despise me or ridicule me for my ignorance of your ways. Prove to me that you respect me and what I represent, as much as you respect the things you have learned elsewhere."

"Have I not done that already?" John's voice was now raised, less than a shout, but verging on it. "Would I ever have returned to this place if I bore no respect for you or my people? Could I have not simply stayed where I was, in England, and simply forgotten that you existed? I had a fine life. I had and still have a fine family, a wife I love and a wonderful daughter. I had money, a fine house and a car. I gave that up because I wanted to contribute something here, something that could help my people. What more do you want of me?" John's stance was now imploring recognition, his outstretched arms looking like a confession of innocence.

In Musyoka's eyes there appeared great understanding. Seemingly without needing to think, he spoke quickly and quietly, as if the words had been rehearsed, practised in private until perfect. "A man harvests what he plants. You come here because you want power, my son. Only here amongst your own people can you achieve your aim. The Englishman might offer you a share of his riches, but he will never allow you to control. Here you can win and control people's ultimate respect. Here you can aspire to become a leader. You think that they will respect you because you are educated and you are rich. Here, my son, you can have access to the power you crave. So be it, but be sure to use it for everyone's good, as well as for this," he said, gesturing again towards the generality of his son's project.

"Tell me, father," asked John with a calculated innocence that only just excluded cynicism, "if this is not good, then what would be?"

Again Musyoka's words were quiet and assured. "Allow your daughter to do as she wishes, to become a woman as a Kamba." He paused for a moment and stared at his son, eager to assess his reaction. When none came, he continued, "I have tried to tell her much in these last few days of what young girls of her age are expected to do in the home, and what is expected of them outside the home in the community. I have told her of the respect she should always show to her elders and of her duty always to follow her father's wishes as she grows older. She has understood. I am sure of it. She then asked me what she should do, so that she could become accepted as one of her father's people." Surprise suddenly shone in his son's face. "Yes. That is what she asked me. A calf with no mother must lick its own back. I told her that she should become a woman as Kamba women do, that she should be initiated into adulthood in the way that her future sisters expect and accept. I told her it is the way to make herself ready for maturity. She told me that more than anything else in the world she just wants to be like other girls and do as they do. Unless she is ruled by the same laws and responsibilities as the other girls this can never be so. An uncircumcised child can never mix with those already mature." Musyoka then said no more for what seemed like some minutes, during which the windless silence of the afternoon grew heavy around father and son. John, deep in thought, could not look at his father. He stared, as if bearing the guilt of some great abuse, dejectedly at the ground. Finally, Musyoka spoke again, his authority demanding his son's attention. "I have spoken to Katuunge. I have not tried to trick her. I have even had the words translated by your sister who knows English. I tell you that this is her desire that I speak of, not my own. Ah yes, my son. 'Yes' can never harm." With that the old man bid a timely goodbye to his son, turned and set off to retrace the rising path towards Kamandiu. He walked with the strength of one still young, swinging his stick and whistling quietly.

Some hours later, with darkness surrounding and encapsulating the isolation of the house, John sat opposite his wife across the table where earlier Musyoka had shared their food. Lesley and he had sat, it seemed, for hours and drunk innumerable cups of coffee. The night, however, was still young. Crickets and cicadas had yet to awake and the air was still undisturbed by night's breezes.

John's mind was made up, but he felt a great inner sadness. Finally, he had realised that the changes were irreversible. Ideals he had tried to live had been revealed as no more tangible than dreams, no more attainable than fantasies. He had learned, that afternoon, to hate his father, but still these feelings could find no expression, so deeply did his fear of the old man restrict his words and silence his lips. He was not left totally without hope, however. As Lesley had pointed out, there was still herself and Anna. If he really believed in what he was doing, she had asked, why should this setback change his plans? If the farm would have succeeded before, it would still succeed. If his job was worth doing, it would still be worth doing. If he still loved his family, what had changed? No aspect of their family life, John's career or ambition or, indeed, his project needed the cooperation or blessing of his father.

Lesley, however, could not begin to understand how deeply the father's suggestion had bitten into her husband's conscience. In his own mind were painful recollections of the hospital bed where he had lain as a child. Deeper than that were memories of the malice in his father's eyes on the day Father John had taken him home to rejoin his family. Since that day, he had never again felt a true son to his father, something that over the years had caused him great pain and much soul-searching. The matter, however, had been decided. Without being prompted, Lesley had spoken her mind and he had immediately and sincerely agreed. The matter was settled.

"Never!" said Lesley, almost shouting the anger that distorted her face. The very idea of her daughter going though an initiation rite, being physically mutilated and frightened into a conformity she did not want, filled her with abhorrence, a mixture of nausea and guilt. "No one is going to doctor Anna. She is my daughter, not your father's."

Sixteen

April 1976

A stranger is a passing stream. His coming changes the land through which he passes, sometimes germinating a memory which will live alongside the people he leaves behind, sometimes bearing fruits to enrich their lives. But he will pass on his way. His influence might last a season at most, but his words flow away with him, remembered today, forgotten tomorrow.

No more than a day separated the juxtaposed scenes in Bill's eyes. Through rain and a driving wind he had sat, sprawled, resting on the suitcase at his side, across the back seat of a London taxi. Through the crawling traffic of the westbound rush hour the cab had stopped and started along the Cromwell Road apparently compressed by a combination of darkness and the enclosing buildings on either side. The driver, a Londoner by birth, travelled this route to the airport every working day and yet he appeared to become ever more frustrated with other road users the further he travelled, his cursing and swearing effectively punctuating the snatches of conversation he shared with his passenger. He had swapped lanes several times, braked, accelerated, done everything he knew to try to cut the journey time, everything possible to get one car ahead and had accomplished little except raise his own frustration. On hearing that Bill was bound for Kenya, he had sucked hard on his smouldering stub of a cigar and offered words of confident advice.

"I'd be very careful, mate, if I were you," he said. "The same goes for anywhere in Africa nowadays. You should hear some of the stories people tell me after coming back from some of those places! It's a white man's grave is Africa, mate. And watch you don't get ripped off. They seem to think that we are made of money – Lord knows we give 'em enough in charity and aid as it is. I've stopped giving, myself. As far as I can see, there's more money over there nowadays than there is here. They ought to be sending their money back here, if you ask me. I suppose I shouldn't complain really because some of 'em, some of them Arabs, keep me in business. Mind you, I don't like 'em. Yes, if I were you, I'd be very careful. Have you got a hotel booked already?" He offered a snatched glance towards his passenger via his rear-view mirror.

"No," replied Bill, his reticence implying at least some disinterest and distaste, "I'm staying with friends."

"OK, that's all right then," said the driver with apparently relieved, if rather overdone, concern. "They'll take care of you. They'll know the ropes, I suppose, won't let anyone get at you. Been there long have they, your friends?"

"Not really," replied Bill, "they went out there about three years ago."

"Well they must have a nerve and a thick skin, that's all I can say," said the cabby sarcastically, apparently drawing on experience he clearly did not have, "to emigrate to Africa and stay. I suppose they are getting rich on some contract job or other?"

"No," replied Bill, almost encouraging further confusion, "they're working with the government."

"God Almighty, they're tempting fate, aren't they? You tell 'em from me to watch their step," he said. "I hear so many stories from people who've gone out to these places and they've been promised the earth. When they've got back here, they've climbed into my taxi and cried because they've been so glad to get back. I've had people saying that they've been cheated, humiliated, robbed – and loads who have said they've never been paid what they were promised."

And so the one-sided conversation continued as far as the airport where, still ignorant, the taxi driver took his fare and wished Bill a good flight, before repeating his warnings in the same seemingly experienced voice. So he drove away and returned to the job he had done all his life in the only home he had ever known.

Laid on top of and melting into this scene was the sight now before his eyes this evening. It showed a barren landscape where people seemed to disappear into the earth's anonymity. This was an apparently empty world, which human beings had never tried to tame, and certainly never controlled. The night before had brought rain – a lot of it – which had destroyed the road to Miambani, along which John had hoped to travel in the last stage of his journey from Nairobi to his farm. Thus, skidding and sliding on the treacherous mud, they had diverted to Migwani having decided to stay there for the night. The mountain roads were gullied and awash with run-offs, and numerous small flooded patches along the way had threatened to glue John's car to a halt, but they had now reached their changed destination and, relieved, had gone straight to the mission house to see if they could have a bed for the night. Disappointment, however, was all they found. The house was empty and betrayed no sign of life as the two men walked around the outside, peering through every closed window. For some minutes, John had been undecided as to what to do. He felt sure that even if Father Michael were not around, Mutua, the cook, would still be in town, since the only day he usually took off was Saturday. So, leaving Bill alone in the car, he turned to walk the short distance to the town to see if Mutua was in the room he rented at the back of Ngandi's shop.

By now, Bill felt quite stunned by what he had seen since his plane touched down in the dull half-light of a Nairobi dawn. In the London taxi, he believed he knew what to expect. In the event, reality did not exceed expectation, but merely bypassed it. He emerged from the airport by nine and for the next five hours he and John battled against the remnants and effects of last night's rain to travel a mere hundred skidding miles, with the constant fear that they might have to turn back and try again the following day. Having completed the bulk of the journey, only a few miles separated them from their intended destination but, if John's fears proved real, there was utterly no chance of reaching his farm that day, either by car or on foot. How would I have reacted at home, thought Bill, if I had made such a journey only to find a sign across the road a few miles from my destination saying, "Road washed away – no other route"? How soon one might be disappointed, he thought, if one came to this place to impose one's own standards rather than discover its own.

How could one react to this, thought Bill, as he looked around from the vantage of the mission drive. Behind the house, a bare field rose up an incline, thereby denying any view of what lay beyond. In front of the house the land dipped into a shallow valley only to rise again to the slopes of a long flat rock, apparently compressed beneath the sky. Further to the left a taller, greener mountain, rising from the crest of a vast ridge, tapered to a neatly pointed summit.

The rest was a barren lifeless rust of earth, today saddened to mud by rain and bearing only a few tattered yellow maize stalks, obviously the uncleared and now lifeless remnants of a pitiful crop from last season, and everything was apparently trapped beneath the vast weight of a wide, glaring sky. The wind gusted fresh and cool, blowing from behind the pointed mountain, rippling the surface of pools of water standing on earth still too hard to absorb it.

In this landscape there were none of the familiar, recognised elements, none of the landmarks one expected to see, none of the fingerprints that mark human activity or work. Here, people seemed to live unaffected by the delusions of their own grandeur that controlled, artificial landscapes can cajole their observers to believe. Here, it seems, human beings were merely one of the many creatures prying the earth for survival. And here people were not succeeding, were not the dominant force. They seemed held in a kind of bondage not, like the European, by the grip of his own hand, but by the land, the sun and the rain. An animal, here, was still free to wander, to search and to find the comfort of food, but humans were now rooted to their farms, unable to leave fields fast dying from what appeared to be their own misuse.

Bill's contemplation was ended by the rasping of a motorcycle on the nearby road. He watched as the bike whined through a change of gear and turned towards the mission. Riding it was, to his surprise, a young white girl dressed in a T-shirt and jeans. Her long brown hair flowed and twirled in the wind. Though unexpected and incongruous, Bill was already so immune to further surprise that he could merely stand and watch as she drove up to and alongside John's car.

"Are you looking for Father Michael?" she asked after nodding her head in greeting. After Bill confirmed, she continued, "He's gone home to Ireland. He left today and certainly won't be back before July. It could even be as a late as September, because I heard the other day that he might do a fund-raising trip before he comes back."

"My friend has gone to the town to look for the cook," answered Bill, after a moment's surprise at being offered so much information about a man he had never met. "I think you should tell him when he comes back."

At that very moment John appeared from behind the tall euphorbia grass hedge, returning from the town, where he had been told that Mutua had gone home to his farm in Thitani after Father Michael had left Migwani. The appearance of Janet immediately solved his problem, however. Of course he could simply have taken two rooms at the back of the Safari Bar, but he had not wanted to subject Bill to the hard metal-framed beds, with their creaking wire frame springs and flea-infested foam mattresses, which were the only facilities the town's only hotel could offer. Immediately he saw Janet, he smiled and waved, and greeted her warmly with a handshake and a gentle hug. Bill could see in that instant, perhaps in the way she did not automatically arch her body away from his, perhaps in the way that he assumed she would move towards him in the encounter, that the two of them were something more than acquaintances. He explained their predicament in a few words and a moment later they were on their way to her house, Janet having offered them beds for the night.

Later, after dinner of roasted goat and chapatti, the two men relaxed for the first time that day. Bill produced a bottle of whisky he had bought on the plane and the three of them set about its destruction. Though Janet at first said she didn't want any, because she had quite recently been stupid enough to have drunk too much of the stuff and got quite drunk, she did relent and joined in on the third round. John took only a little, diluting it with Sprite, but Bill clearly enjoyed his drink, his already ruddy complexion glowing a little brighter with each glass.

"I didn't want to come here," explained John, "because I thought you might have gone away on a trip."

"Not this time," said Janet, self-consciously fiddling with a cigarette. She had not yet been smoking long enough to have shaken off the need for self-retribution each time she succumbed and accepted an offered cigarette. The revelation tobacco had delivered her some months before had been sorely needed when she had smoked for the first time, but by now it had become something of a commonplace. "I decided to stay at school this holiday to finish various things I had let run for weeks. I'm due to leave in a few months so I may not get another chance to do them."

"You are a very conscientious teacher, Miss Rowlandson. I wish you would consider staying here. Our school would be the richer for it," said John.

Though flattered and rather embarrassed by the strength of the compliment, she smiled, but it was with a distinct tinge of frustration in her voice that she acknowledged the words. "Thanks. If only I could make up my mind…" How many times had she pondered the question during recent months? And how many times had she sternly resolved not even to consider it further, only to find it again at the forefront of her mind an hour later? To leave would be to give up a life she had grown used to, had even grown to love, to leave a place which had grown to become the happiest home she had ever known. Here she felt thoroughly alive, liberated from Europe's neuroses and allowed to live a life of true freedom, immune from perceived pressure. She now seemed to rely on the freedom that Africa endowed. To leave would necessitate another new beginning and she was still unsure whether she wanted to teach in Britain. Such a decision bore too much of an air of inevitability, of potential respectability, feeling more of a termination than an opportunity. She was qualified in her field, but as yet had no particular skill or experience to offer an employer and had little desire to make what she saw as the retrograde step back into a college of some sort to seek new and different qualifications. To leave Migwani would mean coming to terms again with a society and its associated attitudes that she could no longer respect. To stay, on the other hand, would be to forego the chance of making relationships on equal terms with people of her own age or beliefs. It was also to commit economic suicide. Each year the return was deferred would make it ever harder to leave. She would have to reject not only the seedy side of English life, which was easy, but also the side she liked, the chance to visit friends, theatres, cinemas, concerts and galleries which, in her student past, she had enjoyed so much. To stay would mean that she would have to learn to live with, rather than flirt with the sides of Kamba life she could not accept. To stay and teach in the school might destroy her sanity, so deeply did she doubt the worth to these children of the academic education their nebulous aspirations demanded. Always to be remembered was the chance that here and now she might by sheer default take one of life's irreversible decisions in the light-headed manner, which life in this land encouraged, only to realise some time hence that she had made a mistake and be terribly, deeply disappointed and unhappy.

"I haven't really thought about it," lied Janet, unconvincingly, to John's question.

Bill, who had listened rather than spoken after the introductions had been completed much earlier, spoke next.

"I can't help feeling great admiration for someone like you, Janet. It must take a great deal of nerve and lot of guts to come to a place like this to work and live alone."

John smiled and looked at Janet, who hardly knew how to begin to address the contradictions in the words. Though they had seen one another just a couple of times since the closure of the Munyolo case, they felt they now shared a bond. On the few occasions they had met, they both felt as if they had taken up their conversation at the point where they left it, usually focusing on their shared experience and love of London. As John Mwangangi and Janet Rowlandson eyed one another, Bill Goodman instinctively and immediately knew they were at least good friends. After a long silence, during which she helped herself to more of the whisky she originally said she would avoid, she said in her soft, now consciously flippant voice, "Well, I'm not actually alone. There are twenty thousand people in Migwani location."

Bill looked suddenly enlightened, then embarrassed and then delighted by Janet's answer. He began to laugh at himself, saying, "You know, I really had never thought of it like that. Isn't it strange that even when we think of ourselves as enlightened, liberal thinkers, we can still say something like that? I suppose it's part of our culture to assume that black people don't count. Everything I have said about this place has assumed someone like yourself is apart from the rest of the community, something different from 'the people'. In fact," he continued, lightly coughing the words after a sip of his undiluted drink, "that kind of distinction can only be made by someone who has utterly no concept of actual experience."

Janet, impressed by Bill's willingness to eat humble pie, began to take more than a polite interest in the conversation.

“What about yourself?” asked Bill. “If you don’t mind me saying, you’re a very attractive young lady. You must have a very limited social life here. Have you had many difficulties adapting?”

Janet’s pursed, suppressed smile as her eyes met John’s was immediately noticed by the questioner, who interpreted correctly that his assumptions again had been misplaced. There was obviously more than mere acquaintance between these two. “You pre-suppose that I have adapted,” she replied. Two years before she would have blushed and mouthed a quiet, inconsequential reply. These days, however, her shell was harder, her will stronger and, as a result of her contact with John Mwangangi, her experience wider.

Bill was becoming very impressed with Janet, in very much the same way he would with a new student who showed signs of being more than run-of-the-mill. “One must assume,” he noted, “that you must have adapted to some extent, otherwise your life here would have become unbearable some time ago.”

Janet agreed and continued by answering his original question. “The amount of difficulty a person experiences in adapting – the degree of culture shock one suffers, if you like – is determined only by one’s staidness: the depth of one’s refusal to modify the demands one makes of others. A person who accepts this place as it is will have no problems. A person who comes to impose conditions of friendship will feel estranged.”

Somewhat stunned by Janet’s words, both John and Bill looked at one another and smiled. Then, as John began to state his point of view, there was a knock on the kitchen door and they all instinctively turned toward the sound.

Janet got up and, after closing the door connecting the kitchen to the lounge behind her, went to answer the call.

With Janet out of the room, the two men immediately began to discuss who would take the spare bed in the house and who would sleep on the plastic-covered settee. Bill, adamant that his tourist visit should cause no one even the slightest inconvenience, said that he would take the settee. John, laughing at his exhibition of characteristic overt politeness, which he had not experienced since leaving England, refused Bill's offer, telling him that now he was in Kenya he would have to get used to the local custom of accepting whatever offers of help were made. To refuse here, John explained, was to insult. To say 'Yes' said the Kamba proverb, could never cause harm, though he accepted that these rules might not apply in Janet's case – she was, after all, English. John pointed out that it was he who was actually making the offer and he was a Mukamba, so Bill had better accept that John would be sleeping on the settee. "Furthermore," John continued with a laugh, "I promise to take any refusal one hundred per cent personally." Thus Bill would take the bed.

Janet's caller had been unexpected. In Migwani, Solomon Musee was still a young man, regarded as immature and irresponsible by his father. Only rarely now did he ever visit his family home in the Kaliluni area of the location and each time his visits were proving ever more trying, because he had grown tired of what he interpreted as his parents' constant nagging. They were forever telling him that he should be saving to buy a parcel of land, that he needed to start building a herd of cows so that he might be able to marry, that the life he was leading in a rented room in Kitui town was bound to lead to trouble, bound to leave him poor and alone. He had gone to the town as a school leaver without qualifications two years previously. His intention was to seek out any available work. His goal was simple: to earn some money so that he could buy for himself a few of the symbols of modernity, a transistor radio, a bicycle, perhaps, and some colourful shirts to go with his flared trousers and *platiform* shoes.

Privately, he had longed to go to Nairobi, where he could find work and then forget that he had ever lived in Migwani, but none of his relatives lived in the capital and the cost of establishing himself there was too great for his meagre resources. The risk, therefore, was too great. He knew that if he were forced into the shanties, the chances were that he would never get out. No, he was not that stupid! In Kitui, on the other hand, he had a cousin who was a primary school teacher and who was willing to feed him for a while until he found a job.

Eventually, after some months of asking and some weeks of offering bribes to be paid from future earnings, he had lowered his sights and legitimately persuaded the Asian owner of the timber yard to employ him as a labourer. His pay, a mere forty shillings a week, seemed like a fortune at first, but later, as his taste for spending grew, it had to be supplemented by any casual job he could find. The options available were not always legal, but he had been lucky up to now. Janet had met him at a dance in the Umoja Bar, Kitui town's fabled nightspot where, on Friday evenings the Kitui Town County Council Band played on a regular basis. Janet had gone to the last dance there to convince herself that Father Michael's imminent departure and absence would not change the way she lived. She had a wonderful time and danced the bump with all and sundry, the men at one stage forming a queue to have the privilege of the next hip and bum touch.

Late in the evening and by then rather drunk, she was asked to dance by a tall slim young man with fair brown skin, a characteristic that had led to his being called 'that brown boy' by most of his acquaintances. He danced as flamboyantly as he dressed. He was, in fact, the model of the new Kenyan, an attempted copy of the characters that adorned the adverts for beer or cars in Drum magazine, with his imported platform shoes, red flares, yellow shirt and coloured baseball cap, set off by the reflecting dark glasses. These were just a little too big to create the image, since they had a tendency to slide down his nose, the correcting push up with the middle finger of the right hand having now become such an automated action that he did it even when the glasses were in his pocket. Apart from his ragged working clothes, these were his only possessions and he clearly prized them greatly, feeling inches taller when he wore them, more inches, that is, than those added by the clumping platforms of his soles. Dressed in the tattered khaki of the lumberyard, he was reticent and respectful, only ever doing precisely and exactly what he was told and never, never speaking out of turn. In his dance clothes, however, he stood tall, proud and upright and spoke with the volume of one slightly arrogant in his self-confidence, sure that others would take notice.

He saw Janet as soon as he entered the courtyard at the back of the bar where the dances were always held. He did not arrive until late, waiting at home until the time when the entrance fee was reduced from ten shillings to five, so that he might have enough money left for a couple of beers. Holding the dumpy Tusker Export bottle at an angle while lodging the thumb of the hand holding it over the broad plastic belt of his trousers was just another element of his calculated image. Once inside the Umoja and charged with his bottle, he paused on the steps that led down to the courtyard to survey the scene or, perhaps, to invite those already in attendance to note his presence. As ever, he was far too self-obsessed to notice that no one ever looked his way. The first thing he saw, however, was Janet's white skin. It was his greatest ambition to have a white girlfriend and even better if, like Janet, she also had straight hair and was good-looking. Having found himself at the front of the informal queue for the next dance with her, he set about the bump with what he thought was an enthusiasm and energy that would impress both her and the other competing males, and then, by complete coincidence, the music stopped. She told him she was rationing her partners to one song each. He protested, saying that he had only a part of a song with her and insisted he dance the next one as well. She shrugged her shoulders and agreed.

When the band struck up again, however, it was not a tinkling Zairois melody, but a slow American soul ballad, a song by a black man called White. Solomon needed no encouragement and grasped his opportunity, otherwise known as Janet, with both hands. Normally, of course, she would have resisted the pull of a stranger's arms, but tonight she felt she had cast her fears to the wind and, after a momentary self-conscious pause, she warmed to his embrace and held him closer. By the time Solomon suggested they sit down, they had danced almost motionless like this for more than ten minutes. Janet's queue had dispersed out of lack of opportunity and so the two of them chatted over a couple of beers that she bought. Soon they kissed, but Janet's head began to spin and suddenly her natural reserve reasserted itself. Before Solomon had time to react, she got up to go, telling him that he could visit her in Migwani if he ever went there. She did not need to tell him where she lived. Everyone knew that this woman taught at the town's secondary school. Tonight, with John Mwangangi and Bill, his newly arrived visitor from England in the other room, Solomon had shown up to accept the invitation.

"What on earth are you doing here?" she asked.

"I have come to visit, like you said," he replied. Janet's impatient expulsion of breath told him he was not welcome. He looked confused.

"I have friends here," she said. Solomon could hear men's voices from inside. He looked at Janet, offering an expression of pathetic disappointment. He had misjudged her, perhaps. "Come inside for a moment."

The embarrassed, but curious young man followed her through the kitchen and into the living room. On entering he was suddenly transformed. Though dressed in his confidence-endowing colourful clothes, he suddenly dwindled into a subservient boy. John Mwangangi recognised him immediately, though at first he did not remember his name. In recent weeks it had not been uncommon for John to attend the Umoja dances, at least for a while. He tended now to spend most of his weekends in Kitui to supervise the development work on his farm. Kitui town was on the way, since he was travelling from Nairobi, so it was a good place to pause before setting off into the bush and the Umoja had the best food in town. He had met Janet there and talked with her several times, though he had missed the previous week's event, having stayed in Nairobi to prepare for his friend's arrival, so he had not witnessed Janet's extended smooch with Solomon.

After a moment of petrified silence, when Solomon tried to take in the presence of a man as important as John Mwangangi and also a white man as well, he turned abruptly and left, without offering a word. Janet did not even have time to offer him a drink. He just fled.

Janet tried to follow, saying, "Solomon, I have Father Michael's motorbike. Can I take you somewhere?" But he had already gone, was already walking briskly and determinedly away from the house. These were surely men to be feared. He could not stay.

Janet re-entered the living room and offered a confused shrug of the shoulders.

"That's the fellow from Kitui," said John, "the boy who goes to the dances. I didn't know you were such good friends."

"We aren't," said Janet. "Last weekend we danced and I said he could visit me. I never thought that…"

"You must be careful, Janet," said John, interrupting forcefully. "You are alone here and now Father Michael has gone on leave. You should be careful not to encourage boys like him."

It was Bill who mused that John was now assuming that only white people qualified as possible companions for Janet.

After closing the kitchen door and, unlike most other nights, locking it, Janet returned to her drink and her visitors. "Are you going to the Umoja next weekend?" asked John. Janet nodded. "Well, I'll be going as well. I'll call in on my way to the farm. If he causes you any trouble, remember that I'll be there by about eight thirty or so. So don't worry."

None of them, neither Janet herself, nor John, nor Bill had the slightest inkling that, on their next meeting in Kitui's Umoja bar, it would not be Solomon Musee that would make a pass at the young English teacher, but John Mwangangi, who would go well beyond a mere pass.

Seventeen

April 1976

Opinion had it that he had always been a rebel. Some say it was the revolt of a Christ, while to others it was that of a bigot. In reality he might have been both, but the truth – that which is true of no one – lies somewhere between.

John was thirty-five, or thereabouts. His birth date is unknown, but most people are sure of the year. It had been during the torrential rain, the year when rivers still flowed after the maize had ripened. Even the oldest men agreed that this had happened only once in their lifetimes. Had John not been the first-born son of his father, his name would certainly have been Wambua, born of the rain. Many men of John's age bore that name but, according to tradition for a first son, John took the name of his father's father, Mwangangi, the one who has gone away. It was also in the year of the rain that a white man came and paid people to build a house next to the holiest land in Migwani. The man had lived unmarried in the house for many years and it was he who gave the name 'John' to Mwangangi son of Musyoka. Since that year, many said that the rain and the harvest had steadily grown worse. The cattle had weakened with each new generation and goats had learned to browse upon thorn bush. Once green hillsides had scorched brown and even old men's farms had grown sandy and dry.

John's father, Musyoka, was still the most revered man Kamandiu had ever known. His career had been long and distinguished, outshining even the memory of his own forebears. In his language, there are two words for respect. One embodies fear. This is the respect a son has for a father, or a man has for a snake, or the community has for the family of Musyoka son of Mwangangi. The tradition was long established and grew stronger as each generation had given another, more skilful doctor to the community.

Musyoka took three wives and they gave him just six children. John Mwangangi son of Musyoka was first-born and was the only boy to survive the hardening drought. Four other children had died, three of them before they had lived a year, but the boy who could learn his father's craft grew as healthy and strong as his father grew proud of him. This was the sum total of Bill's knowledge of John's background and how little it was, Bill thought, after such a long acquaintance.

That morning was to be Bill's introduction to Musyoka. John had tried to tell him much of his father. John's manner, throughout their friendship, had grown consistently more laconic, even reticent. But slowly, over the years Bill had known him, he had divulged enough for the friend to piece together the fragments he thought he had understood and thus he believed he knew what to expect. In his mind was a tall, dignified man dressed, probably, in a goatskin. His hair would be ochred, his feet bare and in his hand he would carry a walking stick made from no more than a trimmed branch of thorn. Thus, as they took the last strides of their walk down the valley from Migwani to Kamandiu, and the clustered huts of John's ancestral home came into view, Bill felt quite nervous and apprehensive of the picture in his mind. In fact, he was showing the greatest respect:

he was afraid.

A few minutes later, the picture was redrawn. The man who shook his hand with such force was thin and small. He was dressed in a scruffy black suit and wore no shirt. His bare chest seemed lost inside the cavernous jacket and the legs of the trousers finished high above his ankles. A frayed straw hat with no top, sandals made from old car tyres and a plain black umbrella – clearly a cherished possession endowing status – completed the picture. In appearance, Musyoka was nothing like the man Bill had envisaged, but it was the old man's character that gave him the greater surprise. Having anticipated a severe, serious, perhaps imposing man, laconic like his son, he met a warm, friendly, almost excited old man, who was clearly overjoyed that Bill had accepted his invitation.

To collect the prize you must be first in line. The first man ever to leave Kamandiu to take up a foreign life had returned. He had returned, though, not to claim his prodigal's prize, whatever that might have been, but to display openly to his family, as well as himself, that he had come to reclaim those aspects of his life that he had once rejected. He had not come to discover his past, merely to reclaim it. But he remained aware of the dangers. He had no niche in this place he could no longer call home. He returned as a stranger, an outsider, whose presence might ask questions, rather than answer them. If you pull a branch, the tree bends.

Bill began to feel like an innocent accessory at his accomplice's trial. John had always admitted that the prime guilt had been his own. Bill's role, he said, had been secondary but nevertheless important. In rejecting Africa in favour of Europe and the age-old laws of his people for the Church, he now believed he had committed the most mortal of sins. Thus three years ago he had returned, determined to offer any penance demanded by those whom he had abused.

This was how Bill regarded John's decision to leave England, as if the decision had been totally conscious and rational. In fact, though he would never know, Bill himself had planted the seed of discontent in John's mind. John had returned to college to visit his tutor after attending a case. In his idealism he had assumed that he would be able, as a graduate, to enter the legal profession in Britain, but he had encountered a wall of discrimination barring every path. It had been Bill who had said candidly, "I don't think you will ever be accepted as an equal. It's not because you're black or because you're not qualified, but simply because you're different. In Britain we don't like it when people rock the boat." John had worked for several years and had even become successful within his firm, securing his own client base and earning considerable fees, but he never forgot his tutor's words. He would always be an outsider.

They set out from Janet's house before dawn. Night's chorus of insects had gone, save for the odd cricket clicking beneath a cactus. The air was curiously still and clear. Sounds seemed muffled and faint and borne of the very air itself. A cow lowed somewhere deep in the darkness of the valley. A moment later, a child played gentle trills on a bamboo flute. John stood and listened intently to the near silence. These notes grew clearer as they listened, intensifying like the light in the eastern sky. Was it a herd of cows beginning their daily trek to water, shepherded by a child, or was it a trick of sound played by the echoing valley? Gradually, the sky grew grey overhead and then an orange glow warmed the wispy clouds above the horizon. Dawn had come and, as the misty darkness of the valley dissolved, the sounds died to silence.

Then, close by, a donkey began to scream its greeting to

the morning. Within seconds others had answered, cocks began their crowing and birds took their songs to the air. From a homestead by the road came a woman carrying a baby wrapped in a cloth on her back. John greeted her and she replied, so loud and enthusiastic in her innocent welcome that John began to smile. A little further along the path, he stopped and turned to face Bill. He was laughing out loud. "That woman used to look after me when I was a boy. She is just five years older than me. She sometimes fed me. Now she greets me as 'old man'."

As they walked briskly along the dusty ridge, John began to speak of childhood memories of the mountains and valleys. He spoke coldly at first, with a matter-of-fact disinterest, rather like a prisoner recalling his detention. He told Bill about the largest of the valleys, the one on their left, beyond the next ridge. Its name was Ikoo and its depth more than a thousand feet. Bill asked him if the name had a meaning. John nodded. "It means 'valley'," he said. Slowly, however, the words brightened and the stories began to glow with laughter. He spoke with an almost self-conscious candour, as if the fear of his origins, which the Church had instilled in him at school, had been aroused and was trying to seal his lips. But then, through his words, Migwani and his memories came alive. Since his first meeting with John, Bill had thought of this place as a dot on a map, somewhere foreign, different, and perhaps, according to the modernising assumptions of his time, a place to label 'primitive'. Now he was here, he surprised himself in finding the experience as prosaic as walking a London street.

Nzauni, the place of bulls, was a long low hill to the west of the main road. At one end, separated from the rest by a deep depression, a large grey rock thrust skyward. During the day this gap is a missing mouthful of rock bitten out long ago by a wandering giant driven mad by thirst and hunger. At night, the hill becomes the giant. He lies on his back where he fell after dying of thirst in this land that God neglected. The great bare rock becomes his petrified chin and the trees at its base the remains of his hair.

Kea, the prick, is a sharp, twin-peaked hill behind them. Boys and girls would pass between the twin peaks before their initiation to adulthood. John told Bill of the boy's race on the day of the ceremony and how he had finished hours after his peers. He had felt duty-bound that day to visit the priest in the mission, a detour no other boy took.

Bill had never known him like this. In these surroundings, it seemed that John was the stranger he had been on their first meeting. Urged on by an almost childlike excitement, he began to speak more quickly and was soon engaged in an almost unbroken monologue. He was talking non-stop, bursting into laughter at his own stories, most of which Bill either did not understand or did not find amusing. Bill did learn some useful survival tips, though, as John rushed from one bush to another, both to instruct his companion in their properties and, so it seemed, to renew an acquaintance with them, a familiarity rekindled by a visitor's interest. The root of this one, for instance, when powdered and swallowed, will cure stomach ache and diarrhoea. The leaves of that one have antiseptic properties. Rub the sap into a wound to prevent infection. Above all, this one is the finest. Its bark is pounded and mixed with water to form a paste. There followed a description of an infant being cured of a serious malady after this balsam had been smeared on its head and incantations spoken over a pile of feathers from a newly slaughtered cock.

In contrast to John's vitality was the land about which he enthused. Bill had never seen a more barren, desolate, dusty place. It reminded him of a disused and worked-out quarry, exhausted not only of its resources, but of its life as well. Bill's cultured Englishness was not yet able to appreciate the beauties of nakedness and he could see none of the glory which John enthusiastically tried to reveal.

"When God created the earth he worked without food, drink or sleep. First he made the land and, while that baked hard in the sun, he made water and cut rivers for it to flow. But there was still much to be done. The land had to be finished, just like a carpenter must plane, polish and paint a table. His work was still not done when he was suddenly gripped by a new idea. He made insects, animals and birds. And then he made man. He became so excited with these new things that he forgot about the land which still lay unfinished, and so it remains today." John lifted his arms and pointed at the rugged mountains and deep valleys that were his home. "This is the land that God forgot."

The antithesis of the Jews. This had long been John's favourite description of his own people in his college days. Bill had once read a paper by him, written for the college Africa Society, in which he had paralleled the two races. Jews, God's chosen people, are persecuted by their fellow men. Akamba, God's forsaken people, are persecuted by God. They were never meant to inhabit the land that remained God's failure, and so they must accept His vengeance in the form of famine, drought and disease. Bill's comment at the end of the paper had been to ask why they simply didn't move away. "It is not our custom," had been his student's reply, a reply that had not satisfied the teacher. At that stage, Bill had no idea how strong an answer that was. So, with their four-hour walk complete, they approached John Mwangangi's ancestral home, hanging on the side of the great valley.

On that morning, he began to see that custom unfold. John's words to his father seemed uncomfortably formal, like a string of set answers to set questions. Then it was his turn. John had taught him just two words of Kikamba. When prompted by Musyoka, he said them, and to his astonishment the old man reeled with laughter. He laughed so hard he had to steady himself with his umbrella and hold his side. Feeling quite embarrassed and growing more ill at ease with the passing of every second, Bill was doubly shocked when, still laughing, John's father drew himself up to his full height, threw his head back and shouted to the sky. Now terrified of what he might do next, Bill started to retreat, as if to put distance between himself and this unpredictable being that confronted him.

In fact, Musyoka was simply announcing Bill and John's arrival to the rest of the family. One by one they came running from the nearby fields. Two women were first to appear, followed quickly by a girl, much younger than John. All converged upon the group of huts, some stumbling over the uneven ground. There were no formalities this time. All three ran straight to John and immersed him in their embrace. The old man smiled and came forward again. Taking Bill's hand, which he did not let go, he led him to the entrance of one of the huts. Holding aside its sackcloth door, he went inside, still pulling his companion by the hand.

After coming straight out of the sun, the hut's darkness was blinding. Inside, the air felt cool and fresh. As shapes began to appear out of the blackness, Bill saw an old iron bed in the centre of the space. On the uncovered foam mattress lay a crumpled piece of printed cotton cloth. Musyoka bent down and picked up a large calabash from the uneven floor and then stormed straight back outside with Bill still in tow. Obviously one of the women had anticipated his intention and she returned sporting two handfuls of dappled enamel mugs. With these distributed, she took the gourd from the old man and, approaching Bill first, turned it upside down over his mug. It gurgled once or twice and he felt something heavy drop into the mug. Bill raised a hand to try to say "Enough," but her only reply was to brush aside his gesture and continue shaking the gourd until his mug was filled to the brim. Bill decided to adopt a passive role and set about examining the contents of the cup. The contents were white, or thereabouts, and seemed to have the consistency of cottage cheese. Thus an increasingly uncomfortable-looking Bill stood motionless, apparently trying to stare through the bottom of his cup. The girl hid her giggling behind a cupped hand. Looking up, he found that the entire family group, John included, had gathered in a semi-circle to watch the spectacle. Bill's eyes scanned his audience with an air of faintly amused acceptance of his appointed position as jester. The women laughed and slapped their thighs. The young girl giggled some more and again hid her face. John smiled and made drinking motions with his right hand. The old man scratched his head through the hole in his hat.

"You are to be our guest," said John. "You must be the first to drink."

Bill had begun to laugh in sympathy with the others until John spoke. Then, as his smile faded to concern, he again bowed his head to peer into the cup. There were flecks of black showing through the white. "What is it?" he asked, somewhat plaintively, and the uproar started again. John said something to the woman holding the gourd and she came forward to fill his mug. He drank the contents in one and urged Bill to do the same.

"It's milk," he said. "Just milk."

Bill looked unconvinced. Then he drank, or perhaps ate, a mouthful. The taste was rather like sweet yoghurt, but it was aromatic, almost as if it had been flavoured with rum.

He liked it, despite being rather put off by the dark flecks, which floated like detached enamel amongst the dregs.

In the hour or so that followed, they all sat together in the shade of an acacia tree, some on small low stools, others on tree roots, the rest on the ground. Words flowed in torrents, but Bill understood not a single one. Never before had he been in a position whereby he held not a single handle of what was being said. Occasionally, John would nod in his direction, say his name and then revert to words he could not even distinguish, let alone decipher. This feeling of helplessness, of total dependency on another to be his mouth and ears was something Bill had never experienced before.

As time passed, Bill's attention moved from the people to the surroundings. The homestead was a cluster of a half a dozen almost identical huts. Each had red earth walls and a thatched roof, neatly trimmed in steps. A gap in the wall was its entrance, lightly covered by a sackcloth door. Set apart from the rest were two other huts, but these were made from thin wooden laths and stood on legs a foot from the ground. There was not a blade of grass to be seen. The whole area had been cleared of all vegetation apart from the tree under which they sat and a group of thin straight pawpaws near the huts. Small breast-shaped fruits clustered around the tops of some of the trees, whose brilliant green, fingered leaves contrasted strongly with the general dull brown of the landscape.

On all sides the land had been tilled and cultivated. There were a few dry brown maize stalks in a nearby field. A donkey, tethered to a large stone, gnawed at one of the crinkled leaves and then stripped it off the plant. Chewing its prize, the animal seemed to return Bill's gaze with interest for a few moments until it again turned aside, apparently uninterested in this mere white man, to renew its search for food. Each field was bounded by a hedge of cut twigs, which carried slender but sharp white thorns, each at least two inches long. Poking through the hedges at apparently regular intervals were sisal plants, whose petrified stems rose twelve feet to sprout pathetic little twigs at the top. Standing in lines, they might have been natural telegraph poles, so regular did they seem. The whole farm nestled neatly halfway up the valley side and felt as if it might slide down the slope at any moment. But above all a feeling of stillness pervaded everything. If one listened through the conversation, sounds were few. A bulbul knocked out its call and left. The donkey crunched on a maize plant in the field. Far away a cow sounded angry and close by a pair of tethered hens scratched for food in the dust.

The silence was vast. He heard a conversation, listened for a minute or more through the words of his nearby companions. Then he realised that it was coming from another homestead on the far side of the valley, at least half a mile away.

Eventually one of the women got up and went into one of the huts. As she pulled back the sacking to enter, to Bill's surprise, smoke came billowing out through the gap. On closer inspection, Bill noticed that there was a constant hint of smoke percolating through the thatch. Then John got up and walked over to his former tutor, leaving his smiling father to sit and watch. "Shall I show you round?" he asked. At that moment, Musyoka's first wife appeared. She was walking up the valley side with her head bowed and her back bent by the weight of her load. Supported by a thick leather that passed across her forehead, the bundle of firewood nestled neatly in the small of her back. As she bent forward to take the strain, it seemed that her buttocks became the highest point of her body. With her head bent low and swinging her arms to ease the effort of each tortuous step, she climbed the hillside quickly and efficiently. Her bare feet found solid ground at every step and her tread seemed convincingly light, despite the obvious weight of her load. Quite unused to such a sight, Bill instinctively went forward to intercept her, with the intention of helping her off with her load. He pointed at the bundle of wood, took hold of the strap and started to lift. The load, of course, did not move. She shouted something, bent her legs and then flicked the wood from her back with a jerk of her hips. In one movement she had unloaded her burden and stepped aside to let it fall. Unfortunately, Bill's hands were still clinging onto the leather strap and he was dragged somewhat involuntarily by the weight and was still holding the strap after the load hit the ground. For his own peace of mind, he gave a tug to see if he could lift the load, but he could not even drag it to the side. He found he had again become the centre of attention and everyone seemed to find the sight very funny. His hands were now perfectly trapped between the tightened cord and the wood it bound, and the smile he still displayed looked ever more forced, as he fruitlessly tried to free himself. After a moment of merrymaking, when the entire family stood back and wallowed in the improbability of his predicament, the woman stepped forward and, after reducing its tension with a plunge of her foot onto the wood, loosened the cord.

His fingers were grazed. He tried to hide the obvious discomfort and shrug off the whole incident. Musyoka would have none of it, however, taking his hand and pulling him towards another of the huts. From a box under the bed the old man retrieved a roll of sticking plaster and tore off a length with his teeth. Over the graze he placed a single cool leaf and then bound it with the plaster. "Finish," he said in English, much to Bill's surprise.

John and Bill then walked down to the sandy river bed at the bottom of the valley. Rocks of all sizes jutted through the fine grains and on one of the larger boulders Bill sat and smoked a cigarette.

"Your father speaks some English?" he asked.

"No," said John curtly. "He served in the British Army for a while – as a cook, would you believe? He learned a few things there: a few words of English and the practice of shaking hands with his left hand clasping his right forearm." He had finished the phrase as if in mid-sentence, glancing to see if there was any reaction from his friend. "That was to ensure that he was not holding a knife behind his back."

"You're not serious!" scoffed Bill.

"Totally," John replied. "There were times of tension between the races, and there were times of calm. My own people, for instance, generally welcomed the white man and collaborated with the new rulers right from the start. But in some areas, especially where the settlers took land for themselves, there was always conflict. I personally don't believe that the white settlers actually distrusted their own servants to the extent that the existence of this custom suggests, but the example was set and the tradition survived."

He obviously wanted to continue, but did not. For the first time, Bill began to feel self-consciously white in John's company. It was John who eventually broke the silence.

"I am in a privileged position. I have lived, as a child and as a young man, in a land ruled by immigrant whites. I have lived for eleven years or so as a black immigrant in a white country. As a student I arrived in England convinced that the white man was a kind of 'superman', capable of anything, and unwilling to allow any obstacle to come between him and his vision. Filled with stories of our ‘motherland’ by my teachers – of its beauty, its perfection and wealth – I went to England to learn what I still saw as the white man’s knowledge, so that I might return to educate my own people. I really did believe that! My father told me to beware of thieves and to remember him and his ancestors every day. My mother feared that my skin would be turned white by the cold weather. I knew stories of the white man’s cruelty and exploitation of defenceless people, but I chose not to believe them and hoped – sincerely hoped – that I could help to make Kenya into another Britain.” From his own memory, Bill knew that John was being unfair to himself, but he did not interrupt.

“It took me some time to appreciate my mistakes. I saw, for instance, that the riches of England were not for all to share. But it took me longer to understand that the whole way of life, the religion, the institutions, were merely different answers to the same questions posed by life anywhere. The fact that those answers are different is no more significant than the fact that your skin is white and mine black.

“Then, as you know, I became convinced that colonialism was just another word for conspiracy, a master plan to enable the white races to exploit all parts of the world for their own ends. We were to be pushed to poorer and poorer land to make way for progress, perhaps just another word for someone else’s interest. In our new settlements, our communities would wither and die, thus leaving all for the colonial masters. The ways of my own people, which I had learned to despise and insult both in school and in church, were suddenly no longer mere primitive, pagan rites. They became part of a romance infinitely more attractive than London in midwinter.

“Then I changed my mind again! The colonialists, and the government which backed them, were neither supermen nor crooks. They were merely stupid. They did not think that the solution they applied with such verve and without exception might be only one of a number of equally viable possibilities. Their guns allowed them to believe that that they were always right. They settled here, took what they wished and were defeated, all because they were ignorant. I hoped that our struggle for independence and freedom would make them realise this, but, alas, it did not, just as it will not change the image of the white man in the eyes of these people. He is still the master, because he can build tractors and make music come from a box.

"So when people talk to you and ask you questions, you will tell them that you own a car and your house is built of bricks. You work with paper in an office high up in the air in a building where there are hundreds of others like you. Each year you travel thousands of miles just to see different places – a practice quite unknown and utterly incomprehensible to people here. And people will laugh at you in wide-eyed disbelief. They will call you a rich old man and give you great respect, but it will be the kind of respect reserved for a freak. They will not understand why you took only one wife. A man with such obvious riches should have at least four, but your divorce will raise no problems of explanation. The woman bore no children, so you sent her away – a common practice and quite understandable."

"And what about you, John?" asked Bill. "How white are you?"

John laughed and paused before answering. He looked Bill in the eye and said, "This is my home. I was brought up here. The customs and beliefs are my own. I have lived away and now I have returned. No matter how long you chew, you must eventually swallow." There was another long silence before he spoke again. "Frankly, I don't know."

Eighteen

August 1976

August is the month when little boys piss. Day begins not with the fanfare of sunrise but with a melting of grey through mist. The air is wet, but the earth stays baked concrete hard after three months of scorching sun. There is always this damp, but never, never rain. Clouds envelop the mountains, rolling soft in grey waves over the peaks and then sinking low, as if leaden, into the valleys between. Standing in the river bed, where the sand now sticks to shoe leather, look around and the air is clear and clean. But look up and you are trapped beneath a wall of mist, compressed between the dewy acacias on the valley sides. The only way is to follow the sand between the crumbled and scarred earth banks of the winding dry river. Some twenty miles or so along this apparent tunnel, there is a miracle awaiting. Surely the head of the valley is here. The sides grow steep and the dry river suddenly narrows to no more than ten feet across, squashed between rocks rising through cloud a thousand feet on either side. Turn the corner expecting to see a wall across the path and find emptiness, utter emptiness. The earth becomes a placid sea, without rise or fall, wave or tide. Distance is an even line between earth and sky, an unblemished boundary between apparent infinities. Clouds are higher here and softer than the heavy swirl of the mountain mist, still so close at hand. And the dampness has gone, and with it the sense of cold. With only thorns and cactus straining from the hard red soil, this land is now only a memory of the scorching days between the rains, when dust flies high on the wind and the fields lie bare.

This land lies a thousand feet below the hills of Migwani. Here the heat is deadly and the breeze is light, but there are wells that never run dry, fed by the seepage that runs like sweat from the mountains, down through the faults in the rock, the wrinkles in this weatherworn land. It was here that John Mwangangi bought a hundred acres of desert, or so it seemed, determined to build a model of what could be achieved. It almost adjoined his ancestral home, but the difference in altitude between the two and the lack of a path made it virtually impossible to walk directly from the family *shamba* to this new experimental farm. Now almost two years after the purchase, through this August mist, Father Michael retraced the hike he had made with John in October's heat on that inaugural day, and how different the place now seemed.

On the edge of the plain, resting beneath the towering mass of Museve, where before there was only thorn bush, couch grass and euphorbia cactus, there was now a large concrete building surrounded by tanks to collect and store rainwater from the roof. Near the river bed, a small brick-built pump house with weld-mesh over its unglazed window next to a bright yellow door, provided the real marker, the true identity of this place, for without the water it provided, no part of this project would have survived. John's firm belief that a borehole in this spot would yield year-round sweet water had been perfectly judged. Electric pumps and their associated diesel-powered generators had been in place for several months. Up to now they only needed to run a couple of hours a day, and that had been enough to irrigate a large tract of prepared land, which had produced its first crop of cabbages, tomatoes and onions enough weeks before for the same land now to show new seedlings in neat, ordered lines.

Michael tried the door of the main building and it opened easily. Inside he saw a hallucination of life so convincing that he felt unnerved. His shoes squeaked on the newly polished floor. An oil lamp suspended from the ceiling seemed to be about to light itself, so perfectly did its highly polished steel reflect the daylight in the sudden darkness of the room. Curtains swayed gently in the breeze beside a barred window, whose louvred panes were left open, the barring in place perhaps only to test the resourcefulness of the thieves. Crooks could now come and go as they wished, he thought, but in fact none had tried to enter or even go near this place. The buildings, especially the areas set aside for residential use were effectively hallowed ground now.

Not that they had ever really been used. Cupboards of clean linen, the incongruous and unused English-style front room furniture, the polished wood of the dining room, all dusted and shined, reinforced the illusion. It was like being in a showroom rather than a house. Had he really heard Lesley use the word 'prison' to describe the place? In that half-heard conversation between John and his wife, had Michael really understood her meaning correctly? Now he had to conclude that he had been right all along. She never wanted to come here. She felt trapped in this place. And now she would never see it again.

Michael opened the door off the kitchen that led into the empty garage and from there took the connecting door opposite to enter the office. John's papers were still on the desk. Someone had been into the house to clean and dust, but no one had come here, and a layer of red powder covered everything. When John left this office to attend Janet's leaving party at the school, he had been working on the accounts and a large ledger was still open across the desk. The cabinets were locked, of course.

And then he went through the office's external door. A few steps more brought him to the large doors that gave onto the storage areas. These were all empty, apart from one which housed the tools of the trade, not the hoes, *pangas* and yokes of the small farmer but a tractor, several ploughs and harrowing discs. They were all still remarkably new. None yet bore any rust.

Michael paused here to mount one of these mechanical beasts and sit in the driver's seat. He smoked a cigarette, moving occasionally to look attentively at each piece of machinery in turn. His eyes scanned everything with great deliberation, but his thoughts were elsewhere, drifting to other places and times. Disbelief in oneself, in one's own perception, in memories which one regarded as time-honoured truths – is this disbelief born of grief or of an unwillingness to grant an unavoidable yet unacceptable truth?

***

"This is the land I will farm," said John.

October on Museve. Here land rises rock-fallen out of desert. Standing with the hilltop church at one's back, the earth becomes motionless sea. To the east an ocean plain, stark, flat and featureless, stretches to a line where it joins with sky in a union of opposites. There are islands. The hills of Endau and Zombe stand together but alone, hills that cannot meet across the vastness. To the west, mountains thrust from the plain in ribbed escarpments with a force the once young earth was too weak to resist. Far hillsides feel green when the eye has rested on the plain. On the summit ridges trees stand in ranks, apparently erect and motionless from this distance, but in reality lashed and swayed by the same gusting wind which holds the bateleur in its lazy tailless curves of flight. High in the sky he feigns indifference only to swoop in an instant to the ground where, in a flurry of dust, his talons clasp and pierce the skin of a ground squirrel, a snake, a rat or a hyrax.

The Vinda is a sandy snake winding dry and yellow through the brown of the valley and plain. Keen eyes can discern the glint of sunlight on the steel of the bridge at Inyuu, the bridge that often seems redundant and is so often ignored, as drivers prefer to cross the apparently safer sand of the riverbed. But the river hibernates like this, ready to awaken in roaring torrents whenever there is rain, and then the bridge is the only choice. But those days are rare.

John pointed towards the base of the hill where, a thousand feet below them, a triangle of flat land nestled across the riverbed.

"That can be no more than desert..." said a disbelieving Michael.

"No," replied John, with eyes fixed on his land and on his imagined future. "Just a few feet below the surface of the riverbed there will be water, sweet water, enough to irrigate that land all year round. The soil is deep and rich and the whole farm will be sheltered from the wind by these hills. I am going to bring a diesel engine from Nairobi to generate electricity so that I can use electric pumps by day and light the house by night from rechargeable batteries. With water, this land will be among the best in the district. Only a mile from here," he continued turning to point along the mountain ridge toward a narrow valley, "there is a man who is lucky enough to have a small river bed running through his land. Not only does he grow all of his own food, but he can also crop sugar cane, bananas and even potatoes, which he sells for cash. What's more, his farm is completely unaffected by the drought because his little stream collects water from all of those hills. He has succeeded because he has been lucky. My farm will succeed because of my engine and my pumps. I will farm this piece first and then expand each season until the whole hundred acres is productive."

"You make it sound so easy," said Michael. "You seem to have no doubt that it will succeed. Why have other people not done this before you?"

"No particular reason other than poverty, Michael," said John. "Drilling for water costs money, as you know, and most boreholes are dry, and most wet ones are salt. But I know that riverbed. I was raised in a farm just above it. I used to go down there as a boy in dry times, sent there by my mother to fetch water. I can remember digging in the sand. I only needed to dig a couple of feet and there was always water. And it was always clean, clean enough to drink. No one has the capital to exploit it, that's all. Of course the place is almost uninhabitable unless you build a European-style house with fans and air conditioning. It's fiercely hot and in the rains there's a danger of flooding, but a house full of electric fans built above the flooding level will work fine. Again, no one has the money to invest. But I have." John turned to face Michael, but said nothing for a while. "But I am going to make the investment for a public good, not a private profit," he continued. "The farm will make a lot of money. I know it will. I have done all the projections any bank manager might want to see. But I am going to make it a cooperative. The people who join me will become part owners, part employees. They will invest in the project via their labour and I will reward them with profit and ownership. I'll recoup my money with a little interest and then I'll move on and do the whole thing again somewhere else."

"Your father wants you to farm his land. Isn't that so?" asked Michael, pausing to ensure that John was listening.

"The old man is the one who is taught new words," answered John glibly.

"But the young cannot educate the old…" was Michael's answer in kind.

The words seemed to infuriate John. Michael was suddenly both shocked and surprised at the reaction. "I do things my way. I am no slave to tradition, whatever that word might mean. If poverty is our tradition, then we must break with our past and make a new life. I am no slave. I will do things my way."

"But you will need to take people with you for it to succeed…"

"They will come with me," said John with impatience. "Its success will succeed. It will be the tangible results that will win people over. There will be no need for me to offer a palliative afterlife to soften the pain of the present, unlike some philosophies that are promulgated hereabouts…" John eyed Michael with a hint of a smile. "The profits will fill bellies with food and through their stomachs it will win over their minds."

"But you are being very ambitious, John," said Michael. "No one has farmed like this; no one has organized the activity around share ownership, and no one has ever tried to hand a successful business over to appointed managers."

There was no hesitation this time. "It will work," said John.

***

John built his house where he said, and built onto that the

office and storerooms, in one of which Michael now sat. The project had been underway long before he took his new job in Nairobi and, as a family, the Mwangangis had lived in the place for only a few weeks before moving to the city. Since then, John and family, initially, and then increasingly John alone, had visited at weekends to supervise the ongoing work and project development. As predicted, his managers and labourers did all that was asked of them and the model farm soon became just that, a model to be emulated. But Lesley and Anna had not visited since the early days and any idea of the family living on the farm had been forgotten. For John, however, this project was more than just a farm to be made productive. It was nothing less than a vision of a new future. It was John's plea to his own people that they should build on what they already had, should develop their homeland using the skills and knowledge that was held in common. But in the end, those who did not understand a complex arrangement such as this simply dismissed it, claiming that John Mwangangi had merely become another landowner, an absentee planter like the owners of the great tea estates up country. And, like all businessmen, the same gossip branded him an exploiter of people, an abuser of opportunity. And now, after she had left for home, only now had Michael understood that for some months it had been Janet's presence in Migwani that had become the true lure that brought John to the bush with such regularity. How remarkable it was, he thought, that the apparent malice of gossip so often encrusted itself around a grain of truth.

John's vision, however, had been real. As Michael stared through the window at the results of nearly two years of John's work, he found it hard to believe that this land had so recently been barren scrub, neglected for an age. Now the wilderness had been tamed. Radiating from the house, pathways defined by loose stone borders led to a matrix of fields hedged with neat lines of young sisal, as yet too small to crop. Near the house were the individually laid out beds of a vegetable garden that Lesley had planned and initially worked on like an English housewife with her rubber gloves and trowel. But of course, she had stayed away for months, unable to come to terms with either bush life or the demands of her father-in-law. The twig-built shades that had been intended to protect the young seedlings from the sun had been built, but nothing was ever raised beneath their shield. They now stood like skeletons guarding the few pockmarked cabbages that had gone to seed in the beds.

But elsewhere it was a different story. The pumps and engine had done their work and a large patch of cultivated land had already produced its crop and new seedlings of the next already showed. Another large tract was levelled and ploughed ready for planting, and the machines had been at work clearing another area on the other side of the plot. At the rate he had been working, the whole farm would have been in production within two more years. It was – or would have been – a prodigious achievement.

Michael was lost between memory and imagination when he heard the back door of the house open, the sound reverberating through the volume of the garage via the connecting door he had left open. A radio was switched on. Someone was in the kitchen. For a moment he was startled and did nothing, fixed to the spot by his own surprise. But it was only John's sister, her familiar voice offering recognition, as she began to talk to herself as she busied herself with some now redundant domestic task.

He left the store and approached the open door of the kitchen. He knew Mwikali's voice and greeted her from outside, before she saw him. She was immediately silent, but it was not with the expected recognition that she greeted him. A look of distance and distrust is what he saw.

"You have been coming here to clean the house?" he asked. Her reply was a simple nod. It seemed that there was no more to say, but while he stood before her, she did nothing, merely stood, rooted to the spot. "Have you been here every day?" he asked. Again she nodded.

After a short silence she picked up the radio and placed it in her bag. She was clearly about to leave, but Michael was effectively barring her way since he had hardly crossed the threshold into the room. "Father, I must go…" she said.

"But you have only just arrived."

His words made no difference. It was clear that she was not going to stay in the house while he was there and, without saying another word, she brushed past him and set off on her way. As this half-sister of John Mwangangi made her way purposefully along the path that led gently at first up the valley side towards her own home, Michael watched her progress unaware of the fact that he would never see her or indeed any other member of her family again.

Michael wandered around the house, buildings and the farm for a long time before he decided to leave. He became lost to time, sauntering apparently aimlessly from one area to another, visiting some places several times, but seemingly inspecting them anew on each visit. Eventually he drank some water from the bottle he had brought in his haversack, and set off in the direction of Museve and its beautiful hilltop chapel, today shrouded in August mist. It would take him several hours to climb the steep paths to the top, but once there he would approach the altar like a pilgrim begging for guidance in this time of crisis.

The climb sapped his strength. During his leave at home in Ireland he had spent too much time in an armchair putting on weight. Stopping smoking had not helped, since he nibbled more as compensation. But that aberration was now behind him. Nevertheless, as he made steady progress over the loose stones of the path, the ascent seemed easier that day than it had almost two years before under the October sun. Both he and John had sweated away every breath from their body to climb the hill in time to reach the top to keep their appointment with the priests from the district. Many had assembled there to celebrate the consecration of this small church by the Bishop of Kitui. For years he had promised Kitui Diocese a small chapel, both intimate and secluded, where true Christians might gather to share retreat. At last it had been built. A group of the more practically minded priests had spent three years designing and then building the small church with their own hands. The town's Village Polytechnic had helped with advice and, more than that, had surprised everyone at the last minute by providing a complete stained glass window, when all they had been asked for was a welded skeletal frame. Though crude, its colour was to become a relief to eyes all too accustomed to the drabness of grey concrete inside and outside to the monotony of the scrub.

That day the chapel was declared open and a sacred place by the words of a solemn mass spoken by Bishop John O'Hara. John Mwangangi, the only layman present, had been invited by the Bishop as a result of a donation he had made towards the cost of the building soon after he had returned to Kenya to become the Mwingi District Officer. John's motives, as ever, had been beyond reproach. He personally wanted to do something to repay the debt he believed he owed to the church for his education and, of course, the even greater personal debt he undoubtedly owed John O'Hara, himself.

The service was short and simple, an unadorned consummation of one man's dream. Afterwards they retired outside to the hilltop to reflect, as only priests can, on a passage from the Bible, a passage specified by O'Hara in his brief sermon. The quiet of the hilltop, the gently wafting cool air and the vastness of the earth below captured the collective imagination and held all in silent melancholy for some time. John, like the priests, found his own solitude while sitting on a rock just under the leeward lip of the summit.

Later, one by one, they all returned refreshed to the church, where a group of nuns had laid out food. Now it was time to talk, to eat and to congratulate one another on the success of the occasion. John, however, was incapable of adhering to such a rigid schedule, and still toiled with the issue he had contemplated during his seclusion. Now he could share it with the others. At his side, Michael spoke from utter innocence in the wide-eyed way that only Michael knew. Facing him, John O'Hara, inhibiting Michael a little by his mere presence, spoke from his intimate knowledge of John's life, the vital quality of which Michael would forever remain ignorant.

"Father John," said John, still unused to referring to his mentor as 'My Lord Bishop'. "I seem to be out of touch with the church's teaching nowadays. Don't misunderstand me," he qualified quickly, "I have kept my belief and both my wife and daughter are believers. But what I want to ask is this. What is the church's current teaching on circumcision?"

A few of the priests laughed a little, while others grimaced at their snacks when John mentioned the word. A few comments passed back and forth, but for John O'Hara the only image that filled his mind was that of the young John Mwangangi, almost bleeding to death while his father almost dispassionately shaved a stick with his knife on the far side of the compound. "There is no written policy,

John," said O'Hara. "In my opinion – and opinion is all I can give – unless a boy is suffering medical problems, well ought to be left alone."

"But here," interrupted Michael, "an uncircumcised boy grows up believing he can never have children. What's more he is mocked by his peers – men and women alike. They call him a little boy, whatever his age."

"I know," O'Hara replied. "That's exactly the kind of idea that we in the church should be trying to challenge."

"I think," offered Michael, "that too many time-honoured truths might be dying out as it is, dying out before any viable alternative has emerged."

"That is why the church sponsors the establishment of schools," said Bishop O'Hara. "That, for instance, is one reason why we teach such things as biology in those schools, so that children will be exposed to some rational ideas that might dispel some of the myths."

"With respect," said Michael, "I feel that what children profess to learn in school and what they do in their lives outside the school are two different things. I sincerely doubt whether any amount of reassurance in biology classes would make a boy think even twice about seeking circumcision and initiation. We know so little about customs such as this. We are still never allowed to witness the ceremony. In my opinion we ought to bring practices such as these into the church..."

Before John O'Hara's temper could burst upon Michael, Mwangangi interrupted forcefully. "My friends, I am afraid I have not been clear. You have rather missed my point." Having paused a short while until assured of the group's total attention he continued, "I was not referring to the practice of circumcising boys. What I meant – and I apologise for not making this clear – was the circumcision of girls."

The entire group was silent for a while. Then Bishop O'Hara spoke. "It's a savage and barbaric custom. I have no reservations whatsoever in saying that, Mwangangi. I would not accept the custom as a young priest and, after all these years, I remain as firmly opposed to it as ever." His voice was strong and, as was often the case with O'Hara, suggested anger. Too many times he had heard of young girls slipping off from school dormitories at night to be circumcised, because their headmistress had refused them the time off school. Some, having limped and stumbled a bloody way back to school, had developed infections and would possibly have died had they not come forward to seek treatment. And how many others bore scars stoically and without complaining, because that was what was expected of them? "What's more," he continued, speaking almost through gritted teeth, "a woman has to live with the scars. I have known many women ruined psychologically, rendered eternally guilty in marriage by this, its precondition. Some are so ashamed they will only speak of it during a blind confession."

Michael, who had remained silent as if listening intently, broke in to speak without interrupting. "I believe," he said softly, "that, like male circumcision, female circumcision is a valuable, useful and perhaps essential part of the life of these people. To ignore that would be stupid. To condemn it might cause as many problems as it might solve. To condone it, therefore, is all we can do. It is part of people's lives. It is important to them and we are not here to strip people of their culture, but to incorporate them as they are into our church. When we receive them, we receive their culture as well. It's a single package. The enrichment of the association will work both ways."

Mwangangi, deep in thought, offered nothing. His question had been answered, but inconclusively.

"Why do you ask, Mwangangi?" asked John O'Hara, who still spoke to the District Officer as if he were a child.

"No reason," he said. "I was just interested."

***

That day, almost two years ago, the chapel and its surroundings had buzzed with celebration and conversation. Today, Michael was alone in that place. The only sound was the howl of the wind across the summit ridges. The small church was deserted save for himself who had approached alone, like a private pilgrim revisiting a place whose associated memories he now wanted to forget. Kneeling before the altar, he recalled his exchange with Bishop O'Hara and John, and begged God to tell him what his future purpose might be. He had been a priest in this area for over six years and throughout he had done what he believed to be right, what he judged to be in the common interest of both the church and the people whom it tried to serve.

Suddenly, the events of that week had brought everything into question. All he had done, all he had thought and all he had tried to accomplish, once so clear and thus passionately pursued, all of this was now in question. Looking back, all the clues to the tragedy were there. Why did he never see them? Why could he never interpret them? He had begun to see himself as a mere fool trying to untie another fool's knot. He needed guidance, and the only place he could possibly search was within.

Nineteen

April 1976

It was good that Bill could see the place like this. During the previous two weeks, when Bill had travelled with his hosts to the coast, the miraculous seasonal transformation of Migwani had again taken place. Rain had watered the earth and begun the cycle of life that for a month would rush ahead with great momentum until over the span of a few days it would come to an equally abrupt halt. Everything was suddenly green. Hard brown earth still showed through the carpet of short blades of grass, but the general impression obtained from a glance was now unquestionably green. Everything had suddenly begun to grow at great speed, as if knowing that time was precious and that life's full cycle had to be compressed into a few short weeks.

They arrived in Migwani at lunchtime, having opted to take a circuitous route from the coast so that Bill could see more of the country. Their timetable had been exhausting, spending no more than a few nights in each place and having visited game parks, beaches, coral reefs and all the other things that the investigative tourist could uncover. All four of the travellers were, in fact, tourists. The places John had chosen so carefully to form his perfectly planned itinerary had been as new to him as the others. John confessed to Bill that he had travelled through more of Europe than his own country. Before departing on their tour, Bill had received this with total disbelief, accrediting the statement to John's eternal modesty and understatement. As the excursion progressed, however, it became obvious to all that John felt as much a foreigner with the Swahili or Somali people of the coast as Bill did. Even with the advantage of sharing a common language, John displayed a manifest apprehension at dealing with these people who, in Bill's eyes at least, seemed a model of friendship and politeness. Most surprising of all for Bill was John's absolute refusal to consider staying in local lodging houses, which seemed to fill the towns they visited. From Mombasa through Malindi and on to the island gem of Lamu, John had insisted on staying in the kind of hotel that catered for foreign tourists – primarily a multitude of loud Germans – at fifty times the price of the small, Swahili-owned counterparts.

At first Bill wondered whether John might be so insistent on his behalf, as if to protect his European visitor from the discomfort of a crouching Arab toilet or the indignity of paying only seven shillings for a night's lodging. But it did not take him long to realise that it was Lesley Mwangangi who was making the rules. She seemed uncomfortable with anything other than Western-style hotels, food or facilities, so much so that he was prompted to ask her directly how she had ever coped with life in Mwingi. A self-conscious smile and change of subject was her clear answer.

The oasis town of Garissa had provided the only problem since, isolated in the desert as the last outpost on the road to an unfriendly Somalia, it was well off the tourist run and possessed no accommodation John was willing to try. Here, however, he had taken the trouble to plan ahead having, some weeks beforehand, written to the District Officer in the area to request his assistance. John had frequent professional dealings with the man, a Mr Makau, a fellow Mukamba, whilst he had lived in Mwingi. Though separated by over a hundred miles, the two towns of Mwingi and Garissa were, by some stretch of the imagination, regarded as neighbours, and this necessitated much communication between civil servants based there. Bill found Makau, a man much older than John and a retired Chief of a town in Kitui District, quite distasteful. Bill was totally captivated by what he regarded as the unspoilt culture and tradition of the coast, especially in Lamu, where the monsoon winds had brought the timeless wooden dhows of Arab traders from Saudi Arabia and the Persian Gulf. Around Garissa, he had photographed anonymous men, their heads and bodies covered in long white shrouds, as they rode camels to market. Makau, however, tried to douse this enthusiasm with his words of experience. Having lived in that place, he explained, for five years, he had come to regard the locals with extreme distrust, almost as enemies. Besides being 'backward' and unwilling to accept the changes which development necessitates, he criticized the Somali pastoralists for trying to assert their own identity on policies for the area, policies that had been handed down from the authority of central government. If these people had their way, Makau had explained in his forceful voice which implored agreement, they would separate their land from Kenya.

Naively, Bill suggested that this might not be altogether a bad thing since the land historically was theirs and was only placed inside Kenya at the whim of the Berlin Conference. Possibly, Bill continued, they simply resented being governed by people they saw as foreigners. Makau, apparently interpreting this as a personal slight, replied in an insulting tone that a visitor to the country, especially an Englishman, whose ancestors had drawn the boundaries in the first place, should not even voice such an opinion, let alone to a servant of the government he criticised. Had John not rescued the situation with his characteristic conciliatory words they might all have been asked to leave there and then. A person is pregnant with his friend, he had said, smiling, thus transferring responsibility for Bill's remarks to himself. Makau, now laughing, heartily slapped John hard on the back and the air was cleared. The evening then continued with the two men, John and Makau, discussing details of the various troubles between the two districts. Somalis and Kambas, it seemed, had repeatedly clashed near the banks of the Tana River and had fought a series of minor battles. Somali swords, they explained, had killed Kambas and cattle had been stolen as the spoils of war. The Kamba, in return, had secured interest on their loan to the Somalis by abducting a number of their women and so the skirmishes continued, until a detachment of Kenya police armed with rifles had been sent to the area to keep the peace. John in Mwingi and Kamau in Garissa had jointly directed the operation and things were much quieter now.

So having politely and pragmatically cut short their stay in Garissa, they set off with another day to fill in the direction of Mwingi and ultimately, of course, Nairobi. Bill suggested that they should call in to see Janet in Migwani to thank her for the use of her house on their first night in Kenya. Back in Migwani, after their excursion to John's ancestral home, they had waited until late afternoon before returning to Nairobi to rendezvous with Lesley and Anna. They had hoped to see Janet again, but they did not. It crossed neither Lesley's nor Bill's mind that the essential trip John had made back to Kitui in the middle of their stay in Mombasa had been for anything other than work. John, in fact, had seen Janet, and quite a lot of her, because that weekend trip to supervise a delivery of materials to his farm was mainly spent in a Kitui hotel room.

John, of course, remembered Janet saying how much she liked to visit the town's weekend dances at the Umoja. What he had also registered, after his recent stay in her house, was how much Father Michael's departure had changed her outlook. She seemed much more vulnerable, somehow. And this was underlined by Solomon Musee's appearance at her door. She had turned him away, but he would be back. He would be there at the dance, intent on publicly associating himself with her. And if she rejected him, he might react.

John also knew Solomon Musee from his time as a magistrate in Mwingi. Solomon had come before the court on three separate occasions, each time with a different co-defendant, but each time on the same charge of threatening someone with a knife after a drinking session. Each time, the case was dropped by the accuser. John knew Solomon Musee, but Janet did not.

And so he made the mammoth trip, leaving their Mombasa beach hotel early on Friday morning to drive to Nairobi to check on work, and then to Kitui that same afternoon, arriving after dark. He made it to the dance at the Umoja, though, and met Janet. Solomon was also there, but because John was around, he kept his distance. The distance between John Mwangangi and Janet Rowlandson, however, significantly narrowed that night. In fact, it shrank to an ecstatic zero several times. When they parted the next morning, they resolved to meet again in two weeks. John asked Janet if she would skip the next dance, because he could not be there, but he did not tell her about his suspicion of Solomon Musee. And so their weekends together took on the air of a regular commitment.

In Migwani, in her own house, she now felt a new strangeness. It was just over a week since her night with John and, of course, the first time since then that she had met Lesley. This new strangeness emanated from the realisation of how easy it was to become devious, even duplicitous. She had never done anything like that before, and yet she was carrying it off like a pro. She and John had become lovers and were due to meet again in just a few days, and yet here she was socialising with his wife and daughter, as if nothing had changed. Having never learned to lie, she felt nervous, ill at ease. It never crossed her mind, of course, that she was not the only woman present practising the art.

And so the travellers contrived the perfect farewell for Bill, who was to return to England the following day, so full of the stories of his holiday, that his new partner would become worried that he would overwhelm their dinner guests with boredom over the coming weeks. For once Anna was allowed to share the happiness and was not sent to bed at her usual time. Janet's invitation to stay the night had been tempered by a warning that they would have to accept what was available, which was not very much. Having told her not to worry, they looked on with embarrassment as first her cook and then Janet herself made repeated excursions down to the town to buy the things their party would need. Migwani's butcher was nearly sold out of meat and could provide only the stomach and intestines of a goat. With some hilarity, Daniel, Janet's young cook, who had become more of a friend than a servant during her stay, seized the opportunity to cook a real meal for her guests. Stewed and served in a rich gravy with thick chapattis on the side, the offal made the perfect meal with which to end Bill's stay in Kenya. "Authentically African" was Bill's comment to Daniel as he collected the dishes. Lesley had found the prospect of eating such things distasteful and had picked at her meat, but had eaten enough beans and chapatti, both of which she found more familiar now, to feel full. The others, of course, had attacked their food with delight, despite the fact that John, having chewed a piece of particularly tasty intestine, had momentarily reduced all the others to helplessness by suggesting that the cook "might have left the shit in it." Their shared hilarious revulsion, however, was only temporary and, aided by significant quantities of the bottled Tusker beer, they all ate well.

It was Daniel, the young man with the name Nzoka, snake, who revealed the real surprise. Unknown to Janet he had made an excursion of his own to the bar near the teashop, whose trademark was bay leaves in its tea. For five shillings he had bought a large quantity of the locally brewed millet beer, *mawa*, which was brought for sale in Migwani from Thitani in large calabashes by the wives and daughters of the man who brewed it, whose family had been brewing beer for generations. When they had all finished eating the small stringy mangoes of which Migwani could always provide a multitude just after the rains, he announced his surprise by setting the beer on the table in a large aluminium cooking pot. Daniel, as he had predicted, found the scene very entertaining, with the sticky sweet mango juice still dripping from their fingers, lips and chins, the diners, Janet included, leaned over the pot and peered into it with expressions of profound disbelief and confusion lost in the expanse of their staring eyes.

"What on earth is that?" asked Bill, breaking into laughter.

Janet turned to look at Daniel, who was laughing very hard indeed. "I think that Bwana Mwangangi can tell you," he said, thoroughly amused.

As they all looked to John for enlightenment, he smiled at Daniel and said, "I've not seen any of this for quite a while. I thought that people had stopped making it."

"I bought it from the Maluki bar. They make it in Thitani and bring it here to sell," explained Daniel, as John nodded his understanding. "Maluki's bar in the market is the only one which can sell it. That is why there are so many old men around that place on market day."

"What is it?" asked Janet impatiently.

"Beer," replied John. "It's a special beer made from millet flour. It's called *mawa*."

"Its origin," observed Bill, still peering with apparently grave interest at the liquid, "would be easier to describe than its appearance. It looks like the contents of a vacuum cleaner, swimming," he said.

"No," said Janet, laughing. "Not here. If you don't hit the dust with a brush, it generally walks away. And there are no vacuum cleaners." From the beginning of her stay in Migwani, ants had always been a problem in her house. As time passed, however, she had learned to ignore them, having learned that once she had carefully picked them out from the marmalade or jam and ejected them to the side of the plate, breakfast tasted the same as it always had. She was thankful for Daniel's initiative. It had provided a focus for their conversation and allowed her the luxury of relegating her recent intimacy with John to the background of her thoughts.

"The best way," announced John, "to find out what it is like is to taste it." With that he told Bill to empty his glass, which he then filled with *mawa* from the pot. This rendered Bill quite speechless and prompted Janet to a fit of laughter, which Anna shared. Even Lesley, though revolted by the sight of the opaque grey liquid, could not help but laugh at the confused expression on Bill's face as he held up the glass to the light of the storm lamp and tried in vain to peer through it.

"Amazing," said Bill, still unable to bring himself to drink. "It's totally opaque, like porridge."

Remembering the milk at his father's house, John smiled and poured a glass for himself, saying, "You seem to be making a habit of this. I'm sure you'll enjoy it if you try some."

John drank from his glass as the others watched, struck dumb by their conviction that he would choke. When he did not, Daniel poured some of the beer for Janet and Leslie and also some for himself. Anna protested, but no one was going to allow her to have a share. "Cheers," he said, raising the glass and drinking.

The others now decided to try the experience. All three winced. Lesley coughed and spluttered through her laughter and replaced the glass on the table, pushing it forcefully away in a single movement. A moment later, after wiping her lips with her handkerchief, she looked at the others in disbelief, saying, "How can you possibly drink that?"

"I am not sure whether to drink it or chew it," said a concerned-looking Bill, as he watched the thick liquor stick to the glass, repeatedly turning and twisting it to get a better view of the contents.

Janet's reaction was different. After approaching the exercise with great caution, she had cast fear to the wind and taken a sizeable gulp of the liquid and swallowed it. She was helpless for a second or two, gasping like a fish out of water. After slamming the glass hard on the table, she rushed to the kitchen to get a glass of cold water, which she drank in one. Returning to the others, much to the amusement of Daniel, who was quite beside himself with laughter, she sat down, wiping her now running eyes,

"Wow.. it's like drinking neat gin with flour in it!" This comment apparently renewed Bill's interest to try more and he drank again, this time with more conviction.

Before long, they had all overcome their initial problems and went on to finish the pot. Lesley, who declared with some conviction that she did not like it, was the only one to remain with a glassful in front of her. Eagerly, Bill took it from her and finished it off. He announced that he had really started to enjoy it. They did not have long to wait before they all began to realise just how strong it was. The word 'beer' was clearly misapplied, since a few minutes later they all knew they were quite drunk and filled with euphoria. All, Lesley and Anna included, if only by association, much enjoyed the hours that followed. Impromptu parties such as this had always been the most enjoyable part of life in Migwani for Janet. In the past, with Father Michael, she had often returned from the bar in such a mood and they had spent some hours telling stories and dancing to music from a radio.

It was after midnight before the euphoria died down and the weariness of a day's journey caught up with the travellers. As quickly as they had begun, the festivities ceased and everyone lolled exhausted in their chairs.

After a while Janet rose from her chair, rubbed her eyes and yawned, saying, "I had better get some sheets and blankets for you. Bill, would you mind sleeping here?"

She was cut short by John who, without a second thought, said, "Don't bother about us. There are too many of us to stay here. We'll go and stay in the Safari Bar in town."

Janet determinedly avoided a glance towards Lesley. This, clearly, was John's carefully calculated way of ensuring there was no risk of extended private contact between his wife and herself, who now, of course, was his lover. The evening had gone well, bypassing, from John and Janet's shared perspectives, difficult terrain, smoothed by Daniel's perfectly timed injection of local brew.

Suddenly revitalised, Bill looked up and smiled. At last he would spend a night in a local hotel and find out just what one might receive for the meagre fee. They left Janet, truly grateful for the hospitality she had shown. Lesley, leading the very sleepy Anna by the hand was the first to leave, thanking Janet again and kissing her goodbye, telling her that she must come to Nairobi soon to stay for a weekend.

After Lesley and Anna had walked off towards the car, Bill and John remained with Janet in her kitchen, still trying to express their thanks. Janet maintained that there was no need for them to go to the hotel, but John would hear none of it, stating that he thought they had overstayed their welcome already. Quickly, Bill scribbled his address in her address book and told her that if ever she might need somewhere to stay in London, she would be more than welcome in his house. Bidding a fond goodbye, they left and joined Lesley and Anna in the car.

"She has become a true African," said Bill, whose admiration for Janet was clear.

"Indeed she has," said John in a calm, measured tone.

Twenty

June 1976

Janet looked on and laughed, laughed so much she almost cried. This unknown man dispersed a cloud which began to gather. She was on the road, on the way to recovery. His performance, skilled as well as spontaneous, entertained her like nothing else had done for months passed. Its true joy was its unexpectedness. Sitting on this bench in the shade of a concrete canopy in Nairobi's Kariokor bus station, awaiting the arrival of her bus, the last thing she expected to see was a performance like this. Unannounced at first, a young man dressed in a threadbare primary school uniform of khaki shirt and shorts, and wheeling a bicycle, crept slowly out into the centre of the large expanse of tarmac, where idle buses were parked. Then, beginning with a bow to his distant audience, he displayed his skill as a trick cyclist. He offered real circus, spinning the front wheel, standing on one foot on the saddle and doing headstands on the handlebars. For ten minutes his cycle described lazy circles on the tarmac, as if propelled by some perpetual energy. Easing himself from one trick to another, from handstand to headstand, from balancing on the crossbar to swaying from side to side over the rear wheel, he entertained a gathering crowd, holding their attention, provoking them to laughter and applause. Had he not appeared by chance to entertain the waiting crowd, among them Janet, she would have sat alone with her discomfort and thus meditated herself nearer the depths of depression, which had threatened to envelop her for several days.

As ever, Nairobi was a stuffy and uncomfortable place, a city Janet found easy to detest. It seemed to live an independent life, a life far removed from any other part of Kenya. Everyone in the city, even a visitor due to stay only a few hours inside its influence, was transformed by the obsequiousness of its life, and tricked into mimicking the false grandeur of its façade. Even the beggars, who each day shuffled the length of Kenyatta Avenue on hands and knees, dragging behind them their waving polio-shrunken legs, even they seemed full of the city's infectious false pride. A beggar in Kitui was part of the town, a showman whom people knew and recognised, like a landmark in the town's character. For instance, the old man who sat in the road opposite the Standard Bank in Kitui completely covered by a large black blanket crying, "Don't forget the leper," had become an involuntary traffic island. The one-way system that operated around his pitch was known and honoured by all. Traffic in Kitui, of course, was somewhat limited in quantity. Only a handful of vehicles would pass the spot each day, but all followed the direction marked by the old beggar's bent arm, which stretched out from beneath his blanket to hold the chipped enamel bowl in which he collected the average salary for his job. At sunset he would emerge from under his shroud to count the day's takings. Then, wrapping the blanket around his shoulders, he would walk to the bar in perfect, if wrinkled health at a great pace, with the weight of pennies jingling inside the knotted handkerchief he used as a purse.

The one they called 'the tinker' was simply a showman, a zany one-man band who looked less like a musician than a walking advertisement for kitchenware. Completely covered in tin plates, enamel pans and *sufurias*, the giant shining aluminium cooking pots used for making *ugali*, which he tied with strings and hung around his neck, he possessed no permanent pitch, electing to dance his way through the town, sometimes past the cathedral, sometimes through the bus station, syncopating with his steps the rhythms he played on his bamboo flute. Since he was entirely naked save for his swinging pots and pans, people looked upon him as a *mwana wa mungu*, a child of God, a madman, rather than a beggar.

Even the smaller towns had their resident eccentrics. Kabati, the ugly town between Kitui and Migwani, which had grown in five years from two mud-walled shops to a town the size of the District centre by virtue of having been founded at the junction of two bus routes, even Kabati possessed its own *mwana wa mungu.* Rejoicing in the name of King Kabati, he was surely a child of God, for his words, his actions, his vision seemed governed by some rationale, some unconventional wisdom, which was immediately apparent, and yet both absurd and forever indefinable. He was utterly irrational, but so completely that he created his own reality. Janet had met him many times, had sat and talked with him over a tea in the shop where most travellers who changed buses in the town took their refreshment, where they would spend the blank hours around midday awaiting the arrival of their connection. Unlike most other acknowledged madmen, King Kabati was young, tall and quite handsome too. He claimed to have left secondary school only a few years ago, having completed his studies, like so many others, by obtaining an unclassified, and therefore useless, result in his examinations. His great ambition had been to work as a clerk in a government office and then seek promotion until he had become "a big fish in the net like Bwana Mwangangi in Mwingi, a man who could command his own fleet of Land Rovers and give orders to everyone else in the District, save for the Commissioner in Kitui and a handful of rich people." Even his dreams were realistic enough to recognise that this particular office could be most easily attained by birthright. He certainly suffered no scattered confusion in his madness.

Some months ago, when she met him for the first time, he had accosted her in a way similar to the spitting old man in Migwani. By then more experienced in how to deal with such people, she had suffered no fear and invited him to take some tea with her. Then to her great surprise, he had interviewed her in English across the table, as if he were some strangely warped tax collector. She had laughed at the incongruity of this business-like tone coming from one so absurd, dressed, as he was, in shirt and shorts with his head topped by a silver crown made of aluminium cooking foil. Entertained, she had played his game only to be presented, to her astonishment, with an apparently authentic and blank British Inland Revenue tax declaration form. Listening intently to her answers, he had filled in the form with a stub of a pencil he carried on top of his head within the confines of his crown, held by a knot of his close-cropped hair. Having competed his interrogation of her, he declared the meeting closed and left her, pausing, as he stood, to take a large knife from the waistband of his shorts and complete the sharpening of his pencil, before sliding it into its place along his scalp. The knife he held on to for just a little too long, she thought, before returning it with a show of blasé speed to his shorts.

She had gone on her way, that day, having changed from

the Nairobi-bound *Uhuru na Kazi* that had brought her from Migwani, to a Nairobi-Kitui bus of the same company, with her list of errands to be accomplished in town again at the forefront of her mind. Indeed, she had completely forgotten her meeting with King Kabati until the very next time she found herself waiting for a connection in the same teashop. It was some weeks later, but King Kabati strode directly up to her and introduced himself, referred her to their previous meeting and politely asked for a few minutes of her time so that their business might be concluded. Again over a tea that she bought for him, he announced that there had been quite a lot of work to complete on her behalf since their first encounter. He announced that the ministry had fully reviewed her case and had decided that she had overpaid her tax. Therefore she was due a refund of one hundred shillings. This could be paid, he told her, as soon as she paid the five shilling investigation fee, a charge made to discourage spurious claims for rebates.

Everything about the man was a contradiction. His English, his manner, his logic, within its own context, seemed perfect, but the whole was so absurd as to be rendered completely surreal. Faithfully, Janet complied with his request and handed over a five-shilling note. Then to her surprise, he produced from his pocket the tax form she had filled in those weeks before, still crisp and neatly folded, as if it had been filed for future reference. After sticking a ten-cent stamp at the bottom of page three, he asked Janet to sign over it with what appeared to be the same stub of a pencil. Then, pocketing the five shillings, he produced a wad of hundred shilling notes and presented one of them to his client. Janet was rendered speechless. The note, of course, was not genuine, but every detail of a real note had been painted in a dark red hue on to a piece of paper torn from an exercise book to produce a child-like, but strangely accurate forgery, despite the portrait of Jomo Kenyatta looking distinctly pop-eyed. Smiling, as she scratched at the colour in an attempt to convince her eyes that it was real, King Kabati had proudly stood up and bid his goodbye. As he turned and literally skipped out of the door, clutching his five shillings of earnings, less the cost of a stamp, he pointed to the wad of fake notes still in his hand and said, "Goat's blood." With that he set off ostensibly to honour his next appointment.

But Nairobi beggars, thought Janet, mirrored the schizophrenia of the city. Along Kenyatta Avenue crawled the handicapped, but they seemed to regard their predicament as a business, accosting only the white or obviously rich with their often gnarled, misshapen hands. They knew that these people would rather discard ten shillings than suffer the embarrassment of being followed along the street by one so obviously destitute, so desperately ugly. Here, in what the well-to-do called the native sector, a beggar was again the mixture of madman and circus act one could encounter and enjoy anywhere in the country. Here, the child of God performed, sometimes for himself alone. He never crawled; there was dignity in his madness. Only when his act was completed would he visit the groups of people at each bus stop to collect the pennies they would willingly give and the thanks they would voice for the entertainment he had given. What would happen, she thought, if this trick cyclist had chosen to give his act in the road outside the veranda of the New Stanley? There, tourists met to laze away the hours between sightseeing and shopping over exorbitantly priced coffee, served by proud white-coated waiters. "What would they think?" she thought, as she watched him wheel his bicycle, still counting his money, over to the side of the bus station, where he bought a slice of pineapple for twenty cents from a street vendor. Surely, she concluded, a tourist would not even regard him as a madman or even a beggar. No, for the tourist he would be an example of the street theatre that page two hundred of the guidebook probably labelled and described.

But had she, herself, not operated this double standard without a thought for the alternative? When sick, why had she assumed that she must travel to Nairobi for treatment rather than visit the health centre in Migwani or the District Hospital in Kitui? She could have gone to the nuns in the mission hospital in Muthale, but then circumstances had not allowed it. She was just thankful to have been swept along by events. It had made her life easier.

Almost two weeks ago, she had rushed away from Migwani immediately after school, bound for Kitui on the bus. The week had been frustrating. Twice she had been invited for dinner at the mission by Father O'Shea, who had been appointed to run Migwani in Michael's absence. She sensed his difference from Michael the moment they met. He was older and more overtly meditative, and conscious of his priesthood. After serving more than twelve years in the district, he had yet to visit a bar, regarding them as places where he was neither welcome nor appreciated. Neither had he ever eaten in a local restaurant, though he never refused the food he was offered when he visited a parishioner at home. He enjoyed a beer, but it was to be shared with his peers, not his flock. She had accepted his invitations and had enjoyed his company to a point, but she found his manner rather strange, discomforting in its intensity. Prematurely grey-haired and with piercingly bright blue eyes, which would stare at her with unblinking clarity during pauses in the conversation, as if he were a tape recorder on a momentary pause, his whole appearance and manner made her feel nervous. She talked to him in the way she might speak to a father, not the religious kind, and not a peer, as she could with Michael. Above all, his deep resonant voice seemed constantly to be offering her advice or admonition, drawn from a direct and long acquaintance with the problems that frustrated Janet's work and locked the people of Migwani into poverty's cell.

So even more than ever she had looked forward to her regular visit to Kitui to seek the company Migwani could not provide. Even the town's bars were deserted these days. It was harvest time and most people including, reluctantly, half of the students from school, were tied to their farms to gather the crop before the dry season's weevils destroyed it. As ever, it seemed the crop had all but failed anyway. There had been enough rain, but it had all fallen on three nights, two months previously and throughout the District the plants had bolted and then, starved of water in maturity, had produced only small, near-grainless cobs. People's disappointment at the harvest seemed to pervade everything. In the town, in the mission, in the school and, though unrealised before now, in Janet, there had developed a propensity toward torpor, toward resignation, toward depression. It was this depression and its promised relief which propelled her to Kitui and the dances at the Umoja Bar. And of course it was the promise of meeting John Mwangangi again each Friday, on the first night of his regular weekend visit to Kitui. Ongoing work on his farm now required that he visit Kamandiu almost as a matter of course, and, since the first time they had slept together on that weekend after Michael's departure, he had made a point of calling in on the Friday night Umoja dance to meet her. They usually spent Friday night together in one of the matchbox-sized rooms at the back of another bar, the Umoja's substantial clientele being perhaps too much of a potential audience for their activity.

Janet looked forward to visiting the place each Friday to such an extent that the rest of the week had begun to take on the feeling of being no more than the prelude to its pleasures. But paradoxically she started to become morose, almost desperate for his company on the days when he was not there. These Friday meetings had become the ecstatic centre of her life, around which orbited a mundane week. She tried to convince herself that it was something more than the sex that she craved, but she knew that was the truth. John Mwangangi, in one thunderous night, when they had not even bothered to turn out the light or, for that matter, sleep, had reopened a closed world within her psyche that had once been populated by a long-standing boyfriend at college. But it was a world she had not visited for almost two years, until John had explored that place, and opened up continents she never knew existed. And with each new meeting it had got better. He was a sophisticated man, this John Mwangangi, and a lover of a kind she had not known existed. With him there were no fumblings, no frenzies, no nervous half measures. To Janet their encounters seemed like a string of her deepest wishes, desires of which she had been unaware, but which he knew in apparently intimate detail. From the moment they met until the moment they parted, she could feel the promise of ecstasy he could give her and, like a drug, she was now dependent on it, and craved more, more than their one shared night per week could supply. Though when alone she scolded herself for falling into a trap she had always resolved to avoid, now even the anticipation of his arrival took her breath away. She was hopelessly and utterly in love with him.

On their previous two meetings, they had not even bothered to stay at the Umoja dances, opting to take their now preferred room at the Kitui High Class Lodging House, whose title could not have been more of a misnomer. But the sheets and mattresses were well known to be clean and free of fleas. There was no electricity in the establishment, but by now John and Janet had learned to sit in the meagre light of an oil lamp on low flame, the wick turned down until it almost burnt a flickering blue. Usually they undressed immediately and made love, and then lying naked together talked. Janet had noted John's scars on their first night together, but did not mention them at the time. She had not seen many naked men, so the obviously unusual extent of John's circumcision was lost on her. But the long scratch scars, showing white and pink on his black thighs, were what caught her attention. When she asked him what they were, he told her they were the result of an accident he had when he was a boy and left it at that. It was the only time she remembered him reticent and defensive, apparently unwilling to divulge more than a minimum. She assumed rightly that he was self-conscious about the disfigurement, or harboured residual guilt at bearing scars in such private places, so she slid down and kissed the whole area, which of course responded as she thought it might and the subject was dropped, as more pressing positions were assumed. But when they parted the next morning, she was rendered speechless when he actually thanked her for being so sensitive. It suggested to her that perhaps Lesley Mwangangi, after more than a decade of marriage, was not as tolerant of his obvious embarrassment. So now there was mutual trust as well.

And so, when John Mwangangi entered the bar at seven on Friday of last week, he suffered no fears of panic when he realised Janet was not there, since their arrangement had already taken on its own sense of normality. Thus they had confirmed their appointment the previous week. Usually,

Janet was the first to arrive at around six, straight from the newly arrived *Uhuru na Kazi,* so when John entered, he had expected to find her already waiting for him. But that night she was not there.

He bought his usual soda, ordered his chicken and chips and waited. She must have gone out to arrange her grocery order for the next day and been delayed, he thought. An hour later, at eight, he was worried. He drove the short distance to Kitui Mission to ask the receptionist if she had been there, but he was not at his desk. Two priests, both of whom knew him well from his days as District Officer in Mwingi, said they had not seen her, and then gave him a look, which he immediately recognised as communicating more than the answer to his question. Janet and he had taken care, but in this small place it was impossible to be that careful. He drove to the sprawling compound of Kitui School, at the other end of town, where he knew there was one particular teacher who had been a close friend of Janet's during the early months of her stay in Migwani, but it turned out that he had not seen Janet for several weeks. John called back at the Umoja before concluding he had no option, and so he set off immediately to drive the thirty miles to Migwani. There were no telephones in Migwani and he could think of nowhere else in Kitui where he might look for her.

He drove into the lightless school compound at around eleven to find Janet's house in total darkness. He tried the kitchen door. It was unlocked. It was always unlocked, even when she went away for the weekend. He had recently tried to persuade her to keep it secure, but she always insisted that in Migwani there was no need. He called her name softly through the darkness. He went through the kitchen and into the living room, the dust on the unswept floor crunching a little under the soles of his shoes. He called her name again. Though he had never slept with Janet here, he knew which of the two other rooms was hers and he pushed open the door. And his heart raced. She was there in the bed.

He bent down by her side and then put his hand on her face. She stirred, but said nothing. He spoke quickly, assuming that she would need the reassurance of knowing that it was him, since the total darkness would render anyone a stranger, but her response was a mere murmur, so uncharacteristic he knew immediately there was something wrong. He moved his hand to her brow. It was hot. There was a fever.

Having located her oil lamp in the living room and lit it with a match from a box that paradoxically was easier to find, because he had previously noticed she always kept it on the kitchen window ledge above her cooker, he re-entered the bedroom with his light. Immediately he saw she was pale. He had spent enough time embracing this body to know it well and the rhythm of the breathing was not hers. It was faster and lighter than normal. He shook her gently and she stirred some more, but still did not know who was there. He shook her again and her eyes opened. She tried to speak but her words were slurred. A glass of water helped, but she was still not completely coherent. She showed not the slightest concern or surprise that he was here in her house, in her room.

He lifted her to a seated position, his arms embracing the body more tenderly and yet more determinedly than ever before. Her youth was a miracle, the slightness of her frame pure perfection. But she did not respond; she was limp in his arms. As he stroked her face with his hand, she roused some more and realised for the first time that it was him. But still there was no surprise. Then she spoke a little, the words barely audible, her voice a croak. She managed to say "Sorry" several times. The obvious lateness of the hour combined with the fact that she was still at home finally registered and she seemed suddenly to realise that John was here in her own room. Another glass of water later she was coherent enough to tell him that Daniel had gone home at lunchtime as usual for the weekend. After eating the lunch he had left, she remembered coming to bed for a nap. She had not felt well for a few days and was sure that her sore throat meant that she was getting a cold. Clearly she had fallen asleep. She had been there since two o'clock. There was a hint of panic when she realised that she had missed her afternoon class and that nobody had noticed.

John tried to calm her. "You've got malaria," he said. "Leave things to me."

Before Janet realised what he was doing, he had excused himself for a few minutes and had returned to his car. Janet felt a little stronger and managed to walk to her sitting room where she watched his progress through the window as he drove through the town towards Mwingi. She saw his car headlights come to a halt about half a mile away, where the road ran along an elevated ridge beyond the town. Within a few minutes he was back in the house, relieved to find that she had felt strong enough to get up. He told her that he had spoken to the headmaster and that she should pack a bag because she was going with him immediately to Nairobi. She had permission to take a week's leave. When she started to protest, just a little, he told her to dress and pack a few clothes. There would be no discussion.

They travelled to Nairobi in John's car, much smoother and quieter, she thought, than anything else she had travelled in for a long time. Janet said little along the way, unable even to express the gratitude she felt, because of the debilitating weakness that consumed her energy. She must have fallen asleep after a few miles, because she awoke the next morning in a beautiful bed with cotton sheets and soft pillows. For some time she had no idea where she was. She ought to have panicked, but she did not have the energy. When John appeared in the open doorway, she began to recall what had happened and tried to get up, but her head filled with blank pain, and she felt sick and faint.

By the Saturday evening she already felt much better. Though she had little recollection of events, she vaguely remembered a visit from a doctor and having had injections and pills. And she had slept. Though she still felt utterly exhausted, she was well enough to get up by seven and ate a light meal before going straight back to bed. She felt stronger again on the Sunday, but stayed in bed. After a light lunch, which John served on a tray, she took some more pills and told him she felt much stronger. He joined her in bed and they made love, just a little. And then she slept again to awake again at seven in the evening, sensing a body settling itself next to her on the bed, a sensation she convinced herself she had felt before. She turned over and was well enough to realise, in the very middle of the action, that her intention to reach out and caress John's thigh was ill-advised, since it was Lesley Mwangangi's female frame that compressed the mattress. John stood aside.

"You look a lot better," he said.

"How do you feel?" asked Lesley.

Janet felt weak, exhausted and mildly confused. Her mouth was dry, her throat sore and her entire body ached. "I feel much better," she said. "Can I go home?"

She wanted to go straight back to Migwani the following day, but both John and Lesley insisted she stay on for a while. After all, she could not be sure immediately that the treatment had worked. She would have to wait and see for a few days and, if necessary, see the doctor again to make sure. Janet felt unable to express her gratitude, explaining that she had no money to buy them a present and no way of repaying the hospitality she had received. They both told her not to worry, that they did not offer help at a price. John tried to put her mind at ease by saying that the medical care cost nothing, because it was provided as part of his job. When she returned to England, he said, she could tell people that she owed a Kenyan a personal debt. It might make them realise that she had been in the country not merely as a tourist or a technician, but that she had lived there amongst people like herself.

She stayed three days, days of celibacy enforced by Lesley's renewed presence. Years later she would regret not having asked Lesley where she had been over the weekend, but, in the circumstances of the time, she was intent on having as little contact with her as possible.

Then, confident that the treatment had worked and that the symptoms would clear up, she thanked her hosts and left, but not before she had given an especially careful goodbye to Anna, who had been allowed a day off school to come and see her. The young girl had spoken of her grandparents, telling Janet that their home was in Migwani Location in a place called Kamandiu in the valley beyond Kea. Janet was quite astounded at the girl's knowledge of the area, its place names and features. As Janet bid goodbye, John, Lesley and Anna all came to the door and stood together to watch her walk off down the main road to get the bus into town. John had offered a lift, but she had refused, saying that she wanted to take the chance to get to know her way around Nairobi a little better. The Mwangangi's house, like all the others in Lavington, was large and stood in its own grounds. As Janet walked away, her feet crunching the driveway's gravel, she turned and waved to the watching group. "I wish I was coming to Migwani with you," Anna shouted, causing Lesley's perfunctory parting smile to fade instantly. It was anger that replaced it, Janet saw, as she turned and waved one last time before disappearing behind the hedge. She was both surprised and somewhat hurt to see Lesley turn and spank her daughter back into the house. John stayed on the doorstep to wave, but inside the house Janet's stay had already been forgotten and Anna, now returned to her mother's discipline, was being given a loud dressing-down, alongside several reminders that she would not be visiting Kamandiu again.

So, feeling much better, Janet waited for the bus to arrive. For ten minutes the trick cyclist entertained the crowd and provoked Janet to thought. Once again, with illness receding and faith in her own strength restored by John and his family, she began to view the journey to Migwani as a real homecoming. For some time the house by the school had felt like a cell and life in Migwani had been like a prison sentence, each day bringing a repetition of work, eat and sleep to be lived through longing for the day that would reunite her with her lover. Already she wished it were Friday. She had only been parted from him for an hour, but had already started to wonder how she would get through the days before their next meeting, when she could begin to repay the debt she felt she owed.

Twenty-one

July 1976

What absolute absurdity! Janet felt like she ought to laugh as Barnabas Maluki wheeled his bicycle out of the school compound and into the road, but it was sadder than that. She watched him set off up the hill away from the town and then turn right at the top and follow the footpath, which bore north-west towards Thitani. She knew the path to be narrow and rough, passing first through the area known as Kaliluni alongside the farm belonging to the Musee family. Here his head was still visible from where Janet stood at the front of the school, just next to the flagpole by the headmaster's office. The pole's affixed rope flapped in the strong wind, rattling against the hollow metal shaft. Then, as Barnabas rode down the first of the many deep gullies the path crossed, he disappeared from her view. Only then did she look down at the sealed envelope in her hand and smile, shaking her head at the irony.

Barnabas was a primary school teacher, and a good one. He had lived in Thitani all his life. His father, a man locally renowned for his brewing skill, kept a bar there and recently had invested the profit it generated over the years in a general shop. Thitani market possessed only eight shops and now two of them belonged to his father.

Whatever he chose to do, he knew he could always return to the family business and receive a good income. Barnabas, however, had become a devout Christian during his stay at the government boarding school in Kitui and had embraced the wisdom of Jesus Christ, as he himself described it. Amid constant self-retribution, he was forever conscious of his position in the community and realised that, if a teacher were to be respected by his pupils, he must be above reproach, a model of discipline and morality. Thus in school he was a hard-working and conscientious teacher. Education, for him, was not merely the accumulation of knowledge, it was the key that would unlock people's lives and free them from the misguided beliefs of traditional society. Since he first entered secondary school as a bright fourteen-year-old, small for his age, with thirty points in the primary school exam – a performance of which he would be eternally proud – his life had been guided by the Bible. Interpreted literally by the preachers of the Africa Inland Church, its advice had provided him with a strict code, a definitive list of rules which, when obeyed, would surely lead to the only true reward.

The way he had chosen, however, had not been easy. The preachers had never said it would be, of course, but always they advised that no one should doubt the word of God as written. Over the years, Barnabas had grown to his maturity, had obtained good results in his exams and had been overjoyed to fulfil his ambition to train to be a teacher. Privately he hoped that on graduation he would be posted to a school in a large town, Nairobi, or Nakuru, for instance, and had been utterly dejected at first to find that his employment would be in his home area. However, he must accept what God provides. It is right.

In the five years since his graduation, he had worked as conscientiously as he could imagine. Besides teaching throughout the day, he had devoted much of his spare time to the local church and hoped that one day he would become a preacher himself. Thitani, however, was still too 'bush' for his taste and people there were not enlightened. Indeed, many were still primitives, because they did not even go to church. His own father, for instance, spent much of his time brewing beer or serving in his shop, which also sold cigarettes. He had told his father many times, and in no uncertain terms, that he would do nothing to help the family business while it practised such sins. So, to keep his options open and to upgrade his teacher's salary, he had studied furiously every evening for three years to obtain his O-levels. His recent success in his latest exam, sat as a private candidate in Kitui, had convinced him that he ought to pursue a better position than Thitani School could offer. It was obvious to him that there was no work in this area for someone with such qualifications. In some years' time, he granted, when people here would be more educated, then there might be jobs to attract people like him, but at the moment there surely was nothing. From the American missionaries at Kyome he had heard that there was good employment in Nairobi in the Bible schools, which their church had founded. People like himself went there from all over the country to study God's word and, for someone such as him, there might be a chance of obtaining a position as a teacher.

Two months ago, with eagerness overflowing, he had taken the bus to Nairobi and had visited the man whose address he had been given in Kyome. He talked to the man and explained his desire to teach in the Bible school. The job would be well paid, nearly a thousand shillings a month, almost as much as a qualified secondary school teacher could earn. Though Barnabas had been told clearly that only people with advanced level qualifications would be considered, he returned to Migwani proud and expectant. The man told him to wait until they had considered his application, a statement that Maluki interpreted as acceptance. According to Barnabas the letter would soon arrive telling him that he should come to Nairobi and begin work. He was still waiting.

It was in a magazine that he saw the advertisement. To pass the time on the return journey from Nairobi, he bought one of the expensive glossies that purchasers would read several times cover to cover before trying to sell it on. Rejecting the Kenyan magazines because he knew them to contain many bad things, he chose an English – and therefore in his eyes respectable – magazine called *New Scientist*. He was attracted by its title and a picture of a white-coated teacher addressing students on its cover. He enjoyed reading it, though it did take him some time. He read all the words and even convinced himself that he understood them. Some of the things he read reminded him of things he learned in his secondary school science lessons. Others he recognised from the words he learned recently to support his studies for his General Science exam and, during the journey home, he took great pleasure in pointing out each key phrase with enthusiasm to the unfortunate sitting next to him and explaining its meaning. He was silenced by a box of words in a narrow column inside the back cover. The words told of courses in computer programming being offered by a college in London. They invited all people to write for details.

With imagination duly fired, Barnabas wrote to the address for details and then waited expectantly for the reply, already trying to imagine what life in London would be like. He knew that another Migwani man, Mwangangi Musyoka from Kamandiu, had gone to study in England, and he had returned to become a District Officer and then a rich man in the city. He resolved to go to see him and ask his advice when the time was right.

Faithfully the agency replied and Barnabas collected the letter just two weeks later. His friend had told him that the letter was there. He had seen it in the cardboard box, which served as the mailbox for all letters addressed to residents of Migwani. Users would sift through the contents of the small box on the shop's hardboard-topped counter to see if there was anything for themselves and invariably decided to take any letters for friends or family with them, but often then forgetting about them in the following weeks. With excited pride Barnabas studied the outside of the envelope before opening it. It had to be genuine because it bore an English stamp with a picture of the Queen and the address had been written with a typewriter. Inside he found a second envelope with the words 'Do Not Open' stamped all over it. A letter pinned to this explained that inside there was a short test which the applicant must complete in the presence of a responsible person, who must then sign to say that everything had been properly conducted. The test was then to be returned to the address at the top of the letter. After some days of indecision, during which he re-read all of his secondary school notes as revision, and after many hours of contemplating the problem of who might be responsible enough to satisfy the people in London, he finally made up his mind to ask the English teacher in Migwani, part of her qualifications being her known proximity to Bwana Mwangangi, his role model.

His encounter with Janet was unfortunate. He rode to Migwani on a Sunday, after attending church in Thitani and went straight to her house in the secondary school compound. Having knocked on the door several times, he concluded that she must have gone to church, but he decided to walk around the house anyway just to make sure there was no one there. Janet, in fact, was spending the day lazily stretched out on a collapsible bed in her bikini within the privacy provided by the euphorbia hedge that edged the whole school compound. Having been told that she would depart for England within a month, she had thought it wise to seek out at least a show of a tan, otherwise her mother would nag at her for looking pale and her friends would never believe she had lived in Africa.

Barnabas was deeply shocked. As he came round the corner of the house and saw her, he could only stand and gape. Having been educated in a tradition that did not allow even a man to bare his shoulders in public, such an array of nakedness left him quite speechless. Had the flesh not been white, he might simply have scoffed damnation aloud and turned away. But this was Janet who lay before him, and he was rendered dumb and weak-kneed by the sight.

Seeing him, Janet greeted him and, calmly donning a wrapper, which still left her shoulders bare, she approached to shake hands.

"I thought you were at church," he said, barely in control of his mouth.

"No. I don't go to church," she replied calmly. The remark served only to anaesthetize further his already numbed senses.

What kind of person was this, he thought, who would go outside wearing almost no clothes and who did not go to church? After a moment's thought, concluding that since she was white Janet must be a Christian, he produced the brown envelope with the covering letter still attached and handed it to her. She read the letter and wanted to laugh. It was only then that she realised that he seriously wanted her to invigilate the exam.

"Can you spare the time, Miss Rowlandson?" he asked. "I have already done my revision and, as you can see from the letter, the test will take only ten minutes. Can I do it now?"

After re-reading the instructions Janet pointed to a series of example questions and answers on the back of the letter. "Have you studied these?" she asked.

"Yes, Miss Rowlandson," he said, "but I have done a lot of other work as well. There," he continued, pointing at the worked solution, "they have given the answers to these questions, so they will not be in the exam."

Janet smiled knowingly. "Are you sure you want to do this?"

"Yes, Miss Rowlandson." Barnabas was adamant.

For the stipulated ten minutes Barnabas sat across the table from Janet with pen in hand, poised ready yet reluctant and eventually redundant. The exam turned out to be a set of extremely complex questions of the kind that were used in IQ tests. At first Barnabas was eager, setting about the task with great technique, reading the question through before attempting his answer. Clearly, however, he had not understood a word of what he read, and when Janet announced that his time was up he was quite speechless in his disappointment. He had not made even a single mark on the paper and flatly refused to comply with Janet's suggestion that he should at least tick the boxes at random. He seemed to be more interested in obtaining her signature on the paper than in attempting to answer any of the questions and, when she had signed it, he offered her great thanks and carefully folded the paper into the previously stamped and addressed envelope.

"Will you post it for me in Kitui?" he asked. "I don't want to give it to the post office here in Migwani because many letters are lost from there."

With that he thanked Janet for her kindness and left. Janet felt a little dazed for a while. She read and re-read the address on the envelope. Then, deciding she had to speak to him, she dashed out of the house towards the school. Having called him, she caught up with him right outside the school's main office in the centre of the circle of bare earth, where the students gathered at each Friday morning assembly to hoist the national flag.

"Are you really sure you want me to send this?" she asked. "The stamps are worth two shillings. If you don't want to send it, I will buy the stamps from you. I can use them to send my own letters. All I have to do is stick a label over the address and I can use the envelope as well."

He seemed more than a little offended, patronised even. Then he answered, his voice almost pleading. "But, Miss Rowlandson, you have signed it… I am sure that when they see your name there they will take me. Please, you must send it for me."

Still standing where he had left her, she watched until he disappeared from sight before she began to laugh, shaking her head in disbelief.

Back in her house, Janet toyed for a while with the idea of throwing the letter into the bin and forgetting the whole incident. But she had given her word and thus she should fulfil her unspoken promise to post it. She placed it, still smiling ruefully, in her jacket pocket. On her next trip to Kitui she might forget the letter, but she would not forget her jacket. Alone again in the house, she set about re-establishing the routine through which she had learned to live most days. First, though, she rocked the blue gas bottle which stood by the cooker to check if it was empty and then lit the stove to make a coffee. Having lost interest in her suntan, she went into her own room to change.

As she began to pull the curtains of her bedroom, she noticed a car standing outside the mission house. It had not been there earlier when she was lying in the sun. It was the Bishop's white Datsun. She knew that Father O'Shea had gone to Nzawa that morning to say Mass and she knew that the monthly trip usually took the whole day so, after Mass at nine o'clock, the mission ought to have remained closed until sunset at least. From the vantage of her house, before which the entire town spread out on the far side of a shallow valley, she could clearly see that the mission door was open. Even the car door had been left open and Mutua, the cook, was taking a suitcase from the boot. With curiosity aroused, she dressed quickly, turned off the gas and as ever without locking the door left her house to walk down to town.

She entered the room without knocking. It looked as if it had been hit by a whirlwind, like a junkshop after an earthquake. Every square inch of living room floor seemed to be covered with an admixture of treasures, some discarded and lying in apparently random heaps, others neatly stacked in the chair. Books, clothes, some folded, others creased in piles, a guitar without a case, a large box in the middle of the floor overflowing with green vegetables and fresh fruit composed a still life completed, with ultimate absurdity, by a set of golf clubs, resplendently and gleamingly new propped up by the wall next to the bookshelves, which Father Michael had never filled. Obviously someone had just arrived from Nairobi and this meant that she would probably be soon presented with a fresh cauliflower, a bag of apples or even a piece of steak which could be fried without being first beaten to a pulp with a mallet.

Picking her way carefully between the piles, trying in vain not to step on anything she might soil or break, she managed to reach the centre of the room when Mutua appeared through the open kitchen door, struggling with a large tattered brown suitcase, which he held against his chest. His eyes peeped over the top and, as he greeted her, he clumsily tried to wave his hand as it struggled to find a hold on the case, which was obviously too heavy to risk carrying by its frail-looking handle. The strain became too much and he let out a warning shout as the case crashed to the floor, spilling out its contents and leaving him unbalanced for a moment, staggering and groping wildly at the air for support. Having regained his balance, he looked at Janet in a way that disclaimed any responsibility for the mess and turned to leave the room by the way he entered. He rubbed his back and muttered in English for her benefit, "Too heavy. Too old."

Her way forward now completely barred by the suitcase and its scattered contents, Janet stood with her hands on her hips and tried to make some sense of the mess, while deciding where next to place her foot. "If you think you're getting your hands on that box of tricks, you're entirely correct," said a voice behind her, causing her to jump. Janet did not turn round. She did not need to. She just laughed. In a moment she was laughing so hard that tears came to her eyes and she finally turned to see Father Michael Doherty picking his way towards her. "Jaysus, girl," he said in his usual exclamatory tone, "you'll do yourself an injury. Here, sit down for a minute and I'll get you a beer." Then, trampling without reserve on the things that Janet had been so careful to avoid, he quickly emptied the last of the contents of the suitcase onto the floor, closed it, turned it on end and invited her to sit on it. Still not quite fully in command of her senses, she sat down and, of course, it collapsed under her weight, spilling her into the middle of the pile of once neatly folded clothes it had previously contained. This just made her laugh harder and she now felt quite unable to stand. "Well, sod that for a lark," said Michael, kicking aside the now multiply-articulated box and creating a space on the floor with his feet into which he could pull one of the armchairs away from the wall.

"I ought to have known it was you, as soon as I saw this lot," said Janet a minute later, when laughter no longer choked her words. "No one else could possibly be responsible for a mess like this. So they finally let you loose again on this poor unsuspecting world?"

"That's right," he answered, kicking shut the refrigerator door, while holding two bottles of beer in one hand and rummaging in the drawer of the chest at its side for an opener. He then issued a quite unexpected expletive and fell down onto his hands and knees to peer around the back of the fridge. "Once before I did that," he said, "and the effing flame went out. I opened it up the next day and everything was spoilt. And the room was full of kerosene fumes. I nearly gassed Mutua when he turned up for work."

"I wasn't expecting you for another few days. In fact I was beginning to think that I might not see you before I left," she said.

"There was a change of plan," he said as he stood and immediately located the bottle opener. He told Janet that two priests from elsewhere in the Diocese had both had to return to Ireland at short notice because of illness. One had been diagnosed with hepatitis and would need to take at least six months off. Another had suffered a motorbike accident and had gone home indefinitely. He was in a bad shape, Michael told her. His hip would need a pin through it and then, after healing, he would probably have to learn to walk again. On top of that another four of the missionary priests had completed their two-year tours of duty and their leave was already overdue. "So," continued Michael, "Bishop O'Hara was left with a difficult choice. Either he had to leave some stations unmanned or he had to bring me back." With that he went to the kitchen for the glasses.

Janet could only burst into laughter again at what

happened next. Immediately he entered the kitchen, Mutua shouted at him in Kikamba, "Don't kick the fridge door. You'll put out the flame!"

"Keep your hair on," replied Michael, as if offended.

Mutua, whose head was invariably shaven was provoked into listing the reasons for not kicking the fridge door shut, paramount among which was his recollection of trying to relight the burners one day, when a minor flare-up had singed his eyebrows. Michael listened to everything Mutua said and then spoke a few words in Kikamba that Janet did not understand. "Only a stupid fly is killed by a falling turd," he translated in an aside for her benefit. Mutua laughed and then patted Michael on the back, a gesture of profound affection. He was obviously more than pleased to see him back in Migwani, despite the reappearance of the madness he brought to life in the mission.

Janet's first surprise came a little later. Now seated amid the mess, she listened to the story of Michael's stay in Ireland. He began by apologising for only having written once during his absence. He had been very busy and assured her that he had not forgotten her. Since he had known for a month that he would return before she was due to leave, he had decided not to write. Where he would go, he would not send greetings, he said in Kikamba, immediately translating it for her benefit. Janet dismissed his apology, telling him not to worry, as she leaned forward to offer him a cigarette. "Ah… this is the first shock…" he told her. His expression was wide-eyed as he patted his stomach. "Didn't you guess from the size of the tub that I had given up?" he explained, nodding towards the cigarette.

Janet apologised for tempting him and lit one for herself, but she found herself drawing on it with a new and surprising self-consciousness, perhaps borne of the knowledge that had it not been for her desire to share things with Michael, she herself would never have become a smoker. During the long hours after sunset in what felt like an interminable dry season soon after her arrival in Migwani, when they had passed so many evenings in conversation over beers in the Safari Bar or sitting in the dark on the mission veranda, it had been Michael who had first prompted Janet to take a cigarette. It had always been part of her nature to appear just a little nervous and agitated, just a little too quick with action or reply, and during that period the demands of her work, with its inherent frustrations and impossibilities had brought the mannerism into sharper focus. Michael had tried to tell her that impatience would solve nothing and that she should learn to put her ideals on a slower flame. He offered her a cigarette as an elixir of relaxation and she had smoked ever since. Now she felt estranged from herself as the cigarette burned between her fingers, perhaps because she now feared that the priest might even disapprove.

After a short talk, they worked together to clear away the debris his arrival had scattered and by the time Father O'Shea appeared from Nzawa just before sunset, only the golf clubs and a few shirts, draped over a chair, remained in the living room. Father O'Shea who, during his visits to Migwani, had always ensured that everything was kept in its proper place, exactly as Michael had left it, as if that indicated permanence, was still a little taken aback. In his eyes the room was still in a state of total disarray and he was prompted to announce his arrival by offering, "What on earth is going on here?" well before any greeting came to mind. When Michael appeared in a doorway to answer his rhetorical question, all was immediately and comprehensively explained.

Just a few minutes later, after Michael's story had been

retold for his benefit, Father O'Shea said that he would return to his own place in Mwingi since, now that Michael was back on station, his presence would be supernumerary. During Michael's absence he had been visiting Migwani only at weekends to say Mass whilst continuing to teach full-time during the week in Mwingi's Junior Seminary. Explaining that he had left on Friday evening with work unfinished and apologizing for rushing away so soon after Michael's arrival, he bid his goodbyes, picked up the haversack he had left by the door and rode off on his motorbike. Within a minute or so the sound of his two-stroke had faded to the north of the town.

"He takes life very seriously," said Michael, obviously regarding his colleague with a mixture of respect and awe. "He'll not be back before dark."

Janet agreed, remembering her abortive attempts at conversation with Father O'Shea over recent months. "He's a very generous man," she said, "but I never really felt that I got through to him, never felt that he was willing to open up and express his own opinions." In the past, in the days when she lived in London and prided herself in her choice of friends and acquaintances, when she had the luxury to choose, she would have probably dismissed him out of hand and decided on first impressions not to pursue further contact with him. She would have seen him as remote, perhaps intellectual, perhaps too obsessed with the accuracy of his few and carefully chosen words – a bore, perhaps. But here, where choice of friends was never an option, she had persevered and, though never entirely comfortable in his company, she had grown to accept him as he was. Over the months, she had developed a good deal of affection for him, for his profound gentleness and consideration for others alongside her respect for his obvious devotion. Unknown to her that evening, she would never see him again. Also unknown to her was the fact that, over the ensuing years, the simplicity of his faith would reconnect her to her own Catholic roots, would plant a seed that would allow her to rediscover what role religion might play in her life. But that was to be the future.

As Michael and Janet talked, the sun set unnoticed and hours passed. They ate some of the food that Michael had brought from Nairobi, Mutua having prepared it and left it on a low oven, prompting them both to comment that a rare steak was an impossibility in this household. They then sat and talked again for several hours. Janet began to realize that there had been significant changes in Michael. Some of the differences were trivial, such as the decision to give up smoking and the equally surprising fact that he had decided not to buy a bottle of whiskey in the duty-free shop. Physically he had changed a little, though not much. As he had indicated earlier, he had put on some weight around the middle and his face was fuller as well. His hair was cut much shorter, making him look older, she thought. Unchanged was his habit of wearing a hat almost constantly, whether inside or outside. Today's version was a peaked cap rather than his usual bush hat. It perched that night on the back of his head, with the peak stupidly vertical, at times making him look like he had a halo. It prompted Janet to smile, as she remembered their many trips to bars both in Migwani and Kitui, where the angle of Michael's hat acted like an indicator, like an absurd barometer of the length of the evening. As he became drunk, the peak would move further to one side, or if it was the bush hat he wore, it would be pushed further and further back until it eventually fell off. She reminded him with a giggle of the night in Kitui when he had a few too many beers and had finished the evening dancing the bump with an imaginary partner, the cap, that night, having worked its way round half a circle so that the peak was down his neck. The moment she finished the recollection, however, she sensed a change in his manner, and this was clearly a profound change. He seemed now embarrassed, reluctant to accept the memory. In the past he would have played up the joke, now he avoided it, as if admonishing himself for a misdeed. Laconically, he changed the subject after muttering, "Well, let's hope there'll be no more of that." She sensed a changed purpose about him, a new rationale behind a retained gloss of absurdity, which, in his own words at least, he now seemed determined to play down. Though still evident on the surface, his easy-going manner had been replaced, deeper down, by a new acceptance of responsibility. Janet sensed it immediately, but only interpreted it as evidence of the change that had percolated to the surface in small manifestation. Her reaction surprised her. It was disappointment that she felt and she was shocked at her own selfishness. Later, he tried to express his changed rationale towards his work and it led them into an argument, an intellectual one, but also a heated one, about his right, anyone's right to come to Migwani or any place they didn't belong to impose values from outside.

Bishop O'Hara's words to him before he left had affected him deeply. He had not believed him at the time, but, after thinking things through, Michael had realised that the man had been right. Drinking in bars and spending a lot of his time with Janet were, of course, trivial things in themselves, but Michael had become more aware that his public image affected the way people received him. He had known all along, of course, that drinking in bars like a primary school teacher or dancing with layabouts in Kitui made him no friends amongst the more pious, but he had always placed great store on mixing with the poor and disadvantaged, and this had been part of his mission. But he now wanted to temper these aspects of his life to see if he might break into wholly different areas of pastoral work. He cited John Mwangangi's ideas as having been instrumental in his refocus, since the projects that John had established needed support, both formal and informal, and on several different levels, to have a chance of success. If he closed access to the more formal links by jeopardizing his credibility, he would spike the projects and that was not a risk he was any more willing to take. It would, put simply, undermine his mission.

"And what is your mission?" asked Janet provocatively.

"Number one is to administer the functions of the Roman Catholic Church to those who desire them," he replied without hesitation. His voice was edged with a sternness that Janet did not recognise.

"And what are the things that people here need most of all?" she continued. "What about those things that the Church cannot provide? What about the people who are not and do not want to be Catholics? Do you ignore them?"

"I've thought about this a lot over the months," he said, his manner and tone offering reassurance, but with also a hint of bitterness growing stronger as he told his story. "I've had a lot of time to think about things. In fact, there have been times over the last few months when I have been so bored I could have screamed, just to try and wake people up. People in Ireland – and in England, as well, because I spent a few weeks there – they live like ants. They wander around in droves filled with illusions of their own wealth..."

"You can't have a drove of ants," said Janet. Her comment rendered Michael silent, he was desperately trying to laugh, but humour was just not in him. "It's a colony of ants, or an army … or even a nest… but not a drove." Michael looked at her quizzically. "It's a thing of mine, as you know," she said.

“Well, they are filled with illusions of their own wealth,” he continued, as if trying to regenerate the gravity that Janet’s interjection had lightened, “their power and their knowledge. At the head of the column there’s some politician, or newsreader or celebrity or expert or some other idiot leading them on with stories so biased and self-congratulatory that they only add to the illusion. I didn’t meet anyone over the last few months who was capable of seeing past the end of their nose! They’re as parochial and simple-minded as anyone, but most people here in Migwani are far wiser than them, because people here at least are conscious of their limitations.

“When I left here, I was ready to give up the priesthood. The whole thing was starting to stink of false values, even bigotry. Take the cathedral, for instance. As far as I saw it, it was sheer madness for professed Christians to build a thing like that amidst abject poverty. The money could have been used for so many more important things. But of course while I was at home in Ireland, it was only then that I truly admitted that it’s not the people of Ukambani, or the Bishop or the priests that demand we build places like that, it’s the people at home in Europe. And it’s especially true of people in the States. They see buildings like the cathedral as evidence of progress, proof that the money they think they are contributing to good causes in Africa is being used properly and is having the effect they wanted. They couldn’t give a shit, never mind money, about things that are less tangible, less obvious. Photos of a cathedral will do the trick. The money will come rolling in. Reports of an adult literacy scheme designed to help married women learn enough to read letters from their husbands, on the other hand, will generate all the right responses, will open hearts, but it doesn’t open wallets. It’s no good showing a field of maize to an old lady in Limerick who puts a pound a week into a collection box after Mass. It doesn't mean a thing to her.

"Some people will get very angry when you tell them that you work in Africa. They resent the fact that aid to places like this might have made some people rich. They argue that the process is corrupt and their governments should stop all payments. Show them a photograph of the cathedral and they'll fill your pockets with money, pat you on the back and tell you what a good job you're doing. I know it's silly, and you know it's silly, but unfortunately that's how it is. And then, of course, there are the sceptics, who think that anyone involved with Christianity is just a Bible thumping bigot, but then we will never bring those people on board anyway. So what to do?" he asked, pausing as if to allow Janet a moment to digest his tirade.

"I could never stay in Ireland and listen to the petty problems that people take to their priests. What's more I don't like life there any more. I've been away for too long now and feel much more at home here. On the other hand, if I was to come back here to continue my work, it was obvious that I was going to have to accept some things I disagree with. I was given an ultimatum, so I have to comply if I am to continue what I dearly want to do. After all, I am a priest. It's what I chose to do with my life. I am devoted to the Church and its expansion to include those people who as yet have never known it. That's why I am here, here and now, and that's what has to become my priority."

Michael's statement, a near confession, was definitive. He had stated his case with such uncharacteristic force that Janet felt quite unable to respond. He had certainly changed.

"Anyway," he continued with apparently renewed flippancy when she did not react, "you seem to have changed, yourself." After again awaiting a reply and receiving only an embarrassed smile from Janet, he continued. "I didn't call at your house on the way here because I thought you would probably have gone away for the weekend – off to a dance, perhaps, at the Umoja."

"I rarely go to the dances now," she replied. "In fact recently I have been meeting up with John Mwangangi at weekends. We have seen quite a lot of each other. We have talked a lot. I think what he is trying to do is just amazing. It's real hope…" She was frowning. She was finding it difficult to speak to him about her relationship with John. His expression gave little away, except a suggestion that what she said was not news to him. She wondered how much the priests and everyone else, for that matter, knew of her and John. And memories were hazy at best. She was finding it hard to remember anything fixed in the indistinct timelessness that was life in Migwani. "And I have done a lot of work in the school. I am trying to get things sorted out before I leave."

"So no more dances in Kitui?" he asked.

"No. I have taken my pleasures in other ways."

Twenty-two

August 1976

Janet went back feeling supremely happy. Though until recently the thought of leaving Migwani had filled her with sadness, she now looked forward to going home, to renewing the relationships which for two years had lain dormant, continued only in letters. Initially, those letters had seemed full of news and the communication had been genuinely two-way, but as time passed the letters Janet wrote told more of her own life in Migwani and she became less able to respond to things her friends in London communicated as news or priorities. She was out of touch with things English and felt out of sympathy with the issues that filled her former friends' lives. At one point she had begun to doubt whether she would ever want to return. But now the time had come, the sadness at leaving Migwani was overridden by new expectations and a determination to go home and work to educate public opinion, by whatever means she could find, about the reality of life in the Third World, in a place like this. If that ignorance could be overcome, she now believed, then it might be possible for people in the richer parts of the world to realise that these places were not 'backward', 'under-developed' or 'primitive'; they were just poor. They were populated with people like people anywhere, not the pathetic recipients of aid, portrayed, therefore, as something less than human. By chance, these people happened to be born in a place that was not as healthy or rich as others. It was not their fault. A rich man does not worry about a poor man, as her Akamba friends had commented many times, and now she was determined that he would, and that she was going to teach him.

Filled with conflicting emotions of contentedness and sadness, the excitement of the journey in prospect kept her awake all night. After some hours of trying to sleep, she lit the candle by her bed and, sitting up to smoke a cigarette, she thought through her time in Migwani and tried to imagine what England – she found it hard to call it home – would look like tomorrow. Would her mother think she looked well or ill? How would she react to her smoking? Would she say that she was thinner? Above all, what would she, herself, do? How would she translate this vague idea of a future into a life, a job and an income? She felt satisfied in the knowledge that she would never forget Migwani. Perhaps she would come back for a holiday as soon as she had some cash and then take up some of the many invitations that she had never honoured. She seemed to have left so much unfinished, so many friendships unexplored and yet by lunchtime tomorrow she would be gone, perhaps never to return. She was glad, though, that she had kept her word and had made at least a gesture towards John in view of all he had done for her. His presence at her farewell party was seen as a mutual compliment by everyone. He enjoyed the gathering very much, it seemed, and, when the guests left, he and Janet had enjoyed their last shared hours doing what they had learned to do steadily better in their weekly encounters. My God, she would miss him, but perhaps now was a good time to call a halt. He was married. He had a daughter to whom he was utterly devoted. Janet had enjoyed him and he had surely enjoyed her, but it could go nowhere from here without much avoidable pain. But could there be just one more chance to share an hour, to place farewells in their appropriate places and thrust one last shudder of pleasure through her conscience?

The party, given that day by the school's governors in her honour, had been a happy and enjoyable occasion. The guests, all of whom Janet had come to regard as friends during her stay, contributed toward the cost of the food and the bottles of soda they all shared. Daniel, for once the head cook in the dark smoky room which served as the school's kitchen, prepared a gigantic feast including the goat and four chickens they had slaughtered that morning. After eating, Janet's headmaster made a speech in which he pointed to the array of people from all walks of life who had gathered there to bid her farewell. Surely this, he claimed, was proof of how deeply the people of Migwani had taken to her and how much they respected the fine work she had done in their school. Suddenly, all Janet's frustrations with her work, all its apparent absurdity and meaninglessness disappeared in the face of the rapturous applause and cheers that greeted her invitation to speak. These people really did want the school to succeed, though they were realistic enough to know that very few of their children would ever be educated in it and even fewer would ever obtain a job as a result. They were, however, sincerely grateful to her for the hard work she had done and for the friendship she had shown.

In a short speech which she wrote, rehearsed and delivered in Swahili, much to the delight of her audience, she thanked everyone for coming to the party, thanked them again for making her stay in Migwani so very enjoyable and begged them respectfully to remember that she was only a teacher and that their true thanks should go to the school's headmaster and governors who were the real driving force behind its success. These few short sentences in stumbling Swahili received great applause and no one went home without shaking her hand, wishing her a good journey and asking her to convey greetings to the rest of her family. Then, by mid-afternoon, the guests dispersed, still voicing Janet's praise, to set off on their various routes home. They would all reach their destinations in the four hours or so of daylight that remained. The party was over and Janet felt not a little relieved that it all went so well. Praise is greater than the praised, she thought as she watched a large group of people walk towards the town. She was glad it was all over. Now she could look forward to a more informal gathering.

As Michael, John and Janet stood together, first in the Form Three classroom and then outside under the covered walkway that stretched the length of the school building, they shared one of those strange, though not rare occasions, when everyone knew precisely what everyone else knew. But, carefully, they avoided any interaction that would involve any reference to the obvious. Michael and John stayed behind ostensibly to help Janet and Daniel clear up. Though the two men had been friends ever since John's return to Kenya, initially to become the District Officer in Mwingi, they said not a word of the past, nor made any reference to it. There was progress on John's farm to describe and details of Michael's travels to log. But Janet's changed status, of which Michael was now clearly and fully aware, made everything stilted and forced, and it had the effect of making her feel she was now the object of the conversation, not a participant. Before Michael's leave, before Janet's liaison with John, Michael would not have waited to be asked if he would like a beer in Janet's house. He would not have remained awkwardly reticent, standing with cap in hand, to see if the invitation would come. In the past, he would have made some idiotic crack about Popes being Catholic and simply assumed the start of the next phase.

But, as Daniel removed the last of the debris from the tables, the room apparently full to echo with the sound of clashing glass, slapping plates and clinking spoons, John, Michael and Janet shared a formal goodbye, complete with handshakes. She thought she heard him say, "I may see you later," as he started his motorbike, but she was not sure, as the first engine fire drowned the end of the phrase. He had changed, she repeated to herself, as she and John watched him ride down the shallow hill and up the other side, his bike seemingly knowing its own way, as it made the slight deviation from straight to find the gap in the hedge and the entrance to the mission compound. A few moments later, her cards and messages collected, she said a final and tearful goodbye to Daniel, who was now ready to leave, to leave Janet for the last time to make his way home to his family. He would be someone else's employee from now on.

And so John and Janet were finally alone. They said nothing as they ambled the fifty yards down the gentle slope to Janet's house. Once inside, Janet locked the kitchen door behind them, an act so rarely done in the past that it seemed to start a new era, her new-found selfishness wanting nothing to trespass on their space, nothing to interrupt what she immediately initiated the moment she turned round to face him. She wanted him so much she ached, and they paused for nothing, neither food, nor drink, nor talk, their shared agenda comprising just one item, a single activity.

So it was with obvious disappointment, but probably not surprise, that Janet listened to John some hours later as he announced that he could not spend that night with her. People would talk. They would notice. Over the previous months they had been careful only to meet in Kitui. This had been the first time they had made love in Janet's house. To stay overnight would invite gossip. He also told her that he had already arranged to meet his father and he had thus already booked a night in a room behind the Safari Bar. He had to see his father. They had things to discuss. He would be alone in the room again from the early morning, of course, after the old man had set off to walk home. She could have a good night's sleep and then come early to the Safari, maybe around eight, and they could have two hours together in the hotel room, an anonymous space once the door was closed, the kind of place in which their relationship had been born. In a strange way, it was the almost communal nature of those places that provided an aspect that Janet had enjoyed. It was like playing with a fire you could control. Now that she was ready to leave Kenya, her two-year commitment almost complete, she was almost compelled to broadcast that she was sleeping with John Mwangangi, but then it was different for him. He would still have to come and go. And he was still married.

But it was with immense sadness that she watched him dress, saw him again become the suited, suave city gent, again in control of every aspect of his being. While naked, of course, she was the one with control, the one who could make him move, the one with the power to put him where she wanted. A simple move of her body, an offering, a widening, a contraction could provoke the precise response she both predicted and relished. He was infatuated with her and she with him, but as the months had passed she had started to recognise how easily she now held him where she wanted. She was surely in control.

And so it was with surprise and not a little challenge that he told her he was afraid that he might be detained in town and not get back to Nairobi in time to see her off at the airport. He did not tell her then of the present he hoped to give her. Hoped, that is, because he did not yet know if it would materialize. At ten o'clock, an hour after checking in to his hotel room, it was delivered.

John retired to his room which, typically for an August night, felt cold and just a little damp. Wind rattled the door. Only in August was Migwani cold enough to warrant a fire in the room. Only in August was a guest in the Safari supplied with a charcoal burner and fuel to warm the night. Today, however, the bar had run out of charcoal and John had been supplied, along with the floor-standing *jiko*, or stove, with several pieces of wood for fuel. He had left the fire unlit, however. He did not want to emerge the next morning with his clothes smelling of wood smoke, so he merely wrapped up in the sheet to keep out the cold.

He passed the hour reading background information on a couple of cases he was currently working on, as well as reviewing plans for the next phase of his farm's development. He had worked exceptionally hard since taking up his new post in the Nairobi law practice and was beginning to feel the strain caused by so much countrywide travelling. He was beginning to think that the jobs furthest from Nairobi were being pushed his way, allowing the other partners to avoid spending onerous time away from home. But he realised that the practice really was, as he had been promised, an elite operation, dealing with the very biggest cases. They were a selective company, but that meant being wherever the work was and, realistically, it suited him. He had been glad at times to render the distance he felt had developed between himself and Lesley into real, countable miles.

At precisely ten o'clock he heard the sound of a familiar voice in the courtyard outside asking the whereabouts of Bwana Mwangangi. On hearing this, John sprang to his feet and rushed to open the door. "Here," he shouted. "I'm in here," he confirmed in Kikamba.

John's father rushed into the room carrying a large parcel wrapped in newspaper under his arm. Having set this down carefully on the small table which stood in the far corner, he wrapped his jacket tight around his body and rubbed his hands together fiercely. "It is very cold tonight," he said. "I set off very late because one of my cows broke its tether last night and your sister and I spent half the day trying to find it."

"You did find it?" asked John, concerned.

"Yes. It had grown thirsty and had found its own way to the dam for a drink," answered the old man, now stamping his feet for warmth. It was then that he noticed the small metal stove and the wood. "Can we make a fire in here?" he asked. Nodding towards the bar he continued, "Or are these people afraid of sooting up their walls?"

John smiled at his father. The man doesn't change, he thought. He still regards the Safari Bar as the height of ostentatious luxury. "I will go and get a *panga* to cut the wood," said John, setting off to the bar.

Ten minutes later he had returned and chopped the wood into sticks with the heavy knife, which now lay on the table near the newspaper-wrapped parcel his father had brought. He built and lit the fire, which kindled easily in the small cylindrical fireplace. His father was already warming his hands. The flickering light of the fire filled the room and slowly, amid continued complaints about the cold, the old man grew warmer and retired to the comfort of the cane chair. He pointed to the parcel and said, "I have finished your gift for the teacher. It is not very good, but it's all I could do in the time I had."

John went over to the table and peeled away the parcel's loose wrapping to reveal a carved wooden figure. It portrayed an old man with his eyes wide open. John studied the figure for a few moments, his great satisfaction momentarily overwhelming his words of thanks. At last he turned to face his father again and said, "It is very, very beautiful. Miss Rowlandson will be very pleased." Smiling at his father, who still looked uncomfortably cold after his long walk, he continued, "It is very funny. I was with Miss Rowlandson and Father Michael earlier. They were both dressed in very light clothes and both of them complained at the heat!"

"Ah," said the old man with a knowing air, "there is cold blood in white flesh."

John smiled at his father with deep affection. For some minutes they did not speak, the old man's still chattering teeth providing the only sound above the breathing of the wind. John slowly peeled away the remaining wrappings from the carving and stood back to admire the quality of his father's work. Janet would surely treasure this, he thought.

"You seem very keen to impress this white woman, Mwangangi," said Musyoka, slowly.

"She has been kind to me and my family," answered John, without moving his gaze from the statue.

There was another silence. John could sense that his father was sifting through a whole series of issues, any of which he might raise, and any of which might cause serious disagreement between them. "And have I not been kind?" asked Musyoka, who had in fact come this evening determined to confront their long-running disagreement once and for all. His son's request had, in effect, brought things to a head. It was one thing for Mwangangi to be a

Christian, another for him to speak English, to study, to live overseas and to marry a foreigner in Britain without his family's consent. But this woman was white, one more step further removed, and it was he, Musyoka, who was carving the present that his son would give her.

"You have, Father," said John. Now leaning against the edge of the table, John eyed his father through the corner of his eye, again not turning to face him. He awaited the words he knew would follow.

"Then you have decided to do as I have advised." Musyoka's voice was full of force and directness. His words asked many questions. "You have already wasted your chance to join this year's group. Next year your child will be a year older…" The old man allowed his words to fall to silence.

John took a deep breath before answering, as if he was giving himself time to compose his answer, though, when the words were spoken, they had a distinctly rehearsed air. Musyoka was perched expectantly on the very edge of his chair. "My daughter is also my wife's daughter and she says it cannot be done. It is contrary to their tradition."

Musyoka was immediately angry. "What kind of a man are you? Are you Mwangangi, son of Musyoka? Or are you a woman married to a man? No son of mine would hide like that behind a woman's words. A man's flour is cooked how he likes it. If you say it must be done then your wife must accept it. Katuunge is also my granddaughter – or have you forgotten? And also any member of my family is also a member of my people. She is yours. You are mine and we are all part of something bigger, something which we have a responsibility to preserve."

"Father, you must understand," pleaded John. "Lesley is not one of our people. She is not even Kenyan. Her people do not circumcise either their men or their women…" The old man scoffed at such madness. "For Lesley the thought of Anna being circumcised is utterly revolting. She says that if it was done, then she would no longer feel that Anna was her own daughter." And there was an unspoken extension to this that both men assumed, that Lesley would no longer be a wife.

"Then she is selfish," shouted Musyoka, getting up from the chair and crossing the room. "And what is more, she knows how to control you. She is a devious woman, who does not tell the truth. Every monkey has a red arse," he continued, waving his arms and making John smile a little, if reluctantly. "There must be customs amongst her own people which are not done here. What about them? I'd bet that your daughter is forced to honour them to the letter!"

"Lesley's people are not a people like we are," said John impatiently.

"Rubbish," replied his father. "If they are a people, then they are a people with customs, traditions, practices. Don't try to tell me that every person does exactly what they want!"

"Father," said John in a voice that offered conciliation, as he took Musyoka's arm and led him back to the chair that his anger had left behind. "Lesley's people are not a tribe. They are very different from us and do not have duties like we have. In the Western world it is the individual that makes the rules that govern their lives. There are laws for everyone, of course, but there are no responsibilities held in common like our people have. The only rule is that one should not question another person's individuality."

"Then they are heathens," shouted the old man, swinging his arm free from his son's grasp and crossing the room.

"As I have said to you before," continued John, desperately trying not to shout, "in the culture that Lesley and I share, it is vitally important that the child should make up her own mind when it comes to matters of religion, marriage and everything to do with her own future. As parents, it's our job to prepare the way, to support her in what she wants, never to make decisions on her behalf. When she is old enough she can decide for herself. It will be her decision. A parent cannot be a child's own heart."

"But then it will be too late!" shouted Musyoka, his words imploring his son to see an obvious truth. "By then she will be a grown woman and well beyond marrying age. She will have a woman's body but still a child's mind. She needs the maturity that only formally and ceremonially joining the adult world can give. A cow cannot be killed by a branding iron," he continued with growing impatience, "but the mark it receives gives it a known place in the world, a place that others can recognise and respect. Without its identity, it is nobody's cow, a rogue, isolated from the herd. She must be initiated into our world as soon as possible. It will not harm her. It never did any harm to your own mother or your sisters. If it is good enough for them then why is it not good enough for your own daughter? If you had married a Kamba woman there would have been no debate. Your daughters, your sons, all would have been circumcised when their time came without a second thought! Why should Anna Katuunge be treated any differently?"

Now John began to show his anger. "Lesley is not a Kamba and we must respect her wishes as well. Anna is her daughter just as much as she is my daughter. As I have said, Lesley and I are agreed that we must wait until Anna is ready to make up her own mind about such things."

"Saying is not doing," mumbled Musyoka without hesitation. "If you ask your daughter now she will give you her answer. I have talked to her and I know that more than anything else your daughter wants to be like other children, to play with them, live like them and be accepted by them, not imprisoned in that palace of a house you are building. A calf with no mother must lick its own back and your daughter knows now what she wants. Ask her!"

"Anna has got a mother!" shouted John, slapping his hand hard on the table.

"One who neither listens nor gives advice," replied the old man as he turned away.

"Your hen's curse doesn't worry a hawk," replied John with great malice, his choice of words a deliberate attempt to hurt. For a moment there was silence. Then Musyoka's expression suddenly changed. He looked up and sniffed the air as his son asked a question without words. "You've been drinking beer. You never used to drink." The old man dismissed his son's attempt at an answer with an impatient wave of the hand. "You always have time for your European friends, especially that white woman from the school. I begin to wonder if you are ready to take another wife?"

John scoffed, turned away and shook his head. So the old man was ready to open another front.

Danger is never anticipated. One minute it is nowhere in sight and then in a flash it is all around, only to disappear again as quickly, having accomplished whatever it wished.

"Father," said John, turning again to face the old man, his voice pleading a favour, "there is something else I must ask."

The old man stood on the far side of the room, his hands on his hips, his face contorted with suppressed anger.

"As you know I am now doing a different job. We moved to Nairobi so that I could take up my law practice again. I am enjoying the work, but I have a lot to do. There is a lot of travelling because my cases are all over the country. Sometimes I am away from home all week. And then there is the project in Kamandiu. I have to be there whenever I can to supervise the work and plan the next stages." He paused for a while before coming to the point. He looked long and hard into his father's face, trying to judge how he might react, but the old man merely returned his gaze, the expression mildly quizzical. "What I ask is very simple," he continued. "Since we are away from the house very often, can you please inform all of our family members that if they want to visit they should send a letter in advance to tell us they will be coming? If they do not do that, I cannot guarantee that I will be there. If they write to me in advance, I can send them a reply to say whether or not I will be around when they come." John again looked into his father's eyes, but now the old man showed no emotion and was utterly silent.

Musyoka had feared something like this ever since his son's return to Migwani. He could show no emotion towards the son, who continued to stand in silence before him. Musyoka had understood. And words like these can only be planned, can only thus be spoken with an intention to offend. It seemed like an age that they stayed in apparent silent confrontation. The old man searched for words, but none came. How was it possible to answer something that was so wholly and completely unacceptable? Musyoka saw in his mind's eye a vivid memory of Mwangangi's circumcision. He knew it would end like this. The thread in the family had finally found something to tie. His words therefore came as no surprise, since this is what he had feared for so long. His son wanted to reject his birthright, his identity, his family, his father. Just as Musyoka or anyone else, including Mwangangi, knew, that wherever I go I do not send greetings. Greetings are not needed when you visit your own family, because they will be given by word of mouth when you meet. A family member will always open the house for you. It is not written, but why write something that goes without question? Whatever the poverty of a family, a relative is always welcomed, always fed, always offered the finest the household can provide. And that is always accepted, always enjoyed, always finished, always expected. Write a letter to find out if my family will be at home to receive me? Of course Mwangangi would not write back saying that he would be present. He would surely always say that he would be away. This surely was the only interpretation of such an outlandish request. It was just a way of making sure that he would never open his doors to his nephews and nieces, to his cousins, uncles, aunts or even his own sister. This was his son's way of saying that he would never pay school fees for other members of the family, despite his riches. This was his way of saying that he would never give presents to honour marriage or birth, despite his obvious obsession with giving presents to that white woman of his. And so Musyoka's head was suddenly filled with images of Mwangangi's circumcision, on the day his son entrusted a white man rather than his own father with the dressing of his wound. Musyoka was filled with self-derision, cursing himself for ever allowing the white man to use some strange magic to bring Mwangangi back to life. He, Musyoka, knew his son would eventually betray. And he had been proved right. Why is it, he thought, that mistakes are only seen when it is too late to do anything about them? Since that fateful day when he, Musyoka, had stood aside and allowed the white man to carry off his own son, since that day his family had been cursed with the trickery. Now that family threatened to disintegrate, broken by the evil his son had harboured all these years. He must do something now, something to make his son see the error of his ways, something to make him see that what he, Musyoka, requested was only right. The one who casts the spell is never the one who breaks it, so I must act, he thought.

"How dare you reject your family?" he shouted.

John looked up and laughed in disbelief. It was a reaction that immediately inflamed the situation. "I am not rejecting my family or anyone else," he said, but the tone was dismissive and struck home.

"You have said," shouted Musyoka, "that your house will not be home for your family, that it will be some kind of hotel, where you have to reserve a place, and, no doubt, pay for it as well!" The old man was now extremely angry and was shaking as he stared long and hard at the son he had long ago come to distrust.

"I did not say that…"

"But that is what I heard!"

"I did not say that," repeated John without a pause, laughing again in an attempt to calm his father, feigned amusement calculated to reduce the tension, but again it was heard as an insult. He should not have laughed.

"A stick can bend only before it is dry," said the old man. He spoke the words like a curse, through gritted teeth, his lips hardly moving. And with that he took up the knife they had used to cut sticks, crossed the room, took hold of the statue he had carved, threw it onto the floor in the same movement, and gave it a huge long-drawn cut across the middle with the heavy blade. The delicate woodwork split in two. He hit it again as he shouted, "And your white woman will have nothing of mine!"

"What are you doing? What are you talking about?" John was pleading as he reached up to try to grasp the wrist that held the *panga* at the hand, his voice laden with a weight of impatience mixed with confusion.

"Don't play with me!" bellowed Musyoka, shaking himself free of his son's grasp with a violence that surprised them both. His eyes now glared with anger. For a moment he was speechless, as was his son, whose expression of disbelief was itself not believed by his father. Musyoka was rendered dumb, unable to find any words. The expression, "He is playing with me," rattled repeatedly through the old man's head. His son had now rejected his family. "You know what I mean!" was all he could say, as he slapped the *panga* blade flat against the table top.

"You know what I mean!" he shouted again, moving towards his son, his voice broken with emotion. Mwangangi jerked his head to one side, trying to avoid the wide swiping arc that his father's arm described, but the flat side of the axe blade connected with the side of his head and he fell stunned to the floor.

Twenty-three

August 1976

August is the month when little boys piss, when mist covers the mountain and drizzle fills the air. This August day had displayed that same unreality. Michael and Janet had left Migwani hoping that the mist which muffled sounds and made breathing uncomfortable, would clear before they reached Nairobi. The rising ground, however, merely clung to thicker mists and their journey seemed interminable. With all landmarks obscured, the brown earth of the road seemed endless. The view from the car that Michael drove appeared timeless and unchanging. The road in front, the road behind and only blank grey mist beyond, all around. There were no landmarks today. Even the long half teardrop of Kilima Mbogo was hidden, so the journey seemed to exist in a cocoon of its own making, protected from an unseen world.

Not until they reached the smooth silence of the tarmac surface near Nairobi was Janet convinced that they had ever left Migwani. She had begun to feel that the day was to be merely a nightmare and that soon she would wake up in her bed in Migwani to start it anew. The city approached, however, and convinced her of its false reality. It was as distasteful as ever, she thought, as the car sped along

Mwang'a Road and the illusory wealth of the skyscrapers came into view. The journey had taken over six hours of crawling beneath the mist which surely shrouded the entire world, today.

Michael had not spoken a single word since they set off. Janet had fought tears all the way, but had felt unable to cry. The shock was too great. Within a few hours it would all be behind her and now she felt truly glad, relieved it was all over. With a minimum of words, Janet directed Michael through the town, telling him that John's house was in the Lavington area. Michael knew it well. Later, with Janet saying no more than 'turn right' or 'turn left', the car threaded its way along the narrow suburban roads which led to the protected and secluded house that was John Mwangangi's family home. Like her first day in Kenya, Janet now felt only a numbness, an inability to feel or react, that the total strangeness created. On the day she arrived, she had seen so much that was new and travelled so many miles that she became immune to all reaction, and her new world just passed by like a dream. Today she could not react because she was tired of it, woefully tired and her thoughts were filled with a new disillusion, which devalued everything in which she had once seen hope. Today the dream was a nightmare.

When Lesley came out of the house to meet the car as it drew up on the gravel drive, it was clear before a single word was said that she knew what to expect. Her face was full of concern and her eyes were already laden with grief. Almost before the car had stopped, Janet swung open the door and got out. Running straight to Lesley's embrace, she burst into tears and cried for a long time. The irony of her crying only when she met the man's wife would not be felt until later, much later.

The morning had begun as expected. She rose early and

finished the last of her packing. As ever in these circumstances Janet felt full of energy and busied herself with her task, trying in vain to get all her clothes, books and souvenirs into the suitcase and travelling bag which comprised the total of her luggage. Eventually she gave up the idea and elected to tie together several items, among them a small gourd, a three-legged stool bought for two shillings in the market and, most importantly, Munyolo's walking stick into a bundle which she could carry under her arm. If she could have known how embarrassed these everyday objects would make her feel on her arrival in London, she would have packed them away and carried her clothes under her arm. Later, they would make her feel like a tourist clutching mementos, and would result in a number of unwanted flippant conversations with fellow travellers, who were capable of talking about nothing deeper than the standard of hotel food and the vagaries or non-existence of Kenyan plumbing. But here, they seemed just like mundane luggage. So, with baggage safely assembled, ready to be loaded into Michael's car that afternoon, she set off to town to her rendezvous with John Mwangangi.

The town was abnormally quiet, unusually slow to wake up. A misty day in August was always like this. People were late in rising and reluctant to begin their journeys to the town when the weather was so cold. Thus the women were only just arriving in the marketplace, only just beginning to spread out their sacks on the earth so they could sit through the day next to their piles of mangoes, tomatoes and guavas. They would await the arrival of the day's buses from Nairobi and Mombasa, hoping that a weary traveller would buy their fruit. The shoemaker, industrious as ever, had arrived at his usual time and already his shoes, car tyres and lengths of rubber were spread about him under the tree that served as his pitch in the town. And the now familiar Munyasya was still asleep at the base of his tree, still clutching the beer bottle he had not yet refilled.

Janet eventually arrived at the corner of the marketplace, outside the blue-painted front wall of the Safari. She had taken much longer than expected to reach there, having called in at several of the shops along the way to bid what turned out to be lengthy goodbyes to people she had known for two years. So now she was rushing and she went alone into the bar and asked if John had gone out. The barman, lazily polishing the glasses left unwashed from the night before, told her that he had not yet seen Mwangangi. He also confirmed that he had not gone out himself since unlocking the doors, so John was surely still in his room. He directed her to number four.

After crossing the courtyard behind the bar, Janet knocked repeatedly on the door but received no answer. After calling the barman and knocking again there was still no reply. Possibly John had left early, Janet suggested. Possibly he might have left via the door at the back. But the barman said in his halting English, it was impossible because the door was always padlocked at night and he had not yet opened it that morning. He beckoned towards the door, Janet cast a glance and saw clearly that the padlock was still in place. He bent to peer through the keyhole of number four and then rose again, indicating with a turn of the wrist that the key was still in the lock. He turned the handle and put his shoulder against the door, but it did not give. Janet smiled and suggested that John might have overslept, probably after having had too many beers. "No," said the barman, John Mwangangi had drunk no more beers last night. He had gone straight to his room and then met his father. They knocked hard on the door, but there was still no response from inside. "Wait," said the barman, raising a finger towards Janet, as if giving a warning. She tried to explain to him that she had arranged to meet Mwangangi. He was expecting her. He would not have left without first visiting her at the school. She was afraid that the barman had not understood her and, when he set off back towards the bar, she followed him. He gestured that she should wait there, but she still followed.

A few moments later, still following him, she was back at the door to number four. The barman, as ever unhurried to the point of apparent lethargy, fumbled with a large bunch of keys he kept on a nail behind the bar until he had found a particular one and then, with Janet in tow, returned to the courtyard. Standing on a chair, he reached into the still dark room through its wire-mesh covered window and, using a piece of stiff wire, he fumbled as he tried to latch a loop around the key on the inside of the door. Still there was no sound from within, not even when the key jangled onto the floor, as it fell from the lock.

"Finish," he said with a satisfied smile. He got down from his chair and then inserted his copy of the key for number four in the lock, turned it and then swung open the door. Having poked his head around the door, he was about to conclude that the room was, indeed, empty. He saw that there was no one in the made-up bed and, as he announced this, Janet almost began to turn to make her way out of the bar to seek John in the town.

Then the barman gasped and rushed into the room, flinging the door wide open and causing it to bang hard against the concrete wall. As Janet followed him, he gave a great shout and she saw him confronting an old man, who was crouched on the floor by the far wall opposite the door. The old man's eyes were wide open, staring and not blinking. The barman bent down and prised the old man's fingers from the handle of a *panga* that he held, it seemed, like a vice. Janet could now see the face clearly and recognised Musyoka, John's father. But still he did not move. He simply stared into space, apparently oblivious of the man who confronted him and who forcefully wrested the *panga* from his grasp.

Now daring to step fully inside the room, Janet looked around. John was not there, but there was a smell, a sweet smell… And then she looked down to the floor by the bed. "Oh my God," she screamed and cried and screamed again, her voice a weight of terror. The barman, startled, turned around, the wrong way, as it happened, to look at her. His eyes followed the line she pointed, but he could not see from where he stood. The bed was in the way. Still she screamed, but no sound came now, only tears, while fear rooted her to the floor. Mwinzi took the two steps needed to stand at her side so he could see along the wall under the window next to the bed. He gave a deep groan, as if breathing out his soul.

John's body was almost under the bed, which Musyoka had clearly pushed against the wall after his son had fallen. Only the remains of his head protruded from under the cover and that was an unrecognisable mass of blood, bone, brain and hair. The first blow the father had struck merely stunned, but knocked the son to the floor at the end of the bed. John Mwangangi, son of Musyoka, had momentarily lost consciousness, but then had tried to stand. As he did, the old man struck again, and this time with the sharpened edge of the blade. Again and again he had struck, cleaving his son's head and ripping the flesh of his face from the bone.

The two could not move for what seemed like an age. Janet felt herself scream and cry, heaving at the air to find breath. But in fact she made little sound, what there was being heard as a laugh. Mwinzi hardly dared to look through the fingers he wished would cover his eyes.

And then he rushed towards the door, pushing Janet with him out of the room. He pushed her so hard he did not even notice she was trying to resist, and then he re-locked the door and ran away. He shouted to her, telling her to follow, but she could not react and she stood where her stumbling retreat had halted by the courtyard wall, opposite the door of number four.

It was only a hundred yards from the Safari corner along the road towards Mwingi to the edge of town where, on top of the hill, the Chief had his office. The barman ran and arrived both speechless and breathless, but so incensed with fear he said everything he needed to say without even speaking. He grabbed the Chief's arm and pulled him from his chair. A moment later he was outside again and rushing to the mud-walled building adjoining the office where the town's resident soldiers brewed their tea during the quiet hours of their duty. He grabbed the arm of the senior soldier and instinctively the other grabbed the rifle it was his duty never to lay down as the barman pulled him to his feet. They all followed without a word. They ran down the hill towards the bar, past shops in whose open doorways people now gathered to see what might have caused the commotion along the street, which usually felt so completely asleep.

Back in the courtyard behind the Safari, a panting Mwinzi fumbled for his keys as the Chief, tall and uniformed, and the soldier with his rifle at the ready by his hip watched in still ignorant anticipation. They remained stoically oblivious of Janet, who stood nearby, still crying, her hands still clutching at her face. Father Michael, who had heard the shouting, now entered the courtyard and immediately took hold of Janet and embraced her. He was trying to console her, trying to ask her what had happened, but she could not speak. When the key was turned and the door opened, the three men went inside and were silent for a moment, and then the groans came again, full of regret. Through the open door Janet saw only Musyoka, the old man she once knew. Still crouched by the wall, still staring blank-eyed into space, only his arms moved, as he chipped away at a stick with his penknife. She did not know, and indeed would never know that it once was part of a carving meant for her.

For five hours, Janet and Michael waited together in the mission under the Chief's instruction not to leave the town. He tried to console her, to lessen the shock, but she was inconsolable. She couldn't speak or eat or drink or believe that it was reality that attacked her. When the District Officer's Land Rover drew up outside and John's successor in the office accompanied by a policeman came into the room, she still could say nothing, nor feel anything, nor show any emotion.

In the town there had been great activity. The Chief had commandeered the town's lorry and ordered its owner to drive him to Mwingi from where he immediately returned with the District Officer and the policeman. The old man, locked away in the soldier's room and guarded by his captor, had sat, immersed in a world of his own, chipping away at his stick. No one had yet thought of taking the knife from him, for he was surely helpless now. John's body, covered by the sheet from his bed, lay on a table in the town's health centre. No one entered the room to look until the policemen from Mwingi lifted the sheet to confirm his death. By then the news had travelled far and wide, conveyed on foot to everywhere within walking distance. It had gone by bus to the west, destined for Nairobi. It had gone south towards Mombasa and north towards Mwingi and beyond to Garissa. Within the day everyone who should have known about Migwani's tragedy would have been told the story as the barman had found it. And all who told or heard the story were to be stunned by it. Old men, young men, women, grandmothers, children, girls, none had ever known a father kill a son.

When the District Officer bid goodbye to Father Michael, still shaking his head in profound disbelief, he said, "I cannot think what is happening these days. We used to say that it is the old man who is taught new things. But make no mistake, what Musyoka has done is unknown amongst our people. From now, Musyoka and his family will only be known for their sin." With that he shook hands with both Michael and Janet without saying another word, took his seat in his Land Rover and drove off into the town. He stayed around Migwani for some hours, gathering what information he could and talking to anyone willing to talk. By the time he set off for Mwingi, Michael and Janet had themselves already left the town, but in the other direction, bound for Nairobi and a meeting with Lesley Mwangangi. In the District Officer's assessment the case was clear-cut. Later, when he wrote up the report, he concluded that the case would go to the High Court, which would find that John Mwangangi, son of Musyoka, had been murdered by his father, Musyoka, son of Mwangangi, an old man who now was incarcerated in the town's only cell at the rear of Mwingi's police station. As he signed the report, he passed it through the hatch in the wall to the waiting clerk, who typed it with multiple carbon sheets, one for his own files, one for the Kitui Police, one for the Nairobi Police and one for the Public Prosecutor. As for Musyoka, neither his name nor a word of sympathy on his behalf would ever again be spoken. He would first be transferred to Kitui and from there to Nairobi to await trial. The case would be judged, his guilt declared and he would hang. Throughout his time in custody, wherever that was, Musyoka would never again see a member of his family, neither his wives, daughter, Lesley nor Anna Katuunge Mwangangi. In death he would be granted an unnamed pauper's grave near the prison outhouse where he was hanged.

It was almost dark by the time Janet and Michael reached John's house in Nairobi. Only a few short hours now separated Janet from her midnight flight to London, but first there was this duty to perform. As she wept in Lesley's arms with Michael looking on, apparently unable to react, she still wondered how she might find words to convey any meaning. And then a young boy emerged from the house. She knew him. He was the son of one of the shopkeepers from Migwani market, a day student in her school's Form Three. It was only then she fully realised that Lesley was not crying. She seemed strangely calm and controlled. As Janet drew back to look at her, she said, "Julius came on the morning bus and brought the news. He arrived about an hour ago." Lesley's voice sounded empty, merely empty.

"Will you be wanting to go to Migwani?" asked Michael after a nervous pause during which he walked towards the still embracing women and then away again.

"No," said Lesley with conviction.

"What are you going to do?" asked Janet, disengaging herself from Lesley's now limp arms.

"I don't know," was the soft, hollow reply.

For some minutes they stood there in the driveway, statically arranged, as if about to deliver a quartet in a tragic opera, but they were all silent. Then, after a simple goodbye, Janet and Michael got back in the car and drove away. Only then did Lesley weep, but it was only a single tear and even that had dried by the time she approached Julius with repeated thanks for bringing the news.

The accommodating waiter in the restaurant that Janet chose was worried throughout by their lack of appetite. He approached the table many times and asked with a broad nervous smile whether the food was all right. Both Janet and Michael said it was fine, but still, it seemed, they did not want to eat. At the airport, necessity ruled as they worked through the formalities of flying. Janet weighed the luggage that Michael had carried and the clerk checked the ticket she presented. Janet paid the tax of twenty shillings and took the stamp without which she could not depart. Then, after kissing Michael once on the cheek, she said what became a hurried goodbye and walked beneath the sign that said 'Departures' without once looking back. She had to begin again.

Mission by Philip Spires

In Mission Philip Spires both expands and deepens the stories that surround A Fool's Knot. Mission is also set in Migwani and features several characters that appear in A Fool's Knot.

Mission begins in 1978, two years after the tragedy of A Fool's Knot, but visits the characters' lives in different eras, covering more than a century of their histories. Again, Philip Spires deals with ideas of culture, identity and personal motivation in a context of rapid social change.

Michael, a missionary priest, has just killed Munyasya, a retired army officer. It might have been an accident, but Mulonzya, a politician resentful of the power of foreign churches, tries to exploit the tragedy for his own ends. Boniface, a young church worker, and his wife, Josephine, have just lost their child. They did not make it to the hospital in time, possibly because Michael made a detour to retrieve a letter from the Mission, a letter from Janet, a former volunteer teacher who was the priest's neighbour for two years. It is Munyasya who has the last laugh, however, when he reveals that he was probably in control of events all along. Thirty years on, the same characters find their lives still influenced by his memory.

Mission is a large and complex novel in which every character is seen to pursue some personal, though sometimes public mission.

Also published by Libros International.
ISBN: 978-1-905988-07-5

Printed in the United Kingdom
by Lightning Source UK Ltd.
131596UK00001B/236/P

9 781905 988488